Daisy, Plucked

C. E. Witherow

Published by C. E. Witherow, 2024.

DAISY, PLUCKED

First edition. October 18, 2024.

Copyright © 2024 C. E. Witherow.

ISBN: 979-8227786654

Written by C. E. Witherow.

Table of Contents

Chapter 1..1

Chapter 2...21

Chapter 3...26

Chapter 4...40

Chapter 5...45

Chapter 6...61

Chapter 7...70

Chapter 8...86

Chapter 9...98

Chapter 10 113

Chapter 11 127

Chapter 12 139

Chapter 13 154

Chapter 14 171

Chapter 15 183

Chapter 16 194

Chapter 17 213

Chapter 18 230

Chapter 19 243

Chapter 20 257

Chapter 21 272

Acknowledgements 285

For my Mom and Dad

Thank you for everything — this book wouldn't exist without your love and support.

Chapter 1

Daisy — June 2019

IF DAISY NEVER GOT out of bed, this day couldn't happen.

If she stayed curled up under her raggedy pink and white comforter, maybe the past two weeks would turn out to be an anxiety fueled nightmare. She could wake up again, *actually* wake up, and Hana would be waiting in her living room with flowers or a poem or some other small gift she would use to win Daisy back. She would still have the last week of classes to face, and she would still be planning her graduation party and getting excited for freshman orientation.

But unless a miracle turned the past two weeks into a fiction, when she got up she would see her high school diploma dumped under her brother's hand-me-down graduation gown and she would have to put on the black dress she had picked out for Hana's funeral.

And, realistically, the funeral of Daisy's best friend and recent ex-girlfriend would happen whether she showed up or not, so she needed to get out of bed. If she didn't force herself to start the day, her dad would come in to get her up soon, and she hadn't properly hidden the love letters from Hana that she had looked at the night before while she was falling asleep. Hana and Daisy managed to hide their relationship for three and a half years, and she wasn't going to break that streak now.

Then again, her dad was so unobservant that he hadn't noticed Daisy and Hana dating the past four years. He thought they were just fighting as friends when they broke up, and he got into the habit of daily lectures about getting over their differences and making up like friends were supposed to. Those stopped once it was too late to take his advice — there was no making up and getting back together anymore. It was hard to get back together with a dead girl.

Hana killed herself on a Tuesday afternoon. Her mom found her after she came home from work.

Daisy's alarm chimed again, and if she lay in bed for much longer she wouldn't have time to get ready for the funeral. She forced herself to get out of bed and hated that she needed to lean against the wall for support. If something as easy as getting out of bed exhausted her, getting through this day would be a herculean task.

Her phone buzzed, and she picked it up to find another condolence text she wouldn't respond to. She shut down her phone and threw it on her bed to deal with later.

She dragged herself down the hall into the shower. After her graduation ceremony the day before, half of her class met up at Gina Yell's oversized house in the suburbs and drank too much. Daisy had only stayed long enough to polish off an entire bottle of wine before she got one of the DDs to drive her home, but she still somehow smelled like a brewery. Luckily, she didn't run into her dad in the hall — she didn't have the energy today to deal with him finding out she'd been underage drinking.

By the time she started her haircare routine for her long, curly, red hair, she could hear her brother shuffling in the hall. She didn't skip any steps, even though he would be inconvenienced by her taking her time. The ritual comforted her, and she needed comfort today. Once she was done, she started loudly collecting her things, and his steps disappeared back into his room. He always gave her space when she needed it.

"Bathroom is all yours, Will," she called. He walked out of his room and gave her a small sleepy smile on his way past her.

Back in her room, she blow-dried her hair with the overpriced hair dryer Hana got her for Christmas a few years earlier and let the white noise lull her. She put on the dress she bought for Hana's father's funeral and hated how it fit her. She hadn't thought to try it on before today, and now she was forced into the too-tight, itching A-line that constricted her chest.

Hana had worn pants to her father's funeral three years before. Her mother, Noriko, threw a fit over it, saying that she was taking the "being a lesbian" thing too far. Hana snapped back that it was ridiculous for her mother to worry about what she looked like when her father had been shot dead by a psychopath, and that shut Noriko up for a little while. Daisy hated witnessing those little squabbles, but now she missed them. Every moment with Hana felt more precious now that there would be no more.

She considered not wearing makeup since she would probably cry it off, but she didn't want to worry anyone with the bags under her eyes. She swiped on mascara and concealer and a hefty dose of setting spray and hoped for the best.

She stared at herself in the mirror on the back of her door and wished she could go back to bed. The dress didn't fit right, her curls were frizzy despite the care she took, and the concealer wasn't doing enough to hide the bags under her eyes. She turned away and resolved to avoid mirrors for the rest of the day.

Her dad already had a cup of coffee ready for her when she got downstairs, and she gave him a small smile of thanks before taking a sip.

"Good morning, Daisy. I made it just the way you like — lots of hazelnut creamer," Henry said proudly.

Daisy actually liked her coffee with just a small splash of milk, but Henry still only knew the overly sweet way she enjoyed it when she first started drinking it in tenth grade. She never had the heart to tell him her tastes changed, and today wasn't the day to burst his bubble, so she just nodded and choked it down.

"Thanks, Dad," she said warmly. It wasn't his fault she had changed faster than he could keep up with, so she tried her hardest not to resent him for it. She sometimes wondered if he could only love the past version of her or if he would love her now if he really knew her, but she didn't have the emotional capacity to think about that right now.

She was an hour into her day and hadn't cried yet, but her dad gave her a pitying look that tried her resolve.

"No one would be upset if you didn't go today," Henry started.

"*I* would be upset if I didn't go," Daisy retorted.

Hana may have broken her heart, but she had also been Daisy's best friend for almost thirteen years and her girlfriend for three and a half, and there was no way she would miss her funeral.

"Alright, sweetheart. Just let me know if you need to leave early, or if you don't want to go to the graveyard or—"

"I will, dad. Just ... I'm going to go. We'll see ... Well, we'll just see."

He nodded, still somber. Daisy remembered he also lost Hana, just like he also lost Hana's father, Mark, and she felt bad for cutting him off. Was he thinking of her mother's funeral today too? Or was it only Daisy who used it as a mental benchmark whenever there was a death in her life? Daisy wanted to be mad that he thought she was too weak to handle it, but she couldn't muster the anger. Her grief shouldn't be his burden as much as he tried to take it on

They drank their coffee in silence, both reading completely unrelated things. Her dad scrolled through the local newspaper on his tablet while Daisy thumbed through a dogeared copy of Arthur Conan Doyle's Sherlock short stories, skimming her favorites without actually settling on one story.

Hana never liked Doyle's words, but it wasn't until she went away to college and took a women's literature course that she started loudly voicing her dislike of the stories. She would send Daisy PDFs of the stories she thought Daisy should read instead of the "misogynistic crap" Daisy loved, and at the end of the semester Hana gave her all the books she'd read. Daisy skimmed a few pages of each, then looked them up on SparkNotes and lied to Hana that she read and liked them. After Hana died, she tore through them feverishly. She read them as if the words were a message, something that would somehow bring Hana back if she could just decode them, just read them correctly. But Hana stayed dead, and Daisy still hated *The Bell Jar*.

When her brother came downstairs, Daisy looked up from her book to see if he was doing any better than her, but he wasn't. She'd never seen him as miserable as he was the past week, but she didn't know how to acknowledge his grief without being swallowed by her own. He smiled weakly at Daisy on his way to get coffee.

"You should use a travel mug. We have to leave in a few," Henry said.

"Oh, yeah. You're right. I guess we are going all the way to the other side of town, right?" Will said. He pulled out an old travel mug and filled it to the brim.

"Yeah, it's in the same place as Mark's funeral. God, Nori must be … You guys make sure you talk to her today, alright? It'll mean a lot to her, I'm sure."

"Of course, dad," Daisy said. Will nodded but didn't say anything. Daisy watched his Adam's apple move up and down his throat with the effort not to cry. She blinked away a few tears of her own and tried to focus on the familiar story she was reading.

A few minutes later, Henry got up and put his mug in the sink, and Daisy followed suit. The three moved in a silent dance, one where they knew the others' steps and where they were meant to be without saying anything. It turned out funeral number three was the one where they finally figured out the right steps to dance around each others' grief. They no longer went through the routine of asking each other how they were feeling — they all knew the answer wouldn't be honest.

The car ride was silent. Daisy tried to read, but she couldn't focus for more than a few seconds before she was distracted by the world outside of her window. She had gone to that restaurant with Hana for their one-year anniversary. She stole a kiss with Hana under that streetlight when they were riding their bikes to the park. That was their favorite bookstore when they were kids.

Hana's funeral was in the same catholic church as her father's, which was the same one she grew up going to every week. Hana's dad was as catholic as they came, but he never hated his daughter for being a lesbian. Even though the rest of the congregation wasn't as kind, she was still confirmed and raised in the religion because she believed in it. Hana pretended to be too cool for organized religion, but Daisy saw her rosary carefully wrapped in a bandana in a desk drawer when she visited Hana at college for Valentine's Day a few months earlier.

Walking into the church was surreal. Hana's body wasn't there yet, so people milled in the aisles and spoke in hushed tones. Daisy always felt out of place in churches since she wasn't raised attending one, and it was unimaginable to her that this imposing structure of wood and glass and prayer was a place of comfort to some people.

The tall ceilings seemed to sweep up the voices, mixing them all together in a cacophony of whispers and murmurs that Daisy couldn't understand. She tried to pick up a line out of anyone's conversation, but they all were distorted aside from a word here and there. The stained-glass windows showed the Madonna and the crucifixion and other stories that Daisy wouldn't know if Hana hadn't pointed them out during her father's funeral.

The Polo family made their way toward the front of the church where Hana's mother and Uncle Dennis were, but before they got there everyone began taking their seats. They ended up tucking themselves into a mostly empty pew about two-thirds of the way down the center aisle and waited in the new silence for the funeral service to start.

Hana's casket was carried in by a handful of distant cousins, ones that lived out of town who she wasn't close to, and Daisy felt a prick of annoyance that *they* were the ones chosen to carry Hana. They barely talked to her, barely knew her, and Daisy knew that Hana would rather Will carried her alone on his back than any of these half-strangers. The only thing she had in common with these boys was their blood, and Hana was a strong believer in found family. If she found this family, she would've returned them to wherever they came from and kept looking for another.

By the time Daisy was done being annoyed at Hana's cousins, the casket was resting next to the altar and the priest stood to speak, cutting off the organ music Daisy hadn't noticed was playing.

"Hello, loved ones. Today we are here to celebrate the life of Hana Holm, a daughter of God that has gone back to Him too soon."

Daisy hated that she was crying already and tried to blink away the tears before they could fall. Will tapped her hand and offered her a tissue, and she took it without looking at him.

All week she kept remembering and realizing that Hana was gone, their love story was finished, their friendship was over. But each time the thought hit her it still knocked her out.

She barely took in the service. All she was focused on was the way that the sunlight bounced off the copper organ pipes behind the altar and onto the shiny, highly polished wooden coffin that held Hana's body. It looked expensive but not as flashy as the one Mark Holm had been buried in.

When she was younger, Hana dared Daisy to jump into the town pool without her life jacket on. She would've figured out how to climb into the sky and steal the sun if Hana asked her to, so of course she did it. She couldn't really swim, and there was a moment after her head went underwater when she opened her eyes and saw the rest of the swimmers in the public pool going on with their days and paying her no mind. This was what this week felt like — the moment before the panic set in, before Will pointed her out to the lifeguard that jumped in to save her. She was just floating and watching the world turn, knowing that as soon as she tried to breathe, she would be drowning.

When the funeral ended, they made their way to the church's foyer, following Hana's coffin with the rest of the mourners. Even though the burial was usually just for family, Noriko had called them the day before and insisted they come as well.

It was a beautiful day, and it felt wrong. The lawn's grass seemed too green, the flowers were blooming too loudly, the sun was shining too brightly, all of it screaming that this day wasn't meant for this.

In another life, this was the day Hana would reach out to beg for Daisy back like she had the other times they would fight. That day outside of George's diner shouldn't have been the last time that Daisy and Hana saw each other. It wasn't supposed to be *the* end, just *an* end.

Will flipped on the radio as soon as they got in the car, and Daisy was glad there wouldn't be silence. The chorus of one of Hana's favorite songs, "Heaven is a Place on Earth" by Belinda Carlisle, blasted out of the speaker, and Daisy couldn't help but burst out laughing.

"The world really has some sense of humor, doesn't it?" Daisy said, curling into herself as she laughed. Will joined in, and their hysterical laughter chorused together.

"This is definitely something Hana would put on after her funeral," Will said, tears in his eyes.

Henry looked at his children like they were insane but didn't comment. He was probably worried about what it looked like to have his children laughing in the parking lot of their best friend's funeral, but he wasn't going to point that out. Maybe it went against the advice of the grieving children books he read in secret after their mom died when Daisy was four.

The funeral procession started, and they stopped laughing. Will turned down the radio until the car was close to silent. When they arrived at the cemetery, Henry turned the car off and the quiet wove between them, growing and stretching until it was deafening. It was difficult to get out of the car, but Daisy managed. One of her heels sank into the grass on her first step off the road, but she trudged forward and kept her weight on her toes.

The casket was on the lift that would lower it into the grave, and Noriko stood next to it, her short frame dwarfed by the hydraulics holding her daughter. The Polos walked over, and Henry placed his hand on Noriko's shoulder. The woman turned and smiled at them before pulling Henry into a hug.

"Thank you all so much for coming. Hana would have—" Noriko cut herself off with a shake of her head.

"Of course, Nori. We wouldn't miss this. You know that you and Hana and Mark are our family. If there's anything that you need at all, you can always ask," Henry said before hugging Noriko again. Daisy saw Hana's uncle talking to the priest, and his eyes flicked to the spot where Noriko and Henry touched.

"Thank you, really ..." Noriko looked lost in thought for a moment before adding, "Daisy, if there's anything of Hana's you want, you can come by the house any time. Maybe some stuff for college."

"That — thank you," Daisy paused, not knowing what to say. "I can stop by sometime soon." Her voice felt small, like a frightened animal skittering out of her mouth.

"Great," Noriko said softly. She seemed to realize it wasn't just Daisy and Henry standing there, and her eyes widened just enough that only Daisy would pick up on it. Hana had her mother's eyes, and Daisy knew all too well how to read them. "And Will, she didn't ... well ... but if you want to come over and get anything to ... to remember her ... you guys can come over. Maybe I can make dinner. You know Hana loves, or loved, I—" Noriko looked pained as she cut herself off. Daisy glanced at Will out of the corner of her eye, and she almost missed the flash of pain across his face, the way he curled his hands into fists like they did when he was trying not to cry. He didn't notice her looking, and she was glad.

"Why don't we come over with pizza soon? Pick a day," Henry said, trying to steer Noriko back. The lost-looking woman gave a nod and glanced past the family where Hana's uncle was walking up. He took Nori's hand and gave it a squeeze before turning to the Polos and hugging each of them in turn. Daisy didn't want to hug him, but she reminded herself that her grief didn't give her an excuse to be rude, especially to other people who loved Hana.

"Thanks for coming you guys. It means a lot. I think they're going to say the prayers now, Nori. Would you like to sit?" Dennis asked.

"Yes, that sounds good. And the flowers have — oh yes, there they are. Great. They brought them from the church." Noriko reached out to Hana's casket to touch the bouquets that were at the front of the church with ribbons that said "daughter" and "friend" on a few of them. Daisy vaguely remembered her dad telling her he was ordering one on her and Will's behalf, but there were so many she didn't know which was "from" them.

Dennis steered Noriko to the front row of chairs and the two of them sat down next to the other members of Hana's family. Will wrapped an arm around Daisy's shoulders, and they walked together to stand behind the family's chairs. She felt like a widow, but Will was the only one here that knew Daisy and Hana were together. Daisy wasn't ready to come out before, and she stood by that, but at Hana's grave, her old problems felt insignificant. She didn't know if any of her fears ever really mattered or if she just convinced herself they did.

The same priest from the church said a few words, but Daisy was too focused on what would happen after he finished speaking to really listen.

How could she say her final goodbyes to Hana's body — the body that held Daisy and loved her and was there for her for thirteen years? She wished this was really the end, that it brought her some sort of closure, but she knew it wouldn't. Just because Hana would be at rest didn't mean that Daisy would be able to sleep at night.

The priest finished and soon Daisy's family was walking forward, though they were relegated to the back of the line of mourners. She didn't want to cry, but she couldn't stop it from happening. Will handed her another tissue, and she held it under her nose with one hand but made no attempt to stop her tears.

When it was her turn, she placed her hand on the casket, and it was sun warm and glossy under her fingertips. She took a deep breath and tried to imagine she was holding Hana's hand one last time.

She wanted to throw herself into the grave, to go with Hana, to never leave her side, but she couldn't do that, especially here where no one knew what Hana meant to her. Besides, Hana had broken up with her before she died. If Hana chose this, chose to die, chose to leave Daisy not just once but twice, maybe Daisy was a fool for wanting to go with her.

She rested her forehead on the back of her hand, saying a silent goodbye to her first love, and stood for a long moment. Will put his hand on her shoulder, and she pulled away, leaning into his side while they walked to the car.

"Dad, can we go home?" Will asked. Relief crashed over Daisy.

If she went to the funeral luncheon, she might start demanding that others qualify their grief. She wanted to ask how they were so hurt when Hana never liked them that much, when they never loved

Hana like Daisy did. Some of the people she saw in the church were outright homophobic to her, some of them barely talked to her, and some of them were just there for the spectacle. To them, the funeral of a rich, pretty, gay girl who killed herself was nothing more than the event of the summer season.

"I'll drop you two off at home," Henry said. "I still want to go to the luncheon. You all saw ... Well, Nori needs friends right now. I mean, God, first Mark and now ... Thank god for Dennis." Daisy held in a scowl at the name of Hana's paternal uncle.

Daisy wasn't a fan of Dennis, but she wasn't going to tell her dad that Hana and Dennis never got along. If Hana could see the way that Dennis was acting, maybe she would think he really cared about her. Then again, if Hana saw the way he was holding Noriko, she probably would've lost her mind.

When Henry dropped them off, Will immediately went for the keys to the car he'd gotten as a gift for his seventeenth birthday. It was used and almost as old as Daisy, but she still envied his ability to go wherever he wanted anytime. She'd failed her driving test two times because she couldn't parallel park, and her dad used it as an excuse to not get her a car. Will caught her jealous stare and gave her a weak smile.

"Come on, let's go get frozen custard," he said. Daisy smiled at him, her first genuine smile in days.

"I'm sorry no one knew," Will said once they were in the car. Of course he knew that part of the reason she was upset was because no one knew why she was so upset. Daisy swallowed back her tears before responding.

"She said that she understood me never coming out after that big fight we got in a few years ago, but I'm not sure ... I mean, maybe the secret wasn't worth it." Daisy tried to figure out how to word her thoughts. Her mind felt like the tin of loose embroidery floss she had used to make friendship bracelets with Hana when they were younger. She couldn't follow one thread long enough to finish untangling it before she started following another, and the mess never got smaller. It just changed shape.

"She knew, you know." Will glanced at her. "She knew how much you loved her. And, I mean, you have to know that she loved you, too." There was something in the way that Will spoke that put Daisy on edge.

"She literally broke up with me a week before she died because she cheated on me. We — it was over. For good that time, and now I feel like ... Maybe if I'd reached out, maybe if I hadn't just gone radio silent, maybe she wouldn't have—"

"Hey, you can't blame yourself. Whatever Hana's reasons were ... she made her choices," he said, his voice thick like he was trying not to cry.

"I wish she'd left a note. I wish I, well, we, knew ... I mean, I didn't think she was struggling so much."

"Honestly, breaking up with you, burning that bridge, giving you the truth about what she did ... Maybe that was her version of a note. For you, at least. They say sometimes when people kill themselves, they start saying their goodbyes weeks in advance," Will said, sounding like he was parroting something he read.

"Where did you learn that?" Daisy asked. She knew there had to be signs she hadn't seen. At first, she hadn't been able to believe it of her best friend. Daisy spent the first few days after Hana's death thinking there had to be some mistake, that Hana actually died from an accident or a home robbery gone wrong or anything other than suicide. She didn't tell anyone about her doubts, and when she overheard her father discussing with Dennis that Hana was killed from a point blank gunshot wound, one that could only be caused from the gun being in her mouth when it went off, she let go of her doubts.

"I ... Well, I wanted to know what signs I missed. So I just looked into it a little bit," Will admitted sheepishly.

"Oh. Well, you know, Hana loved you too. Even if she didn't say goodbye, she did."

"Yeah, I ... I know she did. In her own way," Will said, his voice cracking. He was right, Hana always had her own way of doing everything, even loving people. She might not have said it, but she did always keep Will's favorite snacks stocked for impromptu movie nights at her house, always sent him random care packages whenever Daisy mentioned in passing that he had a hard exam coming up or a long paper to write.

"She did everything in her own way," Daisy said. They were quiet until they pulled into the frozen custard stand's small parking lot. When they walked up to the window to order, a classmate of Daisy's, Jake, was working. She didn't really want to talk to him, but she was already here.

"Daisy! Hey! I like your dress," he said.

"Oh, um, thanks," Daisy said, unsure how to respond. He looked confused by her reaction, but when he took in Will's outfit, and the stormy look on Will's face, it seemed to dawn on him why she was dressed up.

"Oh, shit," he said under his breath before adding, "I'm, uh, sorry about Hana." He said it like he was required to, and the lack of emotion annoyed Daisy. He could choose to say nothing, but instead he brought her up like he deserved to have her name in his mouth.

"Thanks. Can we get two chocolate almonds?" Will asked, saving Daisy from having to figure out how to respond.

"Coming right up. On the house," he said, not even touching the cash register next to the window. Daisy gave him a small, polite smile with no teeth. He disappeared for a moment and came back with their cones.

"Here you guys go." He paused and scribbled something on a napkin. "And if you ever need to talk—" he handed her the napkin inscribed with a phone number.

"Oh. Thanks," Daisy replied, her voice sounding fake and flat even to her own ears. The boy gave an awkward, hopeful smile that fell off his face the moment he saw the glare Will was giving him. He quickly turned his attention to the next customers in line, stammering out a hello while the Polos walked away.

"That sucked," Will said.

"Yeah. Can't even escape the pity at Abbots. Maybe we should dye our hair and change our names?" Daisy proposed, earning a chuckle from Will.

The Polo siblings were pretty recognizable with their matching red hair and freckles, and everyone knew that they were friends with Hana. Daisy was no longer her own person. She was just the poor best friend of that girl who killed herself. Daisy had deleted all her social media apps off her phone the day after Hana died so she wouldn't have to see the posts about suicide awareness that swept through the town, and she stopped responding to a majority of the condolence texts days earlier. The only ones she answered were the ones from Hana's college friends, some of the only people who knew about Hana and Daisy.

On the drive home Daisy used the napkin with the boy's number on it to catch custard dripping towards her fingertips. She should feel bad for dismissing the boy so easily, but she didn't. All she felt was exhausted. Maybe now if she lay down she would finally be able to rest.

When they got home, the siblings relaxed into a comfortable silence and finished their frozen custard on the front porch. They didn't need to say anything to know how the other felt — the grief hung all around them like particles of dust caught in a sunbeam. Daisy was glad for a split second that her brother was leaving for a study abroad trip in a few weeks so she would get a break from witnessing his grief alongside her own.

"I'm going to take a nap," Daisy declared after she finished her cone.

"That's a good idea," Will said, "I might do that too once I'm done." Daisy nodded at him and walked into the house where she was greeted by the cool blast of air conditioning.

She went to her room and pulled on an old sweatshirt that Hana borrowed so many times it was practically hers alongside a pair of SUNY New Paltz sweatpants she bought when she visited Hana at college. Hana was always too petite to have anything that would fit Daisy comfortably, so this was as close as she could get to wearing Hana's clothes to sleep.

She woke up to the feeling of someone brushing her hair back from her face. She sighed and leaned into the touch, and when she opened her eyes, she saw Hana's deep brown almond shaped eyes. Hana was there, lying next to her on the bed, her face inches from Daisy's. For a moment, Daisy forgot that this wasn't right, and when she remembered, she frowned but reached up to hold the hand in place.

"This is a nice dream," Daisy said, breaking the silence.

Hana rolled her eyes. "This isn't a dream, Daisy."

"I was just at your funeral. Of course this is a dream."

"I'm really here. Well, not *really,* but my spirit or ghost or whatever you want to call it is here," Hana said. It was Daisy's turn to roll her eyes.

"Let's not argue. We always argue. C'mon dream-Hana, let's just lie here," Daisy said.

Hana looked annoyed and pinched Daisy's cheek. Daisy jerked backwards and sat up.

"You're awake, Lazy Daisy, and I'm really here, and I need your help."

"Why do you call me Lazy Daisy? You know I hate it," Daisy mumbled, rubbing the sleep out of her eyes. She was still convinced this was a dream, but the usual haze wasn't there. She looked around her room, expecting something to be off, but this dream was surprisingly accurate. She could even read the time on the clock, three hours since she fell asleep, and the calendar on her wall was scribbled with all the right appointments and reminders. She turned to the self-proclaimed ghost and waited for her answer.

"Because you're too good for me, and I feel the need to demean you to bring you down to my level," Hana finally said, looking uncomfortable.

"I ... what? If you're real, you never would've admitted that. Or even thought that. Don't you have that whole thing about only saying things you mean? You've used it as an excuse to insult me enough times," Daisy said.

"I'm dead. It's bringing out a whole new side of me."

Hana reached forward and Daisy leaned back.

"Alternately, I'm just asleep right now and you're saying what I want to hear."

"So you agree that you're better than me? Kind of a dick move, Day."

"Jesus Christ," Daisy muttered.

"Don't take the lord's name in vain."

"What, are you guys buddies now?" Daisy snorted.

"I'm trapped in the in-between. Not sure what comes next. But just in case, I figured I'll stick to the rules."

Daisy sighed and took the bait Hana so nicely put on the hook in front of her. "Why are you in the in-between, Hana?"

"Because I didn't kill myself."

"What do you mean you didn't kill yourself?" Daisy's chest seized before her pulse sped up. This was a dream. It had to be. Only her own subconscious would be aware of the doubts she had about Hana's death.

"I mean I didn't kill myself. Did you go deaf in the last week?"

"No, I didn't. But you — this is just proving that all of this isn't real. You committed suicide."

"No, I didn't. I wasn't done living yet. I wasn't done *with* living yet."

"Sure. That really proves the whole 'not a dream' thing."

"I was murdered!" Hana yelled, standing off the bed and knocking an empty water bottle off Daisy's bedside table.

"You killed yourself!" Daisy snapped back. She held eye contact with Hana and battled a yawn that was threatening to overtake her. Even while she was dreaming, she couldn't rest.

"No, I didn't! And you have to figure out who killed me. If you don't then I have to be trapped in this limbo for God knows how long."

"Don't use the lord's name in vain," Daisy snarked back.

"Oh, shut up. You know what I mean. I just — Daisy, I need your help. Sorry I'm coming across all weird, I'm just ... this place is messing with my mind. And you're the only one that can help me."

"Then just tell me who murdered you," Daisy said.

"I ... I don't know who it was."

"How do you know you were murdered if you don't know who did it?"

"Well, I know I wouldn't kill myself, so even if my last few hours alive are gone from my memory, I'm certain that nothing could've happened that would make me kill myself. I mean, you're still alive, and my mom is too, and there's not really anything else that would've driven me to ... that."

"Sure. Very convincing dream-Hana. Or hallucination-Hana if we're going for some alliteration," Daisy said, lying back down. She longed to go back to her usual nonsensical dreams.

"I can't move on until I know, and you're the only person who can figure it out. Please, you have to believe me, you're my only chance," Hana pleaded. She looked more panicked than Daisy had ever seen her. Daisy looked up at her ceiling in an attempt to avoid the figure in the corner of her vision.

"Well, give me a clue or a hint or *something* that can help me solve your supposed murder. Convince me this is real," Daisy said. Hana was silent for a moment, biting her lip and twirling a strand of her shoulder length black hair as she weighed out each piece of information she held before deciding how much Daisy could carry with her.

"I never knew you were this skeptical," Hana muttered, pausing for a minute before hesitantly adding, "I left clues about what got me killed. Starting with a note. You can figure it out if you turn over enough stones." Hana looked earnest and pleading and a little bit scared, and Daisy didn't know if she had ever seen Hana that way in her life. It was unsettling.

"Alright, I'll make sure to check that out for you, totally real ghost-Hana," Daisy said, trying to come off as annoyed, but falling short. She hoped this wasn't a stress-induced hallucination. She didn't have time to lose her mind right now.

"You're infuriating, you know that?"

"You told me it enough times," Daisy muttered.

"Just ... I can't convince you that I'm real right now, I know that. Just keep me in mind, okay?"

"As if I'm going to forget you anytime soon." Daisy settled back into bed.

"I know. I'm sorry things had to be this way. This isn't what I wanted, I promise. I was going to come back to you."

"That sounds just like something that belongs in a dream," Daisy said, her eyes drooping shut. Hana sighed and sat down next to Daisy on the bed, going back to stroking her cheek. The next time that Daisy woke up, she was alone once again.

Chapter 2

Hana — age 7

THE FIRST TIME HANA met Daisy was at the holiday party for the law firm where their fathers worked together. The lights were bright, the decorations were glittering, and Hana hated the frilly dress her mother forced her to wear. She complained that it was too cold out for something so light, that the lace was scratchy, that she wanted to wear jeans and a sweatshirt like she usually did when she attended her first-grade class. Her mother informed her that she needed to dress like a lady for the event, and ladies wore frilly dresses and didn't complain about it. Hana complained slightly less but made sure her parents knew she didn't like or care about looking like a lady.

The first time Hana saw Daisy, she knew the other girl was something special. Daisy was the only kid twirling on the dance floor that wasn't hiding behind a parent, and Hana needed someone like that.

She walked right up to the dancing girl and said the first thing that came to mind. "Your hair looks like wires."

Daisy stopped dancing and didn't quite smile at Hana's words, but when Hana gave her a gap-toothed grin to show that it was a good thing, the ginger girl smiled back.

"My name is Daisy Polo, and I'm five, but I'll be six in February," she said, sticking out her hand towards Hana.

"My name is Hana Holm, and I turned seven last month," Hana responded.

Daisy grinned at her. "Nice to meet you Hannah."

"No, it's Hana, like sauna, not Hannah like banana," Hana explained. Her mother taught her to say that after she complained about her teacher always saying her name wrong.

"Oh, okay. Nice to meet you, Hana."

Hana reached out to shake Daisy's hand like her father taught her, but Daisy used her outstretched hand to twirl Hana instead. Hana couldn't help but giggle, and she forgot for a second about her scratchy dress and whether or not she was being ladylike. The girls danced for what felt like forever before they were too out of breath from dodging around the legs of the adults and swinging each other around.

"I want water," Daisy said, walking off the dance floor.

"I want soda," Hana countered, and Daisy looked at her like it was a scandalous statement.

"My dad only lets me drink sodas on special occasions," Daisy said.

Hana smiled. "My mom told me this is a special occasion."

Daisy looked like she was thinking about it. "My brother said this was a stupid party, and he didn't want to wear his shoes because they hurt his feet," Daisy whispered.

"Are you allowed to say stupid?" Hana whispered back.

"No, are you?" Daisy asked.

"No," Hana giggled. Daisy giggled back, and the girls worked together to sneak a can of lemon lime soda from the table next to all the desserts. While Hana was supposed to keep watch, she also managed to grab a slice of cake. The girls hid with their treasures under an empty table, laughing and sharing sips of the soda and bites of the cake.

After they finished, they tried to subtly emerge from under the table, but as soon as Daisy stuck out her head, a frazzled looking boy with the same red hair and freckles as Daisy appeared.

"Daisy! I've been looking everywhere for you! Who's this?" he asked. Daisy grabbed his arm and pulled him under the table too, and he gave Hana a weary look.

"This is Hana. She's my new best friend," Daisy said. It was confident and sure, and it surprised Hana. The friends Hana made at school were nice, but none of them were really her *best* friend. She grinned at the boy.

"I'm Will. I'm Daisy's older brother. I'm eight," Will declared, crawling under the table.

"I turned seven last month," Hana said.

"Well, I've been eight since the summer. That means that I'm in charge," Will leveled Hana with a stare.

"I'm only five. I'll never be in charge," Daisy pouted.

"You can be in charge when you're eight," Will assured her.

"That's not how ages work. She'll still be younger than us when she's eight," Hana argued.

"I didn't say that she would be older than us, I said when she's eight she can be in charge sometimes," Will explained.

"It's okay, I don't want to be in charge. But Will, you have to steal a cookie to stay with us," Daisy ordered.

"Did Dad say that we can have sweets?" Will asked.

"No, but Dad isn't in charge under the table," Daisy answered. Will took this as good enough logic, and he disappeared to go steal cookies for them. By the time he got back, Daisy and Hana had started playing fairies.

"I don't want to play this game. It's stupid," Will complained.

"Well, we don't think it's stupid. You can only stay if you're the jester, and that means you have to make us laugh," Hana said. Daisy stared expectantly at Will, and he sighed.

"Fine. But first we have to have a contest to see who can eat the most," Will compromised. Hana nodded in agreement, and Daisy mimicked her a second later. The three gorged themselves on cookies and once there were only crumbs left under the table they stumbled out, their game forgotten, thinking that they were clever. Hana's mother spotted them and clucked while wiping chocolate from their faces and hands. She didn't have to say anything for the three to feel admonished.

"No more sweets before dinner, you three, or I'll have to tell your parents that you were sneaking cookies," Hana's mother said once she was done wiping chocolate from the corner of Hana's mouth. Daisy looked sad while watching, and Hana didn't understand why.

By the end of the night Daisy and Hana had already decided they would be best friends forever. It was the kind of friendship that was born purely out of convenience, but when you're that young it feels like it's destiny or magic or that God brought you and your new best friend together. Hana made them pray together before they left, thanking God for bringing her a new best friend and double checking that Santa received their Christmas lists. Daisy said she never heard of praying before except for in TV shows and movies, and she was confused when God didn't answer them.

"That's not how it works," Hana explained after Daisy had asked how long they had to wait to get an answer.

"Then why did we ask him questions?"

"My mom says that He answers in funny ways," Hana explained. "Like once I prayed for new soccer shoes and then my soccer shoes ripped and my mom had to get me new ones, and she said that it was because God heard me." She didn't say it out loud, but she was thinking about how the girls in her class had been calling her names, and she had been praying for a friend who would be nice to her for once, and it seemed like He finally heard her.

"Oh, okay!" Daisy said as if she understood, though Hana could tell she didn't.

Before they left, Hana's mom took a picture of them. They threw their arms around each other, and the sparkles from Daisy's dress got all over Hana. Her mother was annoyed that night when they got home and kept complaining about how she would have to take the dress to the dry cleaners, but Hana didn't care.

"I think Daisy is going to be my best friend forever," Hana said, interrupting her mother's complaints.

"Oh really? Why do you think that?" her mother asked while removing the bobby pins in Hana's hair with gentle hands.

"I think that because she's really nice and because I prayed for a friend that wouldn't be mean to me, and she was nice to me all night," Hana said.

"That's wonderful, darling. I'll make sure to call her dad so the two of you can play together soon," Noriko said. Her voice was gentle and a little bit sad, and Hana didn't understand why at the time. Still, she let her mom brush her hair without complaint and fell asleep to the familiar action and her mother's humming.

Chapter 3

Daisy — July 2019

BEFORE HANA DIED, DAISY had gotten herself a summer job as a lifeguard at a local day camp. After she got the news about Hana, her dad insisted that she quit, but they compromised by having her switch to only working mornings instead of the entire day. She almost forgot about her first day until Will woke her up, groggily handing off his car keys so he didn't have to get up to drive her to work.

Her dad told her that with her afternoons free, she could take time to find a hobby or get ready for college, suggestions that sounded straight from a self-help book. In reality, Daisy spent the first afternoons lying in her bed and sleeping. She usually woke up before her dad got home because the sun angled in through the gap where the two panels of her curtain didn't quite meet each other around four in the afternoon, but she didn't tell him how she spent her time. He would just worry about her.

However, on Thursday when she left work, she saw a text from her father.

. . . .

Dad

I forgot my lunch. Wanna pick us up lunch from Dibella's and we can eat at my office? It'll be like old times.

Daisy

Haha, sure, always love an office lunch. See you soon!

• • • •

When she got to the office, she parked in a visitor spot and walked up to the front door. The front reception area was spacious and bright with floor to ceiling windows and furniture with sharp, clean lines. The focal point was a large granite reception desk where Sheryl, the receptionist that had been there ever since Daisy could remember, sat clicking away at her computer.

"Hi, Sheryl. How are you?" Daisy asked. Sheryl looked up from her work and beamed at Daisy.

"Daisy! I'm doing well, thank you. And look at you! You've grown up so much since the last time I saw you," Sheryl said. "Are you here to see your dad?"

"Oh, yeah. He forgot his lunch," Daisy said.

Sheryl smiled. "You're such a great daughter. I won't hold you up any longer with my gabbing. Just make sure to tell your dad to get started on that pile of paperwork he has before it gets too tall and topples off his desk, alright?"

"I'll lay on the puppy dog eyes just for you."

"You're a darling. Have a good lunch." Sheryl buzzed Daisy through the door to the offices, which you usually needed a keycard to get through. Daisy began navigating towards the area where her dad's office was, nodding hellos to the people she recognized.

"Lunch is ready," Daisy joked when she walked into Henry's office.

"Daisy! Hi. Thank you, you're the best. Did you remember to get napkins?" Henry asked, barely looking up from what he was working on.

"Oh, no, I totally forgot. I'll go grab some from the break room."

"Great, thanks, I've got to finish up this memo quickly anyways."

Daisy walked to the break room quietly and made a beeline for the area where there was a napkin dispenser, not wanting to delay getting home and falling asleep any longer than she needed to.

While she was pulling out napkins from a dispenser, two younger attorneys, Walker and Heindel, strolled in and headed straight to the coffeemaker, completely oblivious to her presence.

"I just found out that she did it with Mark's gun. I mean what a slap in the face that must have been for Nori, right?" Walker said, pouring himself a cup of coffee. Daisy felt her stomach drop.

"And no note? I mean, you didn't hear it from me, but I have a friend who's a cop, and he said they had a couple of idiots working the scene. I don't know if they even looked for one," Heindel said, picking up a donut. Daisy didn't understand how they could be so careless about discussing Hana's death, but she felt frozen in place and stayed silent.

"I mean, a gunshot wound like that is pretty obviously suicide. And you remember what Dennis was saying about her acting strange for weeks leading up to it."

"Such a tragedy. I'm just sorry that Nori had to be the one to find her. My friend said it was apparently a pretty nasty sight. It always is when someone puts a barrel in their mouth, though. The bits of skull just go every—" Daisy let out a choked noise at the attorney's description, and the two finally looked up to see her standing there.

"Oh, hi Daisy, have you been here long?" Walker said sheepishly.

"Oh, uh, no, just walked in. I'll just be going," Daisy stuttered before bolting from the room, trying not to imagine Hana's skull splattered around her childhood bedroom.

Daisy dropped the napkins on her father's desk and mumbled something about needing the bathroom before rushing back out.

When she got into a stall, she leaned over the toilet and revisited what ate for breakfast. She tried not to picture what the men had described, but her mind flashed the image in front of her over and over again.

After flushing the evidence of the overheard conversation, she walked up to the sink and stared at her puffy face in the mirror.

She'd always hated the roundness of her jaw and the way that her cheekbones weren't sharp like Hana's were. She was all soft edges and gentle touches, a flower petal when she wanted to be the thorns on rose stems. Daisy wished for a moment that she knew what the other girl looked like, the one Hana cheated on her with, and whether she was thorny and sharp-edged or petal-soft like Daisy. Not that it mattered now.

She turned on the faucet and splashed water on her face before sipping some out of her palms to rinse her mouth. She felt raw and unbalanced, and she stared in the mirror to try to motivate herself to walk back to her dad's office. She took a deep breath, and it dragged through her lungs like a rush of water, thick and unwelcome.

The door opened, and Daisy bolted upright, reaching for a paper towel. Sheryl walked through the door with a look on her face that told Daisy she somehow knew everything.

"Your dad saw you rush in here, and he wanted me to check on you," Sheryl said.

"Oh, yeah, sorry, I didn't mean to make him worry," Daisy said, "I'm okay, I just … overheard something."

"What was it?" Sheryl asked.

Daisy started washing her hands just so that she didn't have to look at Sheryl's concerned face. She wasn't used to the maternal worry, so she didn't know how to respond without telling the truth.

"Just some people talking about how Hana … how she died." Daisy could barely say it, but Sheryl understood.

"Oh, honey, I'm so sorry. Who was it? I'll talk to them about it." Sheryl's genuine concern made her voice feel warm and silky. Daisy swallowed down the sob that threatened to break loose.

"It's okay. They didn't know I was there," Daisy said, deciding to go headfirst into the conversation instead of skirting around it.

"I saw the way the two of you were," Sheryl said, and Daisy froze. Did Sheryl know the way the two of them really were?

"Yeah, we were close," Daisy said, testing the waters.

"I lost my best friend a few years ago to cancer. Even seeing it coming, it was hard. I only got through it because of my husband and the kids. You just have to really lean on your family in times like this." Sheryl placed a comforting hand on Daisy's shoulder. Relief rushed through her, and she gave a small nod.

"Thanks, Sheryl."

"Of course, honey. And I think I know who was talking about Hana. I'll have a word with them. I mean, who knows, Dennis or your father could've walked in on them discussing it too. They should know better than to gossip about something so sensitive." Sheryl shook her head. Daisy gave her a tight smile and followed her out of the bathroom.

On the short walk back to her dad's office, it nagged at Daisy that they talked about the officers at the scene. She'd spent every day since Hana's death wondering why she didn't leave a note, but it would be just like Hana to hide one somewhere that an idiot cop rushing to finish processing a scene would miss it. Maybe the ghost was right, and she did leave something behind, but the ghost couldn't be real. If ghosts were real, she would've seen her mother in the years since she was gone. Daisy put it out of her mind and tried to think of what excuse she would give her dad for her rush to the bathroom.

"Are you alright? I sent Sheryl in to check on you because you seemed to be moving pretty quick," Henry asked.

"Oh, yeah, just ... I think I got too much sun this morning and the heat hit me all of a sudden. I needed to splash some water on my face and cool down."

"Yeah, it's a hot one today. How was it at work this morning?" he asked, biting into his sandwich to show he was ready to listen.

"It was good! I think I'm getting the hang of things already. The kids seem to think I'm special and interesting because I'm only there for half of the day, so they've been listening to me pretty well," Daisy said, trying to think of something other than ripping apart Hana's room until she could look for anything like the ghost described.

"That's good! You know, if you do go into teaching, this will be great experience," Henry said.

Daisy tried not to grimace. "Yeah, I'm still not sure what I'll study yet. I might do English or something," Daisy countered noncommittally. She picked at the toppings that fell off her sandwich, but her unsettled stomach begged her not to take any bites. She took a sip of her soda instead, hoping it might settle her nausea.

"You have some time to decide. You'll find what's right for you once you're out in the world a bit more. I mean, you've seen more than you should for your age, but you haven't seen everything. I know what it's like to be young," Henry said. According to Will, he spent the entirety of her graduation ceremony trying not to cry, and she really didn't want to go down that route right now. She was drained enough from acting like she was alright the rest of the day.

"Yeah, sure, Dad. What was it like growing up while the triceratops roamed?" Daisy teased, falling back on an old joke amongst their family to steer away from any more discussions about her day.

Henry groaned. "You wound me. My own daughter calling me old? This feels like patricide," he joked, a smile on his face.

"Wouldn't want that. There are enough fossils down at the science museum already."

Henry let out a hearty laugh and Daisy found herself actually laughing along with him. They'd had a million conversations mimicking this exact one, and for a second she could fool herself into thinking that things were still the same as they used to be. Then she remembered her ideal evening plans included underage drinking and probably crying over her dead secret ex-girlfriend, and she sighed.

"But really, kid, the half days aren't … too much? You can wait another few weeks if you need to. Or even take the summer off. I'm sure the camp can find someone to cover if you need, and I can just give you spending money for school," Henry said the words in a rush, like they were building up and waiting to bubble over.

"I like having something to do," Daisy admitted, leaving out that she didn't want whatever strings would come attached to an allowance from her father. She started counting the lines in the printed on fake wood veneer pattern of Henry's desk to distract herself, and she only got up to seven before her father spoke again.

"I … I can understand that. Just — you'll let me know if it's too much, right? Or if you need a break or anything?"

"Yeah, Dad, I will. No worries." It would take a miracle or another unspeakable tragedy for her to ask her dad for help, but she wasn't going to tell him that. She glanced at the clock. It'd been almost half an hour since she arrived, which meant her dad needed to get back to work soon. She was relieved she had an excuse to leave, but the relief came with an immediate guilt that unsettled her stomach again. But the sooner she got outside, the sooner she could distance herself from the overheard conversation and what it meant for the maybe-imagined ghost of Hana.

"Hey, can I run some errands with Will's car? I just have to run to the store quick." She paused before adding, "Girl stuff," to ensure that her dad wouldn't ask questions.

"Just check with Will first, okay?" Henry said, distracted by an email notification that popped up.

"Okay, I'll text him now," Daisy said.

• • • •

Daisy

DAISY, PLUCKED

Hey I'm taking the car to go to the store so I'll be home a little later than expected thankssss

Will

okay but be fast I want to go out

Daisy

No <3

I will be following all traffic laws to a T can't believe you would encourage me to break the speed limit. Heathen

· · · ·

Daisy stood and gave her dad a quick hug, which he returned with one arm without pausing from whatever he was typing on his computer.

"I'll see you two for dinner. I'm thinking of ordering pizza," he said.

"Pizza sounds good. See you later, Dad."

Daisy wove her way out of the office, walking quickly enough that no one would speak with her. She checked her purse on the walk to the car and found just enough cash to buy her favorite overly sweet pink wine.

When Daisy started the car, she was met with a blast of sound and hot air — clearly she forgot to turn off the AC or radio before she went into the office building. Daisy sighed and reached to turn it down but paused. The same song from the drive to Hana's burial, "Heaven is a Place on Earth," was playing loudly, and Daisy closed her eyes in an effort not to start crying. She shut off the air and turned to see someone in the passenger seat. Luckily the car was in park because she physically jumped back, letting out a startled noise.

"Settle down, lazy Daisy, it's just me. Like the song? I just think it's a nice touch." Hana's ghost grinned at her.

"Still not convinced you're real. I've just finally lost it," Daisy said. If she was insane, speaking with her delusions was almost the same as talking to herself. She backed out of the spot and started driving, trying not to get distracted by the ghost.

"I'm not fake. You're not that kind of crazy. I'm still stuck here, so clearly you haven't figured things out yet," Hana drawled, listing out each point she made on her manicured fingers.

"Very reassuring for the projection of my subconscious to tell me I'm not crazy. Definitely, totally makes me feel one hundred percent better."

"Anyways, back to my murder. Any suspects? First thoughts? Fun clues?" Hana pressed, redirecting the conversation to flow the way she wanted it to.

"Well, I know you were killed with your father's gun," Daisy said after a pregnant pause.

"Oh. That's ... something. Did you get to go look for stuff in my room yet?"

"No, I haven't ... I'm working up to it."

"Working up to it? Just go look in my room." Hana's ghost scowled at Daisy.

"Hana, that's where you died."

"Oh, right. I ... I see why that's hard, but you know what's harder? Existing in the limbo between life and death."

"And we wouldn't want *you* to suffer at all, Hana," Daisy snapped. "Of course not. Of course I'll bend over backwards at your beck and call."

"Come on, I didn't mean it like that."

"What did you mean it like?"

Hana's ghost hung her head. "I saw my mom earlier. She's ... she's not doing well."

Daisy was silent, swallowing thickly around the lump that had appeared in her throat. "That makes sense. Her daughter did kill herself."

"No I didn't!" Hana shouted. The air conditioning flared back on, hitting Daisy with a blast of now-cold air.

"Okay, got it, not suicide."

"Thank you. Now, are you going to look or not?"

"Since I'm still convinced I'm just losing my mind, I don't know what to tell you," Daisy huffed. "Even if you're a real ghost, how do I know you're not just messing with me? It's not like we last parted on good terms." Daisy made a sharp left turn into the liquor store parking lot.

"You're right, and sure I shouldn't have said some of that stuff like that—"

"Love that you're not taking any of it back." Daisy shut the car off. She slipped on a sweatshirt to cover her camp lifeguard t-shirt before getting out of the car, and Hana followed. She opened the door of the car and shut it behind her, and Daisy looked around to see if anyone was around to see a door moving on its own, but the parking lot of the liquor store was unsurprisingly empty at 1:15 pm on a Thursday. She wished the cracks in the sun-worn asphalt could have told her if they saw Hana too.

"Can anyone else see you?" Daisy asked as they walked into the store.

"No. It's another one of those weird left in the between things. I could only choose one person to talk with," Hana explained.

"Why not your mom?" Daisy asked. She would look insane if she talked while in the store, so she hoped Hana wouldn't ask her any questions in return.

"We ... She likes to shut her eyes and believe that there's sun even when she can feel the rain, you know? So I wasn't sure if she would really ... I don't know, actually try to solve my murder." Hana paused.

"Although she probably would've gone through my room by now, so maybe I should've chosen her." Daisy rolled her eyes but didn't respond. Instead, she gave a small wave to the man working behind the counter and started browsing the aisles as if she didn't know exactly what she wanted.

The liquor store was grimy, but that was part of the reason Daisy risked using her fake ID here. The floors were a speckled linoleum that she suspected had once been white, and the corners of most of the tiles were crumbling, making the dirty grout look like it was chipping away at the tiles. Daisy had seen the man who worked here mopping before, but she wasn't sure if that was just for show.

The aisles were organized haphazardly — the bourbon was next to the white wine, and the spiked seltzer was aisles away from the beer. Daisy didn't feel that it was her place to ask what the organization method was, and she had a strong feeling that they simply put things on the shelf this way once and were now too lazy to move the sun-faded signs.

After a few minutes of pretend browsing, Daisy picked up her usual oversized bottle of pink Moscato and walked to the counter. The usual cashier was there, and she braced herself for the interaction. He looked her up and down when she walked up, and she repressed the need to cover herself up despite the fact that she wore a sweatshirt and nearly knee length athletic shorts to comply with the camp's dress code. She shrank slightly under his lingering gaze.

"Hey there, darlin'. That all for today?" he asked, and his phrase was accented by the small beep from the item scanner. She nodded, and he looked at the screen for a moment.

"He's so creepy. Has he ever actually hit on you? Or does he just do this whole talk-to-your-chest-and-call-you-over-stepping-nicknames-thing?" Hana asked.

"Yeah, that's all," Daisy said, fishing around in her wallet for her fake ID before presenting it to the man. A little spike of fear hit her even though she knew it would likely work. He took a look at it and scanned the dates and Daisy's face before nodding. He punched something into the computer and clicked a few keys before announcing her total. She handed him the wad of cash she'd been saving for this, and he clicked more keys before the cash register sprang open, so sudden and loud that Daisy nearly jumped.

"He definitely stared at your ID for too long," Hana said. "Probably thinking about if twenty-two is too young for him. Or deciding to take it even though he knows it's fake because you're cute."

"Got a party or something?" the man asked as he placed the bottle of wine in a plastic bag.

"Celebrating a new job." She smiled, pretending like she was happy to engage with him.

"Congrats! Where are you working at?" he asked.

Hana grimaced. "That's so overstepping," the ghost muttered. Before Daisy could think of how to answer, Hana reached over and knocked the lighters over. The man at the counter jumped back as they fell.

"Wow, I guess these displays aren't as sturdy as they look." He laughed half-heartedly and handed Daisy her wine.

"Yeah, uh, I guess you never know. Have a good day," she said, half mumbling the last few words. He barely paid her any attention on her way out, and she hurried to the car.

"Are you crazy?" she asked Hana's ghost.

"Does that prove that I'm real yet? I'm getting sick of proving myself. It was a funny bit for, like, fifteen minutes max. Now I just need your help," Hana said.

Daisy sighed and relented. "Fine. I'll help. But I'm also not a professional detective or anything, so you really can't expect much from me."

Hana pumped her fist in the air. "Finally. Okay, so you need to go poke around my room and read my journals."

"That sounds deceptively simple."

"Well, also solve my dad's murder. I'm ninety-nine percent sure I figured it out right before I died, but poof, gone. Must be the head wound," Hana explained.

"Whoa, what? Your dad's murder was solved as soon as it happened. What do you mean?"

"There's something more to it. I ... I know I was investigating it. But the details are all fuzzy. My memory isn't ... I don't know how to describe it. It's like I know I was close, but I can't remember a lot about my investigation."

"Great. Perfect. So just solve two murders without also ending up dead. Need anything else?" Daisy asked.

"I would tell you more if I could remember."

"Would you, though? We both know that you love a secret."

"Well, yeah, but like fun secrets are more my speed." Hana tilted her head at Daisy like *she* was the crazy one for not remembering that. "Like the latest drama in Lily Ginym's country club crew and who is secretly flunking half their classes because they can't stop partying. I'm not into protecting the person who killed me."

"You're ridiculous."

"Yeah, but you love me," Hana retorted with a smile at the familiarity of their exchange.

"Yeah, sure." There was silence for a moment, and when Daisy flicked her eyes to the passenger seat, Hana was gone.

When she walked into the house, Will poked his head out of his room with a smile. "You have fun driving according to every single traffic law?" he teased.

She rolled her eyes. "Yes, I did. Thanks for letting me borrow the car." She tossed him the keys. He groaned.

"They go on the hook," he whined, already walking down the stairs to hang them up as Daisy climbed the stairs to her room.

Daisy hid her forbidden goods in her room, already thinking about how long she would need to wait before getting drunk alone. She could toast to the new investigation and the ghost she was beginning to believe was real.

Chapter 4

Hana — age 14

8/16/14

Dear diary,

Today is the day — I'm really doing it this time. I'm going to come out to Daisy.

I know, I know. I've been saying that for weeks, but I really can't back out of it this time. I texted her earlier to see if she wanted to come hang out, and I told her I had something I wanted to tell her. And it's Daisy, so she'll ask about it because she always remembers everything, and she'll definitely know I'm lying if I try to give her some bs excuse. She always knows when I'm lying. Maybe I should ask her what my tell is.

Anyways, I wrote out this whole speech to say to her (which is why there was a page ripped out of this notebook. It wasn't for something stupid this time) and I'm super ready for it. I mean, she'll probably be fine with it. Right?

I mean, even Mom and Dad weren't that bad about it. Sure, Mom made that face that looks like she was trying to get her eyebrows to touch, but she still said she loved me. Dad was super supportive, but ... I don't know. It felt like he was following some "how to react to your kid coming out" handbook and not actually saying what he thought. I could have it a lot worse, I guess. I haven't asked them yet if I'm allowed to have sleepovers with Daisy anymore. I hope I am. I don't wanna lose my best friend over this.

Anyways, Daisy is gonna be here soon. I'm gonna go sit in the backyard and try to relax until she gets here. I doubt I'll be able to actually relax, but oh well. I'll see what I can do.

Sincerely,

Hana

• • • •

Hana breathed in the humid, damp air under the shade of her favorite birch tree. She was lying on the ground in a patch of sun slipping between two trees, closing her eyes against the bright sunlight and letting it bleach the blackness behind her closed eyelids until it felt like she was staring into the sky anyways. She drummed her fingers against the dry grass, unable to stay still with her nerves. For some reason, this felt like a life-or-death moment, like if Daisy didn't accept her the rest of her world would implode.

The warmth of the sun on her face was disrupted, and Hana squinted up to see Daisy holding her hand at just the right angle to block the sun from Hana's eyes. The freckles on her arms and cheeks were dark from a summer spent outdoors, and a sunburn reddened the tip of her nose.

"Hey, Hana," Daisy said. All at once, Hana wasn't nervous anymore. Daisy was her closest friend and the sweetest person that she knew. Just being around Daisy made Hana act kinder towards other people. Her mother loved when Daisy came over for just that reason.

"Hey, Lazy Daisy," Hana replied. Daisy rolled her eyes at the nickname and moved her arm out of the way, making Hana close her eyes and throw her own arm up to stop the sunlight from blinding her.

"I hate that nickname, you know," Daisy muttered, taking a few steps away from Hana to settle on the swing set Hana's dad had built when her mother was pregnant.

"Yeah, I know." Hana ran her fingers over her pocket, feeling the small spot where the corner of the folded note was poking through her jean shorts. She took a deep breath, steeling herself to start talking.

"You okay?" Daisy asked, her tone tense and unsure.

"Oh, uh, yeah, I just — I mentioned I have something to tell you? And it's — I don't know. I think you won't care but, I ... don't know?"

"Did you kill someone?" Daisy teased, trying to lighten the mood.

"If I killed someone, I would've called for help burying the body," Hana quipped. Daisy laughed, and the sound loosened something in Hana's chest.

"I'm a lesbian," Hana said, abandoning her well-crafted speech immediately.

"Oh," Daisy said, her face scrunching up. Hana tried not to hold her breath, but this silence would only be one breath long if she just held on. The silence stretched, and her lungs ached, so she just started rambling.

"Yeah. I don't — Well, I've known for ... a while. Nothing will change," Hana said quickly, thinking back to her original script. The clever words she wrote were nowhere to be found in her mind, but she didn't want to pull out the note now.

"That kind of ... makes sense?" Daisy said, tilting her head to really look at Hana.

"What do you mean?" Hana asked.

"I mean, you haven't even kissed a boy yet. And you're, like 14, so that's not normal ... And you've been listening to that Troye Sivan song on repeat for like a month ... And you were, like super excited when gay marriage was legalized in New York."

Hana felt a pit in her stomach. Was she that predictable? Was the way that her parents reacted because they knew and they just hoped she wasn't?

"Oh," was the only thing that escaped Hana's mouth.

"I didn't mean it like — shit, Hana, thanks for telling me," Daisy said, looking like she wanted to take back everything she said.

"I, yeah, of course. I already told, like, my parents, but I just thought you — you know, you're my best friend. And I just thought you should ... know, I guess. I don't know." Hana stared at her Converse. The girls had bought matching white pairs and decorated them the past summer, and Hana still wore hers often. The marker hearts Daisy drew on the toe of her left sneaker were fading, but Hana didn't want to fix them. She liked wearing a little piece of Daisy with her all the time.

"Yeah, I mean — you said it. Nothing's gonna change. I mean, we never talked about boys anyways." Daisy paused, suddenly looking annoyed. "Is this why your mom told me I couldn't sleep over?"

Hana's head snapped up.

"She said that?" Hana asked.

"That's so stupid. We've been having sleepovers since we were, like, babies. It's not like now — ugh, I can't believe her. I'm texting my dad to tell him I'm staying over. What's she gonna do? Kick me out? She's never mean to me. I can pull the dead-mom card. Do you think this is a dead mom card situation? I can even work up some tears if needed. This is such bullshit," Daisy said darkly. Hana looked up at her friend, her eyes prickling slightly at the loyalty and fierceness lacing with Daisy's words.

"You're the best friend ever, you know that?" Hana asked.

Daisy smiled. "Hey, if I don't play the dead mom card for good things, what use is it?" Daisy asked. Hana got to her feet and pulled up Daisy to hug her. The younger girl's growth spurt had hit her with a vengeance that summer, and she was beginning to loom over Hana's 5'3" frame.

"Want to bike to get ice cream?" Hana asked, still hugging her friend.

"Absolutely. I told my dad we might go to the mall so he gave me $20," Daisy said, pulling away from Hana.

While they ate ice cream, Daisy babbled on about her friends on her swim team, and Hana listened with a smile on her face. She looked at her best friend, and it was like she was seeing her for the first time.

Daisy's hair was frizzing out of a French braid, and a loose strand kept falling out on the left side. She kept tucking it behind her ear absentmindedly, and Hana held herself back from touching it. Daisy's green eyes were bright despite their exhaustion from biking to the ice cream shop, and it mesmerized Hana. Daisy shined like a precious gemstone, like something worth digging up and wiping the dirt from and hiding away from prying eyes.

Something shifted in Hana's chest when her eyes fell onto Daisy's full lips, and —

Oh. That made sense.

She didn't want anything to change, so she decided that she would deal with this later. She pushed the thought as far away as she possibly could, locking it in a gilded box in the back of her mind. It was out of sight, but every once in a while a bit of light would shine on it, and she would be tempted to search for the key.

Chapter 5

Daisy — July 2019

DAISY SETTLED INTO the dull rhythm of her days working at camp and her afternoons spent mostly sleeping. Her coworkers went out of their way to make sure that the kids would have more fun, but she found herself existing mostly on autopilot. It was easier to let her life pass her by than to think about going to Hana's house and searching the room where she died for clues that might not even exist.

She forced herself out of autopilot on the Saturday morning Will left for his study abroad. She wished could help him more with his grief — even in her dissociative haze she knew Will was suffering. He spent too much time with the friends he barely liked from high school, coming home the next morning smelling like a brewery with darker and darker bags under his eyes. Daisy forgot too easily that Will had loved Hana like a sister.

The Polo siblings waited in the kitchen for Will's ride to come, both trying to convince themselves they wouldn't miss each other too much.

"I know that it's hard right now, but you'll be okay," Will said. He made her coffee the way she actually liked to drink it, and she was glad to not have to choke down an overly sweet cup.

"People always say that but conveniently leave out that the okayness won't come for a while," Daisy said, trying for a light tone. Will looked at her with sympathy in his eyes, like the effort made him sadder.

"I know that it can be tempting to ..." Will paused, clearly looking for the right words. "It might be best to be alone right now, you know? Sometimes we're the only ones with the answers we need."

45

"So you're telling me not to get a rebound? Aren't you the one who hooked up with a different girl every day for a week after Jenny dumped you?" Daisy asked.

Will rolled his eyes. "When you say it like that I sound like an asshole."

"Oh, aren't you?" Daisy teased.

She didn't want to think about Hana right now. She didn't want to talk about how she didn't have the guts to go get Hana's journals from her house. Luckily, Will went along with the topic change.

"So funny. Would an asshole give you full reign over his car though? And leave a six pack in your hiding place?" Will tilted his head as he spoke. Daisy smiled — he knew she kept her contraband that she didn't want their dad to find in her broken nightstand. The drawer appeared to be stuck unless you reached into the back of the stand and pushed it at a certain angle. Daisy had told him about it once when Henry almost caught Will with a joint.

"Are you campaigning for brother of the year again?" Daisy asked.

Will laughed. "Of course. When am I not?"

"Last week you ate my lunch because I got home from work five minutes late," Daisy pointed out.

"Alright, alright. Even with the slight sandwich stealing, you know you're gonna miss me," Will said.

"Obviously I'll miss you. You know how to make my coffee."

"You know if you told dad how you like your coffee, he would just start making it that way."

Daisy shrugged. "Yeah, but then he would make that face. You know the one where his eyes drop and his shoulders sag? The kicked puppy one?"

"Yeah, I know the kicked puppy one. I got it when I asked him if I could still go on my study abroad trip."

"Well, he's always told you to go see the world while you're young, to be fair."

"True." He sighed, glancing over his shoulder towards the driveway. "Look, my ride is almost here. Just remember what I said, okay? Be smart about who you let in when you're vulnerable. I won't be here to protect you for a few weeks."

She set down her coffee cup and hugged him. A moment later, her father shuffled down the stairs.

"Will? Are you ready to go? Mrs. Sanders just pulled up. It looks like she's right on time," Henry called from the front of the house. Daisy trailed after Will on his walk to the door, wishing she hadn't wasted so much time moping the past few weeks.

"I'm all set now," Will said.

Henry's eyes flicked to Daisy. "Having a last-minute chat?" He asked, oblivious to the fact they were talking about him.

"Yeah. You know, brotherly advice and such," Will joked.

"Yes, of course." Henry chuckled. "Speaking of advice — you will have to be smart out there, alright? Stay with your class, but don't forget to leave some time to explore the city and see what it's really like. Don't look like a tourist, though. That'll make you a target. And don't get in any trouble, but if you do, make sure that you try to resolve it peacefully. But above everything, of course, be yourself and have fun." Daisy wanted to roll her eyes at the advice, which her father had already relayed to Will in about a hundred different ways the past few days.

"All I got from that was have fun, so I'll just stick with that," Will teased, winking at Daisy over Henry's shoulder.

"Yeah, yeah, yeah." Henry paused, a proud look on his face as he gazed at his son. "Now get out there before Mrs. Sanders leaves without you."

"Sir, yes, sir." Will saluted before slinging his duffel bag over his shoulder and grabbing the handle of his rolling suitcase. Henry pulled Will into a quick hug, murmuring something to him that Daisy couldn't hear. Will nodded in reply and gave Daisy another wave before he strode out the door. The pair watched Will as he packed his things into the trunk and slid into the backseat of the Sanders' SUV. Will looked back one time, waving at them through the window until the car turned off the street.

"I guess it's just us for the next few weeks, huh?" Henry asked.

Daisy nodded, a small smile on her face. "It'll be weird."

"So what were you and Will talking about before I got down here?" Henry said with false casualness.

She panicked, trying to think about an answer that wasn't Hana or Henry. "Boy stuff," she blurted out.

Henry quirked up an eyebrow. "Boy stuff? I thought we agreed on no boys until you're 30?"

"Well, to be fair Dad, you said that, and I never agreed," she joked. Daisy wondered how he would feel about how she took advantage of the biggest loophole in his stupid rule. Technically, he didn't say anything about dating girls.

"Alright. Just be careful. Especially with … you know. Grief can make people act erratic. I just want you to be … safe."

"Dad, I'm not going to do anything. It's fine, you don't need to worry," Daisy reassured him.

"Okay, of course. And you know … I trust you and everything. You can talk to me about stuff, you know that, right?"

Daisy wanted to burst out laughing at his words, but instead she just nodded. "Thanks dad."

"Even Hana. I know that she was your best friend. You know, back when Mark died … I was miserable. I tried not to let it show for you kids, but he was a good friend. A good man." Henry's voice was gruff, thick with emotion, like his friendship with Hana's father was a sludge that he needed to choke down if he wanted to talk about it.

Daisy clenched her jaw to keep her own emotions at bay. "I didn't know you were struggling back then. I'm sorry I didn't—"

Henry waved her off, his wide, wrinkled face fighting gravity to quirk up the corners of his lips. "Of course you didn't. Parents aren't supposed to show their kids they're struggling." He paused. "Did you ever call Noriko about stopping by to look through Hana's things?"

"Oh. No, I forgot with ... everything going on."

Henry had gone over to drop food off at the Holm's house a few times, but Daisy still wasn't able to bring herself to even drive through their neighborhood.

"You should. She'd be glad to hear from you, you know," Henry prompted. He was giving her the perfect opening to go snoop through Hana's room, but the thought of poking around for things Hana never wanted her to see when she was alive felt wrong.

"I'll call her later," Daisy said unconvincingly.

Henry fixed her with a look that made her sigh. "It's too early to call her now," Henry relented, "But you have nothing else to do today. Throw her a bone."

Daisy nodded forlornly and walked back towards the kitchen to place her mug in the sink. "I really want a greasy breakfast sandwich. I'm gonna head to a drive thru, do you want anything?" Daisy asked.

Henry shook his head. "I'm trying to be healthier, remember?" She tried to miss the way his eyes dropped to her body in judgment for a moment before she turned away to slip on her shoes.

"I'll pay for it if you promise to call Noriko later," he said. She sighed and nodded, and Henry handed her a ten-dollar bill along with Will's car keys. The plastic Fairfield University keychain clinked in protest to her quick movements.

When she got in the car, she half hoped Hana would appear as she did on Thursday, and she was disappointed to find that she was alone. The old car's radio puttered out some top forty pop song, and Daisy shook her head, cursing her expectation.

A part of her wanted the ghost to be real so badly just to have the chance to see Hana again, even if it was this version of Hana that just wanted Daisy to solve her murder, even if this version of Hana couldn't love her like the live version could. Even if it was just an echo of Hana's real voice yelled over a canyon Daisy couldn't cross.

Getting a greasy breakfast from the McDonalds ten minutes from her house didn't do much to bring her comfort. She remembered when meals like this were a special treat, but now it just felt like she was trying to fill a void that grew deeper by the second. Driving her brother's car without worrying that he would need it later should make her feel free, not hollow.

She wondered if Noriko was awake now, just past seven a.m. on a Saturday. If Noriko was coming off her nursing night shift at Highland Hospital, she might still be up. Daisy decided to go to the Holm house and started driving before she could second guess her decision.

When Daisy parked her car next to the Holm's mailbox, a few windows were cracked open, and the sound of NPR floated across the lawn to her. Noriko was always careful about closing windows when she was out or asleep, a habit she had drilled into Hana's mind after watching a few too many episodes of 60 Minutes.

Daisy didn't know if the discomfort in her gut was from the greasy food, the anxiety at having to face Hana's mom, or the thought of going into the room where Hana died, but either way she felt out of her depth when she picked up her phone and called Noriko.

"Hello?" Noriko answered after a few rings, sounding tired.

"Oh, hi, sorry if I woke you up, Mrs. Holm," Daisy responded, suddenly worried she'd been wrong. Maybe Noriko was beginning to let old habits slip.

"Daisy! Hello! No, you're fine, sweetheart. I just got home from a shift, so I'm still up. What can I do for you?"

"Okay, great. I was worried I'd woken you up." Daisy paused. "I was in the neighborhood, and I was wondering if I could stop by and look through Hana's stuff?" Daisy heard Noriko's intake of breath, sharp and sudden as the first drops of rain in a sun shower.

"Yes, of course. The door is unlocked — come in when you get here. I'm just having breakfast," Noriko answered.

"Okay, great. See you soon," Daisy said.

"See you soon," Noriko answered before hanging up. Daisy took a few deep breaths, trying to force the tight feeling in her chest to expand. She just needed to rip off the Band-Aid, and then she could stop forcing herself to skip this street during her drives. Maybe she could stop having nightmares about Hana's brain splattered on the walls of the room where they shared their first kiss.

Daisy took another deep breath before making her way to the front porch. Opening the front door was familiar, but when she toed off her sandals, she felt like she was walking across a room covered in broken glass and trying not to let any of the shards tear at the soles of her feet.

Noriko stood alone in the kitchen, looking out at an old oak tree in the side yard. Early morning sunlight poked through the branches dappled the windowsill with spots of gold. She turned when Daisy walked in, and the bright smile on her face contrasted with the bags under her eyes.

"Daisy! It's so good to see you. I've missed having you around the house. Do you want anything? I could make coffee if you're in the mood for—"

"Oh, thanks, Mrs. Holm," Daisy broke in, not wanting Noriko to start offering more things only for Daisy to end up rejecting them. "I just had breakfast, though, maybe another time."

"Oh, yes, of course. How are you doing, sweetheart?" Noriko asked, her own mug of coffee clutched in her hands.

Daisy didn't know how to answer. Her relationship with Noriko was always hit or miss. Hana frequently got in fights with her mother, but at the end of the day they loved each other. Daisy tried to be friendly but not overly friendly so that it wouldn't be obvious that she was just going along with whatever Hana's mood was. Now, without Hana there for Daisy to read, she found herself floundering.

If she told Noriko the truth and revealed that the ghostly version of Hana kept visiting her, Noriko would see Daisy as a grieving kid. Daisy decided on an almost-truth instead.

"I'm doing as well as I can be, I think. It's been … weird without her around," Daisy admitted. She wasn't sure if seeing the ghost of your dead ex-girlfriend could really be considered doing as well as you could be, but she thought it was a nicely ambiguous phrase that would satisfy Noriko.

"I understand that. I thought the house was empty after Mark, but now … I didn't know I would miss Hana's awful taste in music, but here I am." Noriko's eyes brightened with emotion, the black of the pupils glinting with fragments of the reflection of the yellow light bulbs hanging over the kitchen island.

Daisy didn't know how to respond. "Yeah. She did have a weird taste in music. Always a surprising number of eighties pop songs." Daisy laughed uncomfortably.

"Of course, she got that from Mark." Noriko laughed. She fell silent after she spoke, lost in her thoughts, and Daisy stayed quiet too, not sure what to say. Noriko snapped herself out of it after a few long seconds, and she smiled weakly at Daisy.

"You're welcome to take anything in Hana's room. Dennis said they did a good job cleaning things up," Noriko said, sipping at her coffee.

"Oh, okay. That … sounds good. I'll just—"

"What did Hana and you fight about?" Noriko asked abruptly.

"What?" Daisy swallowed hard, trying to recall the excuses she gave her dad about why she wasn't speaking to Hana the week before her death.

"The two of you weren't talking when she ... Was it a lovers' quarrel? Or something serious?"

Daisy's eyes widened, and Noriko gave her a sad smile as though she hoped this wouldn't be Daisy's reaction. As if Daisy was supposed to know that Noriko was in on her biggest secret.

"I, I don't — what are you—"

"Daisy, sweetheart, I've known for some time that you and Hana were more than just friends. I was waiting until you were comfortable enough to share it," Noriko revealed.

Daisy's heart sped up, and she had to remind herself to breathe. "I don't ..."

"I know that when Hana told us she was a lesbian, Mark and I weren't as supportive as we could've been. I know the ways ... I know I hurt her. So I wanted to wait until both of you were ready, but I've known."

Daisy felt like ice was pumping through her chest, infecting all her veins and making her hands shake with the chill. "Please don't tell my dad," she said before she could stop herself.

Noriko looked a little sad at her words. "Of course. I made the mistake of outing Hana to family members before she wanted me to, and she ... told me that it wasn't okay. I wouldn't tell Henry," Noriko said quickly.

"Right. Of course. Sorry, I just ... Hana never said anything about you knowing about us."

"I only talked with her about it a few times, but I wish I'd made it easier for the two of you to be yourselves here. I'm sure I could've done something, said something, but ..." she paused, her eyes turning glassy before she blinked away the tears. "I regret a lot of things I didn't say. A lot of things I didn't tell her."

Silence settled into the room, wrapping arms around each of them like a familiar friend, tucking them into its chest until there was nothing to hear but a distant neighbor mowing their lawn.

"I'm ... I'm gonna go look through Hana's room now if that's okay," Daisy said, filled with a rush of relief when Noriko just nodded at her and released her from the conversation. Daisy was so happy to be away from Hana's mom that she forgot all about her anxiety about going into Hana's room until her hand was on the doorknob.

The last time she was in this room she didn't know a thing about what was coming. She was still with Hana and still thought they'd be together forever.

Everything fell apart so quickly since then. All the memories of this place she knew so well were flickering through her mind like colors in a kaleidoscope, distorted flashes of moments all passing in and out of her vision as she opened the door.

Daisy expected something dramatic and tragic to happen, but it was anticlimactic, the way that these things always were.

Hana's room *was* different, but it was subtle. Daisy knew some things would be gone considering how Hana died, but it was still a shock to see the differences.

In place of the band posters above her bed there were rectangles of darker paint where the sun couldn't bleach the color over the years. Hana had repainted her room in the seventh grade, and Daisy marveled at the fact she never noticed the sun lightening the blue over the years. Hana's mattress was gone as well, just the box spring exposed on her oak bed frame remained.

The changes felt uncanny, like Hana took all the homey, comforting feelings from the space with her when she died here. The spirit of Hana was sucked out of this room.

Daisy pulled open the closet doors and was greeted with an overwhelming waft of Hana's perfume. It was a clean, masculine scent with a bright snap of vanilla, and Daisy half expected for Hana to appear in her real, living form right in front of her. She heard somewhere that smell and memory were closely linked, but she didn't know how closely until that moment. This was the scent that lingered in the corner of her daydreams, the one that held her while they watched movies, the one that she would smell in her bed the day after Hana stayed over. Tears rolled down Daisy's cheeks before she could stop herself from crying, and she cursed herself for breaking down so easily.

She closed her eyes for a moment and let herself pretend that none of this was real, but when she opened her eyes, the mattress was still gone and the posters' reverse shadows were still on the wall. She heaved a shaky breath and reminded herself why she was there. She was on a mission, and she couldn't accomplish it by standing here and crying over the scent of Hana's perfume.

She started rifling through the bottom of the closet where a layer of random odds and ends had accumulated over the years. She passed over old algebra tests, book bags she recognized from Hana's middle and high school years, random pieces of jewelry, and small souvenirs Hana collected and discarded from the vacations she used to take with her parents during school breaks. Daisy opened a plastic bag that was tied shut with a knot, only to find Hana's mud caked rain boots. Daisy scrunched her nose at the smell and closed the bag up again as quickly as she could.

She didn't find anything that seemed like a clue, nothing that could bring her any closer to who killed Hana. Still, she pulled a few sweaters off their hangers, the ones that Hana bought to be oversized but that would still comfortably fit Daisy. Noriko was expecting her to take something, and she could hide Hana's journal in the folds of these sweaters easily enough.

Daisy moved around things on Hana's desk and nightstands until she discovered the constellation covered composition notebook she remembered seeing Hana carry around for the past six months — her latest journal. Hana loved journaling, loved pouring out everything in her head with the thought of being able to look back at it someday. Once Hana caught Noriko reading one of her journals and she was mad at her for over a month, so Daisy never had a burning desire to read them. Daisy upset Hana on accident often enough that she never wanted to do it on purpose, especially not like this.

Daisy looked around the room to see if there was anywhere else she could look, but she didn't have the willpower to look under the bed, gripped with the visceral fear that the professional crime scene cleaning crew missed something. Her eyes caught on the only makeup that Hana ever routinely wore, a tube of lip gloss, sitting on the edge of the vanity. Hana had gotten her first tube from her grandma in middle school and loved it because it tasted minty and made her lips tingle. As Daisy stared at it, debating whether or not she should take it, Hana appeared and picked it up herself.

"I love this stuff. I hope when I get to heaven they have, like, a vat of it. That would be cool," Hana said, tossing it from one hand to the other.

"You sure about that direction?" Daisy joked, but it fell flat if Hana's tight smile was anything to go by.

"I'm feeling hopeful that I get some only-the-good-die-young points. But who knows. I guess we'll find out if God really does hate gay people, huh?" Hana replied dryly. She held out the lipgloss to Daisy, who took it and shoved it in her pocket before gathering up Hana's sweaters and journal.

"I'm doing this now. Sorry it took me so long, but something about Will leaving ... It's like I just woke up."

"I want to be mad at you, but ... you remember how I was after my dad died. So I can't really talk."

"Yeah, if you tried to solve his murder back then you probably wouldn't have succeeded."

"I don't think I succeeded this time," Hana said sarcastically, gesturing around her room, the place where she died.

Daisy felt ill. "Right," she choked out.

Hana grimaced and placed a hand on Daisy's arm, guiding her out of the room. "I have to go. I just wanted to check in quickly, but ... well, I would ask you to tell my mom I said hi, but I don't think that would work out very well."

"No, probably not."

"Alright. Well, good luck," Hana said, fading away again. Daisy sighed and stuffed the journal and sweaters into her bag before heading back downstairs.

Noriko was still in the kitchen, sipping coffee and doing something on her phone. She looked up when Daisy walked in and smiled.

"Well, I'll probably head out. My dad is expecting me back," Daisy said.

"Of course. Tell him I say hello, won't you? And thank him again for the food. He's been so kind." She glanced at her hands, clasped in front of her. "And you know, he may react better than you think. If you wanted to tell him. I'm sure he might understand your grief more if he knew."

Daisy wanted to tell Noriko that she didn't know anything, but instead she just smiled and nodded. "I'll tell him you say hi."

When she opened the front door, Hana's ghost stood there, staring past Daisy with a tortured expression. Daisy glanced over her shoulder and saw Noriko standing there, ready to close the door behind her.

"Thanks again," Daisy said, not wanting to seem odd for suddenly looking back.

"Of course. Come back anytime," Noriko said. She shut the door once Daisy was outside of it, but Hana stayed there. Daisy walked past her and got in the car, where Hana's ghost once again appeared in the passenger seat.

"Is my mom okay?" she finally asked.

"No, she's not okay. She thinks you killed yourself." Daisy handed the ghost the pile of her things.

"So you finally believe me?" Hana asked.

"I don't know, but I want to find out. I mean ... what's the harm in just doing some research?"

"I knew it. I knew you'd help me." Hana smiled widely.

"I did promise I would always be there for you, even if you didn't promise it back, right?" Daisy said.

Hana flinched. "Yeah, you did. I didn't deserve it then, and I probably don't deserve it now."

"Sounds like something I want to hear and not something you would say." Daisy pointedly focused on the road and not Hana.

"I'm dead. New perspective, remember?" Hana said.

If the ghost was real, it was more likely that she was just saying what Daisy wanted to hear so that she would help her, but she didn't want whatever excuse or argument Hana would cook up as to why she was being honest and telling the truth this time. She'd already heard it all before in a hundred different iterations. Hana sighed and disappeared again, leaving Daisy to ride home in silence.

When she got home, she put the bundle of Hana's things on her bed and stared at it like it was a venomous snake. When she finally picked it up, Hana's ghost appeared, looking expectant.

Daisy glanced over at her. "Well, I guess I should start sleuthing now, huh?"

"Yeah. You're smart, Daisy. And I know I gave you shit for all those detectives novels, but I mean—"

"Now it's useful for you so it doesn't seem so stupid?" Daisy finished.

Hana winced. "Yeah, I deserved that one. I'll see you around." She disappeared again, and Daisy went to her desk to rifle around for a pocket-sized Moleskine notebook she bought a few months earlier. She bought the notebook when she visited Hana at college because Hana insisted that journalling would be good for her. Daisy only wrote her name on flowery script on the first page and jotted down one vague entry about her trip to New Paltz in it though. The problem with a secret relationship was that any time you wrote anything about it down, you created the risk of someone finding it and finding out everything. The journal was abandoned pretty much as soon as Daisy thought of her father reading about what she'd actually done when she visited Hana.

She left the journal entry alone and flipped to the next page, where she wrote "SUSPECTS" across the top of the page. She would have to make sure that no one found this as the contents would be pretty obviously about a murder investigation. Somehow, though, the thought of her father discovering she was researching Hana's death seemed less world-ending than him finding out she dated Hana.

Hana's ghost was insistent that reading this journal would help, which probably meant that her murderer, and her father's murderer, was someone Hana knew. Daisy wrote the names of everyone close to Hana, then flipped a few pages and started writing.

. . . .

What I Know
- *Hana is dead*
- *Maybe it was murder?*
- *Mark Holm's gun killed her*

. . . .

She sighed and tucked the notebook into the pocket of the sweatpants she wore. She needed to start a habit of always keeping it with her.

"I hope this isn't a waste of time, Hana," she whispered, not knowing if the other girl could hear her, not knowing if the ghost was even real, and not knowing whether she could solve this mystery with one Moleskine notebook and her determination. She would have to try though, if not for Hana, then to prove it to herself so she might start moving on.

Chapter 6

Hana — age 16

12/31/15

Dear diary,

Well, it's almost 2016. 2015 has been a weird year. I should probably write some resolutions, but I don't know why I would. I mean, what's the point? No one ever follows their resolutions. I have goals for the year, sure, but most of them are sure things. Like, start looking at colleges and get my license so the car Mom and Dad got me for my birthday doesn't keep sitting in the garage unused.

Maybe I'll just have one resolution: get over this horrible, terrible, all-consuming crush on Daisy. It's getting ridiculous, honestly. Not that tonight will help at all. I mean, she's going to be at my house, hidden up in my room for most of the night, all dressed up. Well, I can start on that resolution tomorrow. That's the spirit of resolutions anyways, right?

I should probably go get dressed. I've been writing this while I wait for this stupid nosebleed to stop. Dad gave me his spray, but it can only do so much, and as much as I don't want to dress up, I definitely don't want to see what my mom would do if I got blood on my nice white shirt right now. At least she's letting me wear pants.

I can hear her obsessing over the floral arrangements right now. I should probably go. That's near the end of her checklist. Only a few items away from "make sure Hana looks like a human girl and not a gremlin for once."

Sincerely,
Hana

. . . .

Hana had barely tucked her journal back in its hiding place when there was a knock on the door.

"Hana? Are you ready yet?" Noriko asked.

"Not yet. You can come in," Hana replied.

Noriko opened the door and took in Hana with a scowl. "Why aren't you dressed yet? People will be here in less than an hour!"

"Nose bleed. Didn't wanna ruin my shirt. But I'm dressed besides that." Hana gestured at the dress pants she was wearing underneath her fuzzy bathrobe.

Noriko rubbed at her temples. "Of course you got a nosebleed. Well, anything that can go wrong, right? At least your hair looks nice. Are you doing makeup?"

"Maybe mascara," Hana said.

Her mother nodded. "If you want a little lipstick, I have some that would look nice," Noriko tried.

Hana gave her a look. "Mom, you know how I am with lipstick." It usually ended up smeared across her face because she forgot about it.

"Just for pictures, please?" Noriko asked.

Hana gave a dramatic sigh. "For pictures, sure, I guess," she relented. She would be wiping it off as soon as they were done taking their yearly photo.

"Great. I'll leave you to get ready, but be downstairs in twenty minutes, okay? Your nose should stop bleeding by then. If not—"

"I'll let you know." Hana ushered Noriko back out of her room.

Getting dressed and swiping on mascara only took a moment, and the only accessories she put on were the pieces she wore every day — a small silver cross necklace from her grandmother and a silver ring with a green gem she'd bought at the boardwalk during their family vacation that summer. She got Daisy a matching one, and the pair were rarely seen without them.

When Hana walked downstairs, her mom was speaking to the caterers with a wide, fake smile. Mark stood next to her, his arm casually slung around her middle, subtly claiming her as his. Hana wished she could hold Daisy like that, wished Daisy wanted to be held by her like that.

"I'm ready," Hana said. Her parents turned and smiled.

"You look great, honey. The pants were a great idea," Noriko admitted.

Hana held back a smirk, happy to be recognized for being right. "Thanks, Mom." She hoped her mother would forget she was supposed to put any more makeup on. This hope was, of course, in vain.

"Let me just put that lipstick on you real quick then we can do pictures. People will start arriving soon — you know that the Johnsons are always *so* punctual," Noriko said, reaching into the pocket of Mark's pants and pulling out a small black tube. Hana sighed, resigned to be prettied up by her mother.

"You look so grown up, Hana," Mark said, a bit of emotion leaking into his voice. Hana wished she would've hugged him and told him she loved him. But at that moment she didn't know he would die less than two months later, so she played it off.

"I *am* grown up, dad. I'm sixteen," she reminded him.

He laughed and squeezed her shoulder. "Of course, kiddo. I know that," he teased. She rolled her eyes and stood in place when her mom pulled them to the staircase where Noriko's camera was sitting on a tripod, already connected to the wireless remote in her hand.

Hana kept that picture hanging in her dorm — her dad smiling with one arm slung around Noriko's middle, his other hand placed on Hana's shoulder. Before he pulled them closer, he told a joke that was lost to time, and the ghost of a laugh was in the smile on her face.

Even Noriko's smile was genuine, her eyes crinkling with laughter in spite of how stressed she was every year hosting this party.

Taking the picture was quicker, more painless than previous years, though Hana didn't want to admit it was because she wasn't putting up as big of a fight as usual.

"We should do a last-minute check, Nori," Mark said. "Hana, you're free to go wipe off that lipstick with something that isn't your shirtsleeve." Hana scampered off to the nearest bathroom, annoyed that even after scrubbing at her lips there was still a faint red stain left behind.

Before the party really got started, when there weren't as many prying eyes, Hana walked confidently into the kitchen and plucked one of the almost countless bottles of champagne from the fridge before turning and confidently walking out of the kitchen. Her parents bought cases of expensive champagne for every New Year's Eve party for the midnight toast. There were always leftover bottles that Noriko and Mark broke out during special occasions throughout the year, so the bottle she swiped wouldn't really be missed.

When she passed through the entryway, she saw her father and tried to hurry more, but his always-observant eyes saw the bottle. He held a finger to his lips before tilting his head towards her mother, who was chatting amicably with one of the waiters. Hana smiled brightly at him and took it upstairs.

This was the first year that she'd felt she could get away with sneaking the adults' drinks. Hana didn't really drink aside from when she went to parties, but she only went to a few before she swore off them. The boys there treated her like a novelty, either trying to get her to kiss straight girls who wanted to "experiment" for their viewing pleasure or insisting that she couldn't *really* know that she was a lesbian if she'd never been with a guy before. They never liked when she used their logic back on them and asked how they knew they weren't gay if they'd never kissed a man.

She placed the bottle on the floor below her window, arranging the curtains in a way that hid it from view if her mother were to pop her head in. She glanced outside and saw the Polos walking up, and she bounded out of her room and down the stairs to greet them.

"Perfect timing!" Hana exclaimed as she walked down the stairs, looping her arm through Daisy's. Daisy gave her a dazzling smile in return.

"Great to see you, Hana. How was your Christmas?" Henry asked, handing his coat to the boy they hired to run a coat check out of their front den for the night. This party may have been hosted at the Holm house, but the Holms didn't really lift a finger once the guests arrived. Hana's father insisted on hiring staff so that Noriko could enjoy the night she spent so long planning. Hana was happy with the decision because it meant that her mother wouldn't give her tasks all night like she did when they hosted smaller dinner parties.

"It was good! My parents always give the best gifts," Hana replied easily. Henry smiled at her warmly.

"Wonderful. I'm glad you enjoyed it. Now, do you know where your father is? I have something for him," Henry said before looking over his shoulder towards the rest of the party.

"Last I saw my dad was in the living room," Hana said, trying to be helpful.

"Thank you, Hana. Will, Daisy — you two behave. None of that fighting, you hear me?" Henry pointed his finger at each of his children for a beat before turning and walking away. Daisy rolled her eyes and Will slunk away, probably to see if he could use his height to trick the wait staff into thinking he was of age.

"You and Will get into a fight?" Hana asked, walking Daisy towards the dining room where there were appetizers sitting out to be picked at.

"Yeah. Same old dumb stuff. Mom was big on New Year's resolutions, and I wanted to do that today, but Will said it was pointless because no one keeps their resolutions," Daisy complained.

"That's annoying. Even if you don't stick with resolutions, what's the harm in having them?" Hana asked, though she agreed with Will.

Daisy nodded, shooting a glare at Will's back. "Exactly, it's not about the goals. It's about trying to be closer to Mom. I mean, I barely remember her anymore. He's just being a baby about it."

Hana sighed and pulled her friend into a slightly awkward side hug. "Well, you can keep it alive, and when Will realizes what he's missing, he'll come around. Boys are idiots anyways."

Daisy laughed. "You've got that right," she said, her smile starting to return.

The pair combed through the buffet, taking too many of the small cakes and cookies and a handful of the savory dishes as well in an attempt to keep some form of balance. They ate perched on either arm of an armchair with their feet in the middle, earning a disapproving glance from Hana's mother that they pretended not to see.

They people watched and chatted about nothing important, and when the clock began to wind towards midnight, Hana directed Daisy upstairs, snatching two glasses of sparkling cider on the way.

"Cider? Bold choice, Holm," Daisy joked.

"You know me. I live life on the edge," Hana quipped back, earning a golden laugh from Daisy. When they were sitting in Hana's room, she flipped on her TV to show Times Square glittering away behind a crowd of too many cold faces. The sounds of the party were muted by Hana's closed door, and Hana turned down the volume on the pop singer obviously lip synching on TV. Something settled over them, like a glowing, buzzing aura so delicate that anything loud or sudden would destroy it. Hana knocked back her sparkling cider before retrieving the stolen champagne with a grin.

"I got this before the party started, so it might be a little warm," she said. "I was hoping that being by the window would help, but I'm not sure it did." She tore the foil off the top of the bottle.

"You know I've never had champagne warm or cold, so I have no taste to compare it to. I think it'll be fine," Daisy said. Hana had brought Daisy to one of the last parties she went to a few months earlier, and Daisy had a few drinks, but she hadn't really gotten drunk. Will drove them home after the party, and he sent Hana a very long text saying that Hana was an idiot and Daisy shouldn't have been drinking for the first time at a party. Hana never told Daisy about the text. Daisy hated how overprotective her brother could be.

"I also don't know if this will go everywhere. I watched a tutorial online on how to open champagne, but we'll see if it was bogus advice or not," Hana said. She wrapped a t-shirt around the cork and twisted it, hoping that it wouldn't send a spray of the fizzy liquid across the worn hardwood floors of her room. Luckily when the cork popped, nothing sprayed out. Later, they would call it a sign that the night was meant to be theirs, but for now it was just convenient.

"You're an old pro. Are you sure this is your first time?" Daisy teased.

Hana laughed and poured them both glasses. "Cheers?" she said, holding her glass out.

"What should we cheers to?" Daisy asked, swirling her drink around in her glass and watching the bubbles shoot up in the center of her glass.

"To friendship?" Hana suggested. Daisy gave her a smile tinged with something Hana didn't quite recognize.

"To friendship," Daisy agreed, clinking their glasses together. They both took sips, and Hana was surprised by the feeling that the champagne left on her tongue. Daisy let out a small laugh of disbelief.

"It's like fireworks, isn't it?" Hana said. "Like fireworks on your tongue." Hana took another sip and echoed Daisy's joyous laughter. They both downed their glasses in a few seconds, and Hana poured them each another one, still giggling at the light feeling in their chests and the bubbles dancing on their tongues.

On the screen behind them, the final countdown began. Hana glanced over at it, suddenly aware of the fact that Daisy hadn't leaned back after Hana poured her more champagne, and now they were sitting with their knees almost touching. It wasn't unusual for them to be close; when they were younger they held hands everywhere they went, and as they got older that turned into them constantly draping themselves all over each other. Even after Hana came out things didn't change, mostly because Daisy made sure they didn't. But it usually didn't feel like this, like there was a delicate hum of energy between them telling Hana to lean in, to figure out any and every way that she could possibly be closer to Daisy.

As the crowd on screen counted down from five, Hana swore that Daisy felt it too, the invisible string between them, and Daisy's gaze darted from Hana's eyes to her lips. Hana inhaled shakily, and as the ball dropped and everyone celebrated the New Year, Daisy grasped Hana's cheek and pulled her forward into a tentative kiss. In that moment, every other kiss Hana ever experienced was reduced to a high school production, and this one was a broadway show. Her world was shifting, all her thoughts reduced to the feeling of Daisy's soft lips and the warmth of her hand against Hana's face. The kiss was tentative, a question, and Hana kissed back with all of the hope and love she kept locked away for so long.

The little gilded box where she stored all her feelings for Daisy burst open, and an explosion of longing and lust and desire and *love* all poured out into the kiss. Hana forgot about the glass of champagne in her hand until she spilled some on her lap, and she pulled away with a guilty smile, laughing at herself.

"Happy New Year," she said, barely an inch from Daisy.

Daisy let out a laugh and sat back. "Was that okay?" Daisy asked, sounding breathless.

"More than okay," Hana said, then she had a thought she had to voice, but first she knocked back the rest of her champagne. Daisy giggled and copied her, taking both of the glasses into her hands and placing them gently on the nightside stand. "I mean, it was okay if you actually wanted to kiss, you know, *me*, and not just someone at midnight. Was that what it was? Because if it was—"

Daisy cut Hana off with another kiss, this time using both of her hands to cup Hana's face and pull her closer. Hana placed one hand on the side of Daisy's throat and another on the back of her head, knotting her fingers into Daisy's curls to pull her closer. The hum in the room had grown to a symphony, and Hana's love for Daisy was harmonizing with the fire the kiss ignited in her. There was no going back to friends from this kiss — it was life altering, and Hana's world was changed forever.

This time, Daisy pulled away first, resting their foreheads together. Hana smiled, her eyes still closed from the kiss.

"Does that answer your question?" Daisy whispered. Hana didn't have to open her eyes to know the look on Daisy's face — a small smile quirked up more on the left side of her face than the right.

"I don't know, I think I may need more confirmation," Hana replied. Daisy laughed and kissed her again, and Hana's thoughts slowed to just one word repeating itself, an endless string of *Daisy, Daisy, Daisy* drowning out the party and the thoughts of what the year ahead would hold.

Chapter 7

Daisy — July 2019

DAISY MADE HER LIST of suspects and put off reading Hana's journal while she looked for alibis for all of them. It would probably make more sense to just rip off the Band-Aid and read the journal, but she couldn't get over the feeling that she was betraying Hana's trust.

Without reading Hana's journal or starting to investigate Mark Hom's death, all Daisy could do was try to cross off suspects by imagining possible motives. This mostly involved Daisy trying to remember any petty arguments between Hana and her friends and family as well as a fair bit of social media stalking, but she didn't find anything conclusive.

To be sure of alibis, she needed to figure out exactly when Hana died. Theoretically she could find out by getting a copy of Hana's autopsy report, but the thought of reading it made her sick, so she turned to social media.

There were accounts on Twitter and Facebook that posted about emergency calls in Penfield, and Daisy combed through both accounts looking for calls that could be about Hana. She knew that Noriko had found her, but she didn't know if Noriko called 911. Maybe Noriko screamed so loud that a neighbor heard. Maybe someone heard the gunshot, but Noriko got there before the police. If Noriko wasn't the murderer, there would need to be enough time after Hana died that the murderer could escape.

On Thursday, she found the tweet about Noriko's call.

· · · · ·

Penfield Scanner | @PenfieldScanner

Paramedics and police called to Fiddlers Hollow.
June 18th - 2:07 p.m.

• • • •

Daisy grimaced at the tweet but screenshotted it for her records. She wrote down the time of the tweet in her notebook and wondered how much time passed between Hana dying and someone calling 911. She switched over to look at the account's Facebook page and found the parallel post, but there were comments and replies under this post. She felt disconnected from her body while she read through them.

• • • •

Penfield Scanner
Paramedics and police called to Fiddlers Hollow.
June 18th - 2:07 p.m.
Comments:

Jody Thomas

This is just too sad. RIP Hana

Jennifer Foster

Such a tragedy. I heard a gunshot around 1:30 but thought it was a firework :(I wish I called it in. No mother should find their child like that.

• • • •

There it was. The answer to her question, right there in the Facebook comments. The name Jennifer Foster was familiar — the Fosters lived down the street from Hana. Mrs. Foster wasn't a big gossip or someone who sought out attention, so Daisy believed her comment.

It clearly wasn't a play for personal sympathy, more so a desperate need to share something that was eating her up inside. Daisy understood the feeling.

She crossed out 2:07 p.m. in her notebook and instead wrote "between approx. 1:30 p.m. and 2:07 p.m." She wanted to trust Mrs. Foster's timeline, but she couldn't hinder her investigation on a time that was *probably* accurate.

Daisy was brainstorming how she could possibly get an alibi out of Hana's mom and uncle when her phone buzzed with a text from Chrissy, Hana's best friend and roommate at New Paltz. Daisy opened the text immediately, not sure why the older girl would reach out.

· · · ·

Chrissy

Hey Daisy! So since none of us could make it up to the funeral we were thinking we could come up to visit the grave and have a little memorial just for our group. We were planning to be there around five on Friday, is that cool with you? We can do a different day if it's a bad time for you, we all really want you to come

· · · ·

Daisy stared at the message. She would go, of course, to try to rule them out as suspects. Would she be able to get their alibis without being too obvious about it? She would need to figure out how to ask everyone where they were when Hana died without alerting them to her investigation, but there was still time to consider that.

· · · ·

Daisy

That sounds great. The funeral sucked anyway. Too much preaching and crying. Hana would've hated it. I'm good for 5 on Friday tho, so I'll be there. Need me to bring anything?

Chrissy

Okay, awesome, I'm so glad you can make it. I'll let you know when we're close to picking you up. I think Skippy is driving bc she gets to use her mom's minivan so we can all fit

Daisy

Sounds good. I'm excited to see you guys, it's been too long

Chrissy

I know, right? See you then!

· · · ·

Daisy spent the week looking through the Instagram, Facebook, and even Twitter accounts of everyone on her list. Noriko stopped using social media after Mark died, a decision Daisy was beginning to understand more by the day, so it wasn't helpful for researching her. Dennis was fundamentally against social media, but Daisy still searched for anything from him despite sitting through his latest rant at Thanksgiving. Hana's friends weren't the type to tag their locations, and any stories they posted were long gone. Social media didn't give any easy alibis, so Daisy resigned herself to the most awkward line of questioning in the history of the world at the memorial on Friday.

She tried to think of subtle ways to bring up alibis, but by the time Friday came, she decided to wing it. She just hoped she could be somewhat present — she did like Hana's friends and seeing them would be nice. Her goal was mainly to rule them out as suspects so she could narrow her search, and she hoped she could do that while also gaining more insight into Hana's last year. There was a lot that Hana hid from her, but there were no secrets in a murder investigation.

Before Daisy left for work Friday, she laid out her clothes even though she knew she would have hours of time to get ready later. Facing the difficult decision of what exactly she should wear was a good distraction from the fact she didn't have any leads on Hana's case yet. Chrissy had made a group chat for them all, and Skippy let everyone know there was a party that her friend was having near one of the colleges downtown that they would go to afterwards. So Daisy needed to wear something that was appropriate for both her ex-girlfriend's memorial and a college party.

She ended up opting for a pair of black denim shorts, a dark gray tank top, and a collection of gold rings and necklaces so her outfit wouldn't be so plain next to whatever Hana's friends showed up in. She was sure they would look good.

After getting dressed, Daisy grabbed a random tote bag from the back of her closet and slipped the warm six pack of beer she bought for the occasion into it, concealing it with a sweater. She wouldn't have to worry about driving, so she could drink with other people again.

Just after five p.m. Chrissy texted her that they were out front, and Daisy took a deep breath before going outside to greet the group.

"Daisy! Hi!" Skippy yelled from the open window of a burgundy minivan. Victor leaned forward to wave from the passenger seat, and the back door of the van opened to reveal Aaron and Chrissy. Daisy waved back and watched Aaron start climbing back into the third row. Daisy gave them her first real smile in days.

"This seat is all you," Aaron said, patting the headrest with a smile.

"Thanks! And thanks for inviting me," Daisy said, climbing into the van.

"Yeah, we knew we wanted you to come as soon as we started planning it," Victor said. They turned to look in the back seat, and their smile warmed the cool, sharp lines of their jaw.

"Of course," Daisy said. "Honestly, the funeral sucked. It's good that you couldn't make it — there were all these people that barely talked to Hana in high school there, all acting like they knew her. And it was all really religious — I think you would've gotten hives, Vic," Daisy joked. Victor regularly went on long rants against the actions of the Catholic Church. Daisy caught one the only time her dad had let her visit Hana, but Hana also texted her a multitude of times telling her that Victor was on another one of what Hana deemed their Morally Upright Anti-Church Monologues. Victor knew it bothered Hana, but it didn't stop them from launching into their spiel anytime the Church was mentioned.

"Probably true. Think I'll catch fire as soon as we cross onto sanctified ground?" they joked as if keeping the tone light would stop this from feeling so debilitatingly depressing.

Hana's friends were mostly from Brooklyn and Long Island, so they were convinced that upstate New York was just a hellscape of conservatives and cow pastures. While they weren't entirely wrong, it still bothered Hana, and Daisy by extension, that they judged a place they had never visited. Hana often tried to convince them that even if upstate sucked, the actual city of Rochester had some great spots. The group finally agreed to come visit during the summer, partially because Skippy had an older friend that went to the University of

Rochester, and she wanted to visit him. Hana planned to show them all the sights of Rochester — Daisy helped her when she started planning the trip. Now she wondered if the itinerary was ever finished.

Without Hana here to pull Daisy into the group, she felt like an outsider, despite their obvious efforts to include her.

"So Daisy, how's your summer going?" Chrissy asked. Chrissy had been Hana's roommate for the spring semester after Hana's first roommate transferred to another school.

"Boring to be honest. My brother is gone, and I've just been working. It honestly feels like I'm just crawling through the days until I leave for school," Daisy said. She was excited to go away to college, but she didn't think New Paltz would ever feel like home the way it had for Hana. Daisy hid herself in different ways than Hana did.

"Same," Chrissy said. "I hate working, though. Doing swim lessons for spoiled kids sucks." Daisy laughed, and the group moved into stories about weird customers at their jobs. They laughed like they meant it, but also like they were trying not to think about what was coming.

When the cemetery's gates came into view, the group got quiet. Skippy pulled over to the side of the road outside of the cemetery.

"You can drive onto the paths," Daisy explained.

"This mammoth doesn't corner well. My mom told me not to park outside," Skippy responded. They all got out and turned to Daisy since she was the only one who knew how to get to the grave.

"Right. Well, now I feel like some weird tour guide. Should I walk backwards?" Daisy joked, trying and failing to raise the mood.

They walked silently to Hana's grave, which was marked only with fresh dirt. Daisy asked about the missing gravestone the day after the funeral, and Henry told her that Noriko was still waiting for the gravestone she ordered to be engraved and placed.

Mark Holm's grave was next to Hana's, but his name was already carved into the dark gray granite of his headstone. The polished surface proudly proclaimed him a beloved father and caring husband. Noriko's name and birthday was on the stone next to Mark's, with just the date missing, like it was waiting for the day she would join her late husband.

Daisy had come with Hana to plant flowers and tend to them the past few summers, though their last visit was in May. Daisy didn't notice the flowers at Hana's funeral, but it seemed someone else was tending to them now.

It felt wrong to have nothing marking Hana's grave, but as if Victor read Daisy's mind, they pulled a small lesbian pride flag out of their bag.

"I thought she would want that here. She was proud of who she loved," Victor said quietly, their eyes flicking to Daisy's face and then away.

Daisy held onto her flimsy belief that Hana was murdered and steeled herself to find out where everyone was when Hana died. She needed to do this for her oldest friend, for her only love.

"Why doesn't she have a gravestone? Her dad has a gravestone," Aaron said, staring at the dirt patch of Hana's grave.

"She won't have a gravestone for a little bit," Daisy replied. "I guess they take some time to engrave, and, well ... It's only been a month."

Daisy was the first to sit, a few feet from the end of the fresh dirt, facing where the gravestone would eventually go. The rest of the group sat on either side of the grave, though none of them would look down at it.

"I can read my thing first," Chrissy said, reaching into the pocket of her jean shorts to pull out a small piece of paper. Daisy knew that they were planning on reading things, but she still didn't have anything prepared. Much like her plan to gather alibis, she was hoping inspiration would strike. Hopefully she could wrangle her feelings into a cohesive thought when it was her turn.

Daisy stared at the group. She didn't belong there without Hana. After a year of college, they all seemed convinced they were both infinitely wise and constantly learning. Being around them was like being surrounded by variations of Hana, and Daisy possessed ample experience making herself small to fit into whatever narrative Hana was prizing that week. She got used to being whoever it was that Hana wanted her to be, a liquid personality that shifted to fit whatever standard Hana held her to at any given time.

When she stared around the circle of grief-stricken students, she realized she didn't care if they liked her. She didn't care to be pretty or pretentious or perfect for them. She didn't care to be the *right* image of the grieving girlfriend or ex-girlfriend or whatever they thought she was. She didn't care to pose correctly in their frame of reference. She felt free for a moment before Chrissy began.

"Meeting Hana was like seeing an old friend whose name you'd forgotten ... She — she wasn't a light; she was a flame. She burned so bright and when you got close enough, she kept you warm. I miss her so much, and not realizing she was burning out is one of the biggest regrets of my life." Chrissy paused, clearly trying not to cry. "I miss the way she argued with professors about what she believed, even when they told her she didn't have evidence to support her point. I miss how fearless she was at parties, making stupid guys do dares so we could get free weed or beer or even a hat that one time."

The rest of the group laughed, and Daisy smiled, though she wasn't in on their inside joke.

"When I found out Hana died, it was like a sun went out," Chrissy continued. "The entire night sky looks off without her star there." She let out a wet laugh. "Now I'm just mixing metaphors, so I'm going to wrap it up. Hana, if there's that afterlife you believed in, I hope it's everything you prayed for."

Daisy held back tears, and when she glanced up at the grave, Hana's ghost sat cross legged where her gravestone should be. She looked at her friends fondly, like seeing them together was a gift she couldn't properly thank them for. Hana smiled at Daisy. She wondered what Hana thought of Chrissy's speech.

"I can go next," Victor said, taking a deep breath. "I suck at writing things, so I just brought this poem. It's the one that they read in *Hill House* even though Hana thought that show wasn't good. I mean, memorials are for the living, right?" They went on to read the poem, one about how Hana wasn't gone; she was just *away*.

Daisy watched Hana's ghost, and her expression was something new. It reminded Daisy of the time she broke her ankle playing tag in Hana's backyard when they were still in elementary school. Hana tried to pick her up and carry her into the house to get help, but she just ended up dropping Daisy and hurting her more. Hana still apologized any time it crossed her mind, like she needed Daisy to know how much her mistake hurt her too.

Skippy also read a poem, but it was one that Daisy didn't recognize, and Skippy didn't try to give it context. The poet's name was clearly difficult to pronounce, but it rolled off Skippy's tongue like it was the easiest thing in the world.

"I also have a poem. But I wrote this one," Aaron said, volunteering to go next. Victor quirked up their lips.

"Show off," they teased. The group needed something small to laugh at. Then Aaron started reading the poem, and the lump in Daisy's throat got harder to swallow around. She couldn't bring herself to look at Hana's ghost.

. . . .

The weirdest thing about death
is the way it consumes life.
Making a cup of coffee

is never just making coffee again —
it's one more *I got to wake up*
and she didn't.

Beauty is tainted —
why didn't she get to see this?
Was she not as deserving
of the sight of a fawn
stretching its legs
in the morning light
streaming through the trees?

Maybe somewhere or somehow
she's still here —
maybe she's in the paradise she dreamed of,
or maybe she'll come back as someone else,
a familiar mind
dressed in foreign skin
and a new name.

One day, we'll follow her
to that place beyond the trees.
A place that makes the deer stand still.
A place where, I hope,
she is right now, dreaming.

• • • •

Hana's ghost was crying, and it surprised Daisy. Seeing Hana, who rarely cried, so blatantly breaking down felt more perverse and unnatural than the sight of a ghost sitting on its own grave.

"You have to find who did this," Hana choked out. "You can't let them keep believing I did this. I didn't want to leave them. I didn't *want* to die," she pleaded. Daisy gave the smallest nod she possibly could. She tried not to be jealous, tried not to let the fact that Hana hadn't cried over losing *her* make her bitter. She found it was easier, sitting on Hana's grave, to give her some grace. Later she would worry about it, but for now she was here, and it was her turn to speak. Everyone else had already said something and they stared at her expectantly.

She took a deep breath, trying to steady herself to begin. "When Hana died, I didn't know for a full day because we were fighting. We were always fighting. I think Hana's favorite thing was seeing how far she could push people, how much ground she could cover before the bungee cord would snap her back. But that's not really what you're supposed to talk about after people die, so I'll just keep those fights to myself." The group let out small, nervous laughs.

"Hana might've been the love of my life. She definitely was the love of the life I've led so far. Maybe that would've changed, maybe we were going to outgrow each other, but I always expected that we would be there for each other in some way. But she ... I think I always expected us to grow old together. Maybe as lovers. Maybe as friends that were too close for the comfort of our respective spouses. I looked up the time she actually died this week. I don't really know why," she lied, "but it felt like I should know the exact moment when all of the visions for the rest of my life shattered. The exact moment that meant we weren't making up from this fight. One-thirty p.m. on June eighteenth. A random Tuesday that meant that the entirety of my life was uprooted. I think I was sitting in a final at the time. I was trying to fight through pre-calc questions, and Hana was taking her last breath. God, it makes everything seem stupid now. It makes everything else feel small, insignificant, like I should've spent every moment of the days she was here with her, telling her that she was loved and that her future was stretching out like a promise, not a threat. But even if I did, who knows if she would've broken her promise. She's done it before." Daisy cut herself off, feeling like she was spiraling.

"I always hated pre-calc," she said, "but now that I'm going to always associate it with the moment that took away my best friend, it's even worse. Hana dying didn't just take her away, it took away all the things we loved together and all the things she loved on her own. And I'm going to miss all of it, all of her, even the parts that I probably shouldn't miss. She really was something, wasn't she?" The group was completely silent, all staring at the still-fresh dirt on top of the grave. Daisy wondered how long it would be until grass would grow over it. Would she know who killed Hana by then?

"God, Daisy," Victor said, wiping away their tears. Daisy let out a startled laugh, unsurprised that they were the first one to break the silence she sent them spiraling into.

"Sorry, I didn't prepare anything, so I just kind of dumped out my brain there."

"It was great," Chrissy said. "And I — I don't think it's weird that you looked up when Hana died. I was — I wanted to know too. God, now I have to remember where I was." Daisy's heart lifted. Her stupid, rambling, ill thought-out speech was working. It was doing what she wanted.

"Tuesday afternoons are when I teach stupid private swim lessons to these spoiled siblings that I know from the camp I usually work at," Chrissy said. "Their parents pay out the ass, though, so I always say yes when they open the pool at their house and ask me to come teach their kids. I remember that they were working on dives. The boy, Jackson, split open one of his toes on the edge of the pool and was crying like crazy, and I remember thinking 'Man, when I tell Hana, she's going to get a kick out of this.' But when I texted her, she didn't respond. Afterwards I felt stupid for texting her about something so dumb when she needed a real friend to help her. But now, well, she was already gone when I texted her. Maybe Jackson's toe wasn't even split yet, maybe the whole thing was after she was already gone."

They all sat in silence for a moment after Chrissy finished. Daisy watched her hand twitching toward her pocket where the outline of her phone was, and she felt guilty for making Chrissy think about whether her best friend was dead when she texted her about spoiled rich kids.

"I think I was on my way to pick up my brother from a test," Aaron said after a moment. He looked conflicted to continue, as if he was betraying Hana. "I wasn't thinking about her when it happened. I wasn't even … I don't know if I thought about her the entire day. I don't know if I even thought about her between picking up my brother and going home. I muted the group chat because everyone was annoying me on Monday. What if I didn't think about her the entire day she died?" he asked, pleading for someone to have an answer that would reassure him.

"I didn't think about her," Victor admitted. "Skip and I were at that stupid pre-camp training for counselors. They keep us busy every minute of the day trying to get us ready for camp as if we haven't been counselors there for years. I can't see Hana as the camp type, so there was nothing there to make me think of her, or what she was doing, or what she was going through." They stared at their hands, and Chrissy put a comforting hand on their shoulder.

"Vic, you couldn't have known," she said. "If *none* of us knew how bad she was struggling, she must've been hiding it on purpose. There's no way that all of us could've missed the signs." She tried to comfort them, but Victor didn't seem any happier.

"I texted her that day too," Skippy said softly. "I was asking what she thought about my summer class topic, and she responded. Around noon." The heaviness of the statement settled into the circle. Skippy was probably one of the last people to communicate with Hana before she died.

"And she didn't seem …" Aaron started.

Skippy shook her head fiercely. "No, she was just her normal self. Joking about the fact that being an English major was stupid, and I should've just stuck to being undecided. She thought it was funny I had to read *Frankenstein* again already after just reading it last semester." A few small chuckles broke out around the circle.

"That's just like Hana," Daisy said after a beat of silence. "She never let anyone know anything was wrong until she'd figured out how she was going to fix it. If she didn't have a plan yet, she didn't talk about her problems."

The circle sat in silence, and Hana's ghost disappeared again. Daisy wasn't sure if she had gone back to wherever she was before or just walked away so she didn't have to listen to everyone mourn her. Daisy reached into her bag and took out the six pack, cracking each can out of the biodegradable plastic loops holding it together and passing them around the circle. Victor, who was sitting closest to the grave, gently placed the extra can next to the pride flag, and Daisy smiled at the caring thoughtfulness of the gesture.

"To Hana," Daisy said, cracking her can open and holding it up in front of her. The rest of the group mimicked her actions and words, and her throat tightened at the sight. If only Hana, the real, *living* Hana, were here to join the circle, to complete it and fill the empty spot she left.

Daisy drank deeply, tipping her head back and polishing off her can of beer in under a minute. When she brought her head back to a neutral position, Skippy was staring at her with a small smile on her face.

"What?" Daisy asked her.

Skippy shook her head. "Hana always talked about you in this way like you were magic or something. Something untouchable. It's nice to see you just … be you. Not that you're not magic or anything, just — it's nice to see," she said.

Daisy laughed. "Yeah, Hana always did that with the things she loved. Everything was always on another level with her."

"She was just on another level," Victor added.

Daisy smiled. "Yeah. I guess she was."

85

Chapter 8

Hana — age 16

3/2/16

Dear diary,

Eight days since dad died. In a normal year, it would be seven days, but it's the leap year, so an extra day of shit. An extra day of people pretending to care about how I'm doing when they just want to gossip about me. And Daisy.

Daisy continues to be annoyingly perfect. And yeah, I know that's not fair to call her annoying, but it's like she knows what to do all the time and I hate it. I have no idea what I'm doing! I can barely get ready for the day without breaking down, and she's over there being the perfect girlfriend, making sure people don't talk to me when I don't want them to and collecting all my homework for me (and doing some of it for me when she can. Because of course she can do that).

And obviously I'm so grateful to have her but I also hate that she's doing so well and I'm not. And then I feel guilty for hating that she's okay and then I think about how much it must've sucked for her to lose her mom when she was, like, 4, and then I hate myself for hating her and then I break down again. I'm so lost. I couldn't talk to Dad about Daisy when he was alive, but if he was alive, I still could've talked to him about her without saying it was her. And ... I don't know. If he was here things would be so much better. Everything is worse without him. I'm worse without him. I don't know how I'm going to do any of this without him. How do you go on without the person you looked up to being there for you? How will I figure anything out ever? Who else will give me advice and still be there for me without judgment when I don't take it and everything goes wrong?

I don't know how I'm going to keep going.

Sincerely,

DAISY, PLUCKED

Hana.

. . . .

Hana coasted through the rest of her sophomore year, half out of touch with reality. Her teachers gave her grace, and her friends tried to be understanding but stopped inviting her to most things after she kept having breakdowns and leaving any time she bothered to show up. She spent a lot of time with Daisy, driving around with no particular destination in mind, listening to music, talking, and occasionally making out when they found secluded spots to park.

A few weeks before their sophomore and junior years started, Daisy got into Hana's car looking mildly upset. She still smiled when she saw Hana, though.

"Hi, love," Hana greeted her, already pulling out of Daisy's driveway.

"Hey." Daisy's reply was uncharacteristically half-hearted.

"Everything okay?"

"Yeah. Just — my dad thinks we spend too much time together. I think he reread one of his old books on grief or something and now he thinks that we're codependent." Daisy rolled her eyes.

Hana laughed and laced their fingers together before pressing a kiss to Daisy's knuckles. "Well, on the bright side, my mom has *once again* decided to opt for night shifts this week, so we can stay out as late as we want, and then we've got the place to ourselves. Did Will come through?" Hana asked. Daisy nodded, smiling as she half-pulled a bottle of sparkling wine out of her backpack before shoving it back in. It was much cheaper than what they drank the night of their first kiss, but it was close enough. Will could use his new fake ID when his old lacrosse teammate was working, and he was generous enough to supply them with whatever they wanted as long as they paid him back.

"Sometimes he can be alright."

Hana knew something was off. Daisy basically worshiped her older brother. "You guys get in another fight or something?"

"He figured us out."

Hana flicked her eyes over to Daisy, who looked more stressed than she expected. Hana trusted Will, but maybe Daisy knew something Hana didn't.

"He did? So he knows now?" Hana asked. She was relieved, not that she could tell Daisy. Their secret was fun at first, but it was starting to feel like she was being forced back into the closet. She still regretted never telling her dad.

"Yeah, he knows," Daisy said, "and he said he won't tell our dad, but — I don't know."

"I don't think that he would out you. He's a good guy." Hana squeezed Daisy's hand, and the younger girl squeezed back right away. Daisy was looking out the window, and Hana wished she wasn't driving so she could really look at Daisy, but they were on the highway now and the next exit wasn't for another minute.

"I know he is," Daisy said. "He just … you know, sometimes I'll annoy him and he snaps out something mean just because he can. It's a sibling thing. But it sucks when he does it, and I just hope he has enough sense in that empty head of his to keep this to himself."

"He will. And I mean, if he does say something what's the worst that can happen?"

Daisy whipped her head around to stare at Hana incredulously. "The worst that can happen? My dad knows. And, I mean, when you came out he was all 'I could never be like Mark. If that was my kid I don't know what I'd do,'" Daisy said, pitching her voice to mimic her dad's.

"He'd come around. I mean, when I first told my dad —" Hana cut herself off. She didn't really want to think about her dad.

"Sorry. I didn't mean to bring him up. I'm being dumb, I know," Daisy said, sensing Hana's shift in mood. They finally reached an exit and Hana got off and pulled into a grocery store parking lot. Red tinged her vision, and she took a deep breath to try to fight off the rage running through her veins like a drug.

"You kind of are," Hana said. The breathing method her mother recommended wasn't working, she needed to do something to let out the anger escaping from the black pit of grieving inside her. Everything she felt was consumed by the pit — all the good things and the beautiful things fell in right next to the ugly and bad things. Most days it just made Hana numb, but the pit was turning into a geyser, spitting all her sadness and confusion and anger out in Daisy's face.

"What?" Daisy said incredulously. She turned in her seat to fully face Hana now, her eyebrows pinching together. Her eyes searched Hana's face like she was looking for an explanation to Hana's sudden shift in mood.

"You're being kind of dumb. I mean, really, it isn't like your dad is going to kick you out. What are you so afraid of?" Hana turned to face Daisy too.

"I'm ... I don't know, Hana," Daisy said. "I just don't want everything to change, and everything will when I tell him. You think he'll still let me see you over so much? Do you think we'd be able to have sleepovers anymore? Do you think he'd ever trust me again?"

Hana could tell this wasn't the first time Daisy was asking herself these questions, but she still didn't see why her girlfriend was so hesitant.

"So you're scared to be out? To be seen with me? Is that it?" Hana asked. She wanted Daisy, always mild and tame, to be angry. Hana reached forward and placed her hand on the back of Daisy's neck and leaned in to kiss her. Daisy jerked back from her and looked around the crowded parking lot, and Hana followed the path her eyes took, jumping from a haggard mother to a twenty-something on their cell phone. No one was paying any mind to them, but Daisy was still tense beneath Hana's hand on her neck. It didn't matter that they were twenty minutes away from their houses, that the odds of anyone they knew coming here on a random Wednesday night in August were slim to none, Daisy still had to check.

"You know that's not it. It's not about being ashamed of you," Daisy said, her eyes flicking around once more before tugging Hana's hand off of her neck and grasping it tightly in her own. Hana loved when Daisy held her hand like this — firm but softly like she was precious enough to hold strong to but delicate enough to be gentle with. But Hana was too angry for gentleness to calm her right now. She ran her thumb over Daisy's knuckles, fighting against the rage inside her that told her to pull away from Daisy and leave her alone in this parking lot.

"I don't understand. I don't know if I can. I don't understand pretending to be anyone but yourself," Hana spurred her on.

Daisy let out a heavy sigh, like she was trying to calm herself. "I'm not pretending to be someone else. I'm just not showing my *dad* all of me. He puts a lot of pressure on me, okay? You of all people should understand stupid expectations from your parent when there's only one left," Daisy snapped, drawing her hands back from Hana's grip to wipe at her eyes.

Hana tensed, and Daisy swore under her breath.

Hana didn't know how to respond. Daisy was right, of course. Coming out to her mom after her dad died would have been a lot harder than doing it before. Her parents balanced each other, but things were off kilter now. She could go days without seeing her mom, and sometimes it was like both of her parents died that February night.

"Hana, I'm sorry," Daisy said. "I'm just — it's been a long day, and those guys were at the pool being creeps again, and I'm just, like, an exposed wire. I don't want to fight. Please, let's not fight." Daisy reached out this time to hold Hana's face. She didn't look around the parking lot first, so Hana did it for her. When she saw no one around, she placed her hands on top of Daisy's and sighed.

Of all the people to try to wind up, Daisy was one of the worst. The girl was gentle as her namesake, and just as easy to crumple. She never wanted to fight. Hana always needed to instigate it, and trying to fight with Daisy never started a fire in Hana the way she wanted it to. It just made her see a clear reflection of the ways she didn't deserve the kind, soft girl she loved.

"Of course. I'm sorry, love," Hana said. She wanted to feel normal again, to feel *something* again. She would set herself on fire if it meant she could feel some semblance of warmth among the burning. "I just ... I don't know what's gotten into me. Let's just forget about it, yeah? Why don't we go get some snacks, we can go back to my house, and we can watch that Sherlock movie you wanted to me to see." Daisy smiled and stroked Hana's cheek before removing her hands and wiping under her eyes again. Hana hated making Daisy cry, but she couldn't seem to stop herself from doing it sometimes.

"I just wish you wouldn't push me on it," Daisy said. "I'll do it when I'm ready. It's not about you, it's about me. I promise it's not you. You're, like, the only thing I'm sure of in my life. You're the only good thing that stays." Daisy turned away to rifle through her backpack. Hana knew what she was looking for and handed her the tissue pack she kept in the compartment in her glove box.

"I love you," Hana said. Her voice was gentle, and Daisy accepted the apology and the tissues, her fingers brushing against Hana's.

"I love you, too," Daisy said. Hana wanted to kiss her so badly, but she just smiled at the younger girl instead.

It went on like that for months. Hana pushed Daisy bit by bit, seeing how far until Daisy would snap at her. Hana didn't know *why* she needed to know how far she would have to push Daisy before she would finally get angry at Hana, but she did. Even though it would just make her feel guilty, she kept poking the bruise, harder and harder each time. She pushed Daisy and hoped to see what was in the center when she snapped Daisy in half. She thought it would be like hot caramel, burning but sweet once it cooled. Something still sticky even after you clean it over and over.

The day she finally pushed too far was on a frigid December afternoon when they were alone in Hana's house, laying on her bed. They were supposed to be celebrating the afternoon alone with a Christmas movie marathon, but it turned into another fight about staying in the closet.

"So when, Day? When will it be time for you to come out?" Hana asked. Daisy always played the long game, but Hana couldn't see the visions of the future Daisy crafted. She didn't recognize the person she was a year ago, so how was she supposed to know the person she would be in five years, in ten? Daisy was always so sure of a few things: her and Hana would be together, and everything would be alright.

"I don't know. Maybe college, but I guess it depends. I've been working on my dad, subtly dropping in stuff about bi people. He probably won't catch on because he's as thick as a cement wall, but—"

"College?" Hana exclaimed, sitting up.

Daisy sat up too, staring at Hana like she was a spooked wild animal. "Well, yeah, I mean—"

"Daisy, you're in the middle of your sophomore year. College is *years* away!"

"I mean, yeah, I know that, but we're already so far into this, and—"

Hana shook her head vigorously. "We know this is real. We know already that this works. We've been together for almost a year, Daisy. I'm tired of pretending like I don't love you."

"I've never asked you to—"

"Yes, you *have*. You're practically shoving me back into the closet. I'm not allowed to tell my mom. I'm not allowed to tell my friends. I'm not allowed to hold your hand in public. I'm not allowed to—"

"Hana, it's not you—" Daisy reached forward towards Hana, but Hana got off the bed.

"It's *never* me. It's always about you. But you know what? This is about me too. We're dating. You keep talking about the future we're going to have, but what about now? What are we going to do? Are we ever going to do anything besides sneak around and give each other little looks and have sex when my mom isn't home or with your dad down the hall and hope that he doesn't get curious about why we're watching TV so loud?"

Hana half-expected Daisy to relent like she usually did. But something was different in her eyes this time, and then Daisy was on her feet, face to face with Hana.

"It's always about you!" Daisy yelled, finally angry, finally feeding into the fire Hana had been stoking for most of their relationship. "It's always about *your* grief and *your* stress and how much *you* are hurt by what I do. I want to be here for you, and I love you, but have you considered how I feel? Do you think I *want* to be scared to tell my dad who I really am?"

Hana had been waiting to see what would leak out of Daisy now, so she kept pushing. "You're always afraid, Daisy. Always dreaming about a future when you're not doing anything to pursue it."

"Me? I'm the one not going after my future? What about *you*? You're barely trying in half of your classes even though you know you won't get into Columbia with your grades. Even though you *know* you're not trying your best. Why are you sabotaging everything you ever dreamed about and taking it out on me?"

Hana took a step back, surprised by the sting of Daisy's words. "What are you ... You don't — stop saying that! I'm trying! I'm just

— things are still hard after my dad!" Hana exclaimed, not knowing how things took a turn towards her own issues instead of Daisy's

"You've been calling me indecisive for *months*, and I've tried to ignore it because I know you're stressed and grieving, but I'm tired of this hypocritical bullshit!"

"Hypocritical? You think I'm a hypocrite?" Hana hadn't expected this. Daisy's gooey center wasn't caramel. It was lava, and it would never be sweet on Hana's tongue.

"Yes. You are," Daisy said. "You sit there and tell me I'm not doing anything for our future, but what have you done to help? At least I'm slowly chipping away at my dad. All you do is berate me for not doing what you want. But even if I did what you wanted, would it ever be enough? Or would it just be more of you thinking you know what you want and then being upset when you get it?"

"What do you mean?"

"Did you just want to be with me to see what would happen? Do you even love me?" Daisy asked, her voice breaking.

"What?" Hana said, utter confusion coloring her tone.

"Do. You. Love. Me?" Daisy asked, emphasizing each word.

"Of course I love you. I love you so much. I just — shit. What did I do to make you feel like this?" Hana asked.

Daisy laughed incredulously. "Hana you've been telling me for months that loving me isn't enough. Like everyone has to know for it to be worth it."

Daisy was crying. Hana's grief reached out its greedy hands to grab this moment, and she saw it for the trickster spirit it was. It told her the anger and pain would be worth it, only to sit back with bright eyes and watch Hana rip apart the only solid thing in her life. And now Daisy was crying and Hana was lost and the spirit was opening its black hole of a mouth to swallow the last bits of Hana whole.

"I'm sorry, Daisy."

"Maybe we should take some time," Daisy said, her voice cracking.

"No, I can't lose you," Hana pleaded. "You're the only real thing I have left. You're the one constant I have after my dad."

Daisy ran her hands through her hair and sighed. "Everything would change if I came out. Everything would be different. You can't have it both ways, Hana. You can't want me to change and not want to change yourself."

"You're right," Hana relented. The tables had turned faster than Hana could imagine. Now it wasn't Daisy cooling the situation down, appeasing Hana. It was Hana trying to make things work. All this time, Daisy made it look so easy, but Hana was floundering.

"I know I'm right," Daisy said. "I've — I've been right. For months, you've been saying the same thing and not listening to me. Don't you think that I know myself well enough to know what's the right thing for me to do?"

"I do, I just ... I felt like you were holding something back, and I just wanted you to speak your mind," Hana said, sounding abashed.

Daisy let out a bleak laugh and shut her eyes, tipping her head back as if she was looking to heaven, asking for guidance from a God she didn't believe in. Hana asked Him too, but she already knew what she needed to do. She needed to stop listening to the roaring monster of her grief, stop letting its calls to *destroy*, to *ruin* run her life.

"You know you could just ask me if you wanted to know how I felt," Daisy accused. "You could just *ask*. I would tell you anything you asked. I would do anything you asked of me, and yet you still act like I'm the one holding something back."

"I know that. I know you would—"

"Do you? If I asked you to tell me the truth about something you didn't want to, would you do it?"

"I — I would. I think I would," Hana said. She sounded unsure even to herself.

"I just — sorry. I'm ... You can't do this to me again. I've been feeling crazy for *months* now thinking I was just imagining that you were trying to get a rise out of me, telling myself over and over that you wouldn't be doing that because you love me, but it turns out you've been pushing me this entire time."

"It wasn't ... It wasn't completely on purpose, Day. I'm sorry, let's just have a good night, alright? I'm sorry. Let me make things better," Hana pleaded, walking around her bed to where Daisy was standing. The younger girl tensed, but she didn't push Hana away when she pulled her into her arms.

"Don't do it again. Just ask me next time. Don't make me feel crazy."

"I won't. Never again. I promise," Hana said.

Hana would, inevitably, break this promise. Even as she said it, the words were sour in her mouth, just a sweet nothing to placate Daisy so she wouldn't be upset. Daisy rested her lips against Hana's forehead, not quite in a kiss, and held them there. Daisy would truly do anything for her. Hana didn't know what to do with that much loyalty and sureness when she was barely loyal to herself these days.

"I love you," Daisy murmured, her lips tickling Hana's forehead. Hana turned her head and pressed a kiss to Daisy's cheek.

"I love you, too," Hana said. Daisy held her tighter.

Hana made a vow to herself right then that she would try to be good enough for Daisy. She swore that the vow would last, and she would do her best to love Daisy the way that Daisy loved her. She would love with reckless abandon, like a child reaching their hand onto a stovetop with no care whether the burners were on or not.

"I'm going to do better for you," Hana said quietly. Daisy just kissed the side of Hana's face.

Hana would break her promise again and again. She would figure out the only way to be good to Daisy was to leave her and let her find someone who could love her the way she deserved. But she didn't know it then, standing in the room where she would one day die, holding each other like it would fix everything Hana had broken.

She really hoped that in the end, it would be them. That in the end it *could* be them.

Chapter 9

Daisy — July 2019

THE GROUP OF HANA'S friends were silent on the walk back to the car and for the first few minutes of the drive. It wasn't until Victor connected to Bluetooth and started playing music that Skippy struck up a conversation about where they were going.

"One of my best friends from high school is about to be a junior at U of R, that's University of Rochester, and he stayed here this summer because he got an apartment. They're having a party tonight. I think they even have a DJ. This day has been too much, so it's definitely time to drink and listen to weird mixes, right?" Skippy asked.

"That's been my personal method," Daisy said, staring out the window as the houses crowded into each other, huddling together the further they got from the suburbs. Daisy took in the sights with curious eyes. She rarely went into this part of the city she had grown up in.

"My friend, John, he's great. You're all gonna love him," Skippy said to the mostly silent car.

"Well, there's no way that this party could possibly be more depressing than sitting at Hana's grave, so I'm in," Victor said. Daisy laughed, and any remaining tension simmered away. They all quietly chatted about unimportant things for the rest of the drive, like funny signs and what they thought the DJ would play.

It took Skippy a solid ten minutes to try to find a parking spot, and by the time they were walking into the party, the others were teasing Skippy mercilessly for the "Epic Parking Saga of 2019."

Daisy listened and trailed behind them all on the sidewalk. She accepted that she was an outsider in this tightly knit group and always would be with Hana gone.

Daisy wished she wasn't going to New Paltz in the fall. She wanted a fresh start somewhere, and Hana's friends would hold her back from the clean slate she wanted. Her choice to follow Hana to college felt childish now, but it was too late to change things.

When they walked into the house where the party was being held, Skippy left the group to find her friend, and Aaron pulled a bottle of rum out of his bag.

"Skippy said we're crashing here, so let's all drink up, people," he said. He opened the bottle and smiled with satisfaction at the small *pop* the seal made when it broke.

"We're staying here? Shit, I didn't tell my dad," Daisy said. Victor rolled their eyes, and Daisy choked back a rude remark.

"Just don't mention the rum and you'll be fine," Aaron took a swig from the bottle and handed it to Daisy.

Daisy knew about their group's tradition — all of them would take a drink from the same bottle at the start of every party they attended together. Hana said it was a show of solidarity that they all started the party the same way, that they were forced together for a moment before the chaos of the party took over, but Daisy didn't really understand the importance. Still, she liked being included in it, so she took a hefty swig and tried not to wince.

Daisy laughed to cover a cough at the burning taste of cheap rum. "Yeah, I'll leave the rum out. I'll just wait until later and pretend that Skippy fell asleep and can't drive me home. That's always a classic."

Before anyone could respond, Skippy came bounding back dragging a tall, muscular boy with sandy blonde hair. He wore a muscle tank with cut out sleeves that dipped almost to his waist and a pair of jean shorts with uneven edges that looked DIY. His eyes skimmed around the circle before resting on Daisy for a beat too long. She slid her gaze to the bottle and passed it to Victor to avoid the newcomer's eyes.

"This is my friend John," Skippy said, elbowing him in the side. He stopped looking at Daisy and an easy smile graced his face as he dropped an arm around Skippy's shoulders.

"Nice to finally meet you guys. Skip has definitely told me too much about all of you," he joked.

"Nice to meet you," Victor said. They were clearly trying very hard not to check John out.

"Want a sip?" Chrissy asked. Skippy grabbed it out of Chrissy's hand before John could reach for it.

"After me, of course," Skippy said.

"Of course," Chrissy said, and Daisy laughed under her breath. John's eyes drifted over to hers once again, and Daisy looked back to Skippy, who didn't wince at all while she took a long drink of rum.

Victor started telling a story of another party they all went to together in New Paltz, and the friends all chimed in, skirting around Hana's involvement. The presence of her showed in the gaps, though, and telling the story was like prodding at the skin surrounding a bruise, testing the edges to see how far the damage spread, how far the rot of loss reached. If John noticed, he didn't say anything.

"So what are you guys all going to school for?" John asked, trying to loop himself back into the conversation. Daisy was happy to have another outsider there, another person trying to figure out how to fit into the weave of the group's tight-knit fabric without pulling a thread loose.

While everyone talked, Daisy studied John and Skippy to try to figure out if they were actually just friends or not. Skippy seemed to orient herself around John, shifting with his movements so she stayed in his line of sight, but John wasn't extending the same attention back to her. Maybe she had an unrequited crush, or maybe she was just happy to see her friend after a few months apart.

"Hello? Earth to Daisy?" Aaron said, waving his hand in front of her face. She blushed and the rest of the group laughed.

"Liquor getting to you already?" Victor asked with a smirk. Daisy rolled her eyes and grabbed the bottle out of John's hand, taking a large swig to prove her point.

"I'm just ... out of this world."

"Okay, space cadet. So, what are you going to study in college?" Aaron asked.

"Oh, I don't really know yet," Daisy said. "Maybe history. Maybe writing. Don't I have a year before I have to decide?" The glass of the neck of the bottle felt warm under her fingers.

"You're a freshman?" John asked, clearly surprised.

"Well, I'm about to be. I'm going to New Paltz with these guys," Daisy said with a smile. She loved when people thought she was older than she was.

"Then how do you know everyone? Run into them at orientation?" he joked.

The floor suddenly became as interesting as the Sistine Chapel, and all of their gazes dropped to it. Skippy smacked his arm, and it was clear that she had told him who Daisy was and he'd forgotten. His face sobered, and he looked horrified for a second.

Daisy couldn't stand it. "Yeah, it's a whole thing. Not really feeling like bringing the mood down, so let's just — not?" she said, her voice wandering up into a question. Before anyone could respond, a boy holding a lit joint walked up to the group.

"This is my roommate Harry," John said. Harry gave a half wave and took a long drag from the joint.

"Is this the legendary Skippy?" Harry asked. Skippy laughed and started chatting with him. John took a step back, letting them talk, and walked over to Daisy.

"I'm sorry about that. Skip totally told me, and I totally forgot," John said.

"It's really fine. Honestly, talking to you for a solid five minutes before you put your foot in your mouth is a record for pretty much everyone I've talked to for the past month," Daisy joked.

John let out a laugh. "Can I get you a drink? Like, a real one that's not just a shot. I know the warm rum is a tradition or whatever, but it's nasty."

"Sure, lead the way," Daisy responded.

"I've got Genny Cream. Is that good with you?" John asked. Daisy nodded absentmindedly and followed him into a small kitchen.

The counters were cluttered with a handful of appliances, piles of empty take out boxes, a stack of solo cups, and a scattering of ping pong balls and shot glasses. It would be obvious, even without the party going on around her, that this was a college house. The cabinets were sage green, but the paint was chipping on most of the edges, and a few of them hung like they had been slammed too many times and were no longer strong enough to sit properly.

John handed her a beer, and the warmth of his fingers was a stark contrast to the sudden chill of the can.

"So, are you and Skippy, like, a thing?" Daisy found herself asking before she could stop.

John grimaced and leaned against the counter. "Definitely not. She's like a little sister to me. We met because we both did theater in high school. I only did it because a girl I liked convinced me to do tech, but if you ask Skip you'd think it was my favorite thing," John said with a smile. Daisy hoped Skippy felt the same.

"Okay, great. So we both had our foot in mouth moment for the evening, we'll just move on from there," Daisy said. John let out a loud laugh at that, like he didn't expect her to say something funny and was surprised by her wit.

"Want to go check out the DJ?" he asked. Daisy nodded and the pair wove through the living room to the basement.

There weren't a lot of people down there, but the tiny space still felt crowded. The air was humid and hot from the summer night and the sweaty press of bodies. The DJ was jumping to the beat and singing along in a voice lost to the thump of the speakers while mixing different beats under popular rap songs. Daisy wished the music was good enough to get lost in, but she settled to sway to the overly loud bass reverberating on the cement block walls.

Someone came over and gave John a handshake hug combination before offering him a lit joint. John waved it off with a smile, leaning in to talk to the other boy over the music. He gestured towards Daisy, and she gave a small wave to him, earning a smile and nod of acknowledgement. The boy took a hit off of the joint and held it out to Daisy, and she paused for a second before taking it between her index finger and thumb.

She'd smoked once at Hana's house over winter break and once with Will when he finished the semester, and she remembered how they coached her on making it look like she knew what she was doing. She tried to keep her movements casual as she brought the joint to her lips and breathed in the dry, scratchy smoke. She breathed out and passed the joint back to the original boy, trying her hardest not to cough. He smiled brightly at her. She had passed whatever test she was unknowingly participating in.

John turned all his attention to Daisy, and she fought the urge to shrink away. His eyes were almost black in the glow of the string lights hanging from the ceiling. John took a step towards her, and Daisy moved back into the dancing crowd. John's eyes tracked her movements closely, and he followed a step behind her.

She felt flushed — she wasn't used to the attention of boys at parties. She barely went to them without Hana, and Hana always kept men away with sharp looks, cutting comments, and her reputation. Daisy didn't think she would ever need to learn how to pick up on the signals from people who weren't Hana, but now she realized Hana's protection wasn't as endearing as she once thought it was.

They danced near each other for a few songs and gulped down their beers to cool off in the humid basement. John pressed close to her as one song bled into another, placing his lips so close to her ear to speak that his rough, stubbled chin brushed against her skin.

"You're really cool," he said. Daisy thought he might have dropped his voice to sound more sultry, but she wasn't sure if she was just imagining it.

"Oh, thanks. You too," Daisy said back, unsure how else to respond. They didn't know each other, and they'd only had one conversation that wasn't particularly interesting, but she wasn't going to tell John that. He pulled back, grinning, and placed his hands on her hips to dance with her. His fingers ghosted over the bare strip of skin between the top of her shorts and the bottom of her tank top, and she was surprised at the way her breath caught at the small movement. John smirked and leaned forward, and for a second Daisy considered letting him kiss her.

She wondered how it would feel to have an almost-stranger's lips pressed against her own. Hana was the first and only person Daisy had ever kissed, and she never even considered how she might kiss someone else some day.

Hana and Daisy's first kiss was something Daisy spent weeks dreaming about, and only the tingle of champagne on her lips and the look in Hana's eyes convinced her to make a move. Back then she didn't really know how to kiss someone aside from what she'd seen in movies and heard from her other friends who were already kissing boys, but she didn't worry about being inexperienced. Hana was her best friend, the person who understood her most in the world, and she didn't have to worry about being cool enough to kiss her.

Daisy stepped out of his grip and John looked confused.

"Um, sorry, I'm just going to ..." Daisy gestured vaguely towards the stairs and stepped further away from him, moving between other party goers on her way. She passed by Skippy, who followed her out of the basement.

Daisy leaned against a wall in the hallway at the top of the stairs and willed her hands to stop shaking.

"Seriously?" Skippy asked. She stood in front of Daisy with her arms crossed.

"What?" Daisy asked in return, confused by the question.

"You're seriously flirting with John?"

"I wasn't — I was just being nice. I moved when he tried to kiss me, so it's not like—"

"You mean you stopped when you were about to kiss *him*," Skippy said.

Daisy didn't understand why Skippy was so upset. "Look, I didn't — I'm just kind of messed up right now, okay? I'm ... out of it."

"We were at Hana's grave a few hours ago and now you're trying to kiss someone else? I mean, you don't even want to talk about her. What's up with that?" Skippy asked.

Daisy flinched back. "I — what? What the hell are you trying to say?"

"I'm just saying that if Hana was alive, you would still be with her, so why are you making moves on my best friend?" Skippy asked. Their voices were still low, trying not to cause a scene, but Daisy was sure she was about to start yelling any moment.

"I was literally just dancing with him. And you're sitting there acting like you knew her better than me? I've known her since I was five, and obviously I miss her," Daisy scoffed. "Did you even know that Hana cheated on me last October? Were you even close enough for her to tell you? Don't stand there like there's some set amount of time before it's too soon for me to move on. She was moving on while we were still dating, and she's *dead*. It's not like she's going to come back to me."

"Maybe she cheated on you because she knew you were like … this," Skippy spat.

Daisy opened and closed her mouth, trying to formulate a response, but her mind was reeling from Skippy's slightly slurred words and the anger on her face. Where was this was coming from?

Aaron appeared and immediately started trying to diffuse the situation. "Whoa, Skip, what are you talking about? What is going on here?"

"What's going on here is that Daisy is already forgetting Hana and trying to use my best friend as a rebound," Skippy said.

"Shut up, Skippy." Daisy stood and pushed past the pair. Of course John came up from the basement at that very moment and saw the tears in Daisy's eyes.

"Are you okay?" he asked her, his eyes flicking behind her where Skippy was holding her balled fist like it was taking effort not to lash out.

"I just want to go home. I'm going to call an Uber," Daisy said, trying to push past him towards the door.

"I'll drive you home. I'm basically sober," John said. She should say no, but John was already darting upstairs to get his keys from his room. She walked towards the front door, wanting to get out of the range of Skippy's drunken accusations. She looked back, but Skippy was lost in the crowded party. Aaron looked over his shoulder in the direction she must've gone before walking towards Daisy.

"Are you okay with him driving you home? I know you don't know him very well," Aaron asked.

"Oh, um, yeah. I'm not worried. Is Skippy, like … Do you know what that was?" Daisy didn't care to figure out a nicer way to phrase her question.

"I don't know, dude. I think this was a long day for her. She got up really early to drive us all up here, and maybe she has a crush on John? I couldn't tell you what's happening inside her head. I'm sure she'll apologize tomorrow," Aaron said, but Daisy wasn't feeling sure that Skippy would offer any sort of apology.

"Yeah, maybe. I ... it's not true, you know. I wasn't — that's *why* I didn't kiss him. I mean, I *was* thinking about Hana. It's not like I—" Daisy didn't know how to finish her thought.

"I know. I get it, but Skippy can sometime ... jump to conclusions. I think leaving is a good idea, though. She's weird when she's drunk sometimes." Aaron sounded apologetic, but it just annoyed Daisy.

"Most people cry when they're drunk, not verbally attack people," Daisy muttered. Luckily, she was rescued from the interaction when John came downstairs.

"Let's head out. I don't want to miss too much of the party. Skip will never let me live it down," he said.

"Are you sure you want to drive me?" Daisy asked. "I can call an Uber, it's really not a problem."

"I don't mind," John said before dropping his voice and adding, "I think Skippy needs a minute to cool off anyways." Daisy nodded and said a quick goodbye to Aaron, not bothering to look for Chrissy and Victor. It felt too final, and she knew that even when she saw them on campus in the fall it wouldn't be the same. Hana's friends would always be loyal to a dead girl, and Daisy was just a reminder of what they lost.

"Sorry about whatever that was. Thanks for the ride," Daisy said when they climbed into John's car. It was an older model sedan adorned with a giant dent in the back bumper that she was afraid to ask about, and there was a mysterious stain on the driver seat she tried to ignore. John handed her his phone with a navigation app open, and she punched in her address. The robotic voice told them where to go, and they set off.

"It's okay. Skippy can be intense sometimes. And I know your friend just died, so I get that you don't want to—"

"Girlfriend," Daisy corrected, "My girlfriend just died." She felt it was important that here, in one of the few places that she *could* be out, that she actually was.

"Right." John paused. "Yeah, Skippy ... I don't think she mentioned that. Sorry about the basement, then. I didn't know you were a lesbian."

"I'm not. I'm bi," Daisy countered. She rarely got to talk about her sexuality out loud. She spent so much time hiding it that saying it so plainly made a thrill run through her.

"Good to know. Me too," he said with a playful grin. They were both quiet for a minute, and the drone of a radio host introducing a top forty song was the only noise in the car.

John turned down the radio and glanced quickly at Daisy. "I'm still sorry about the basement. I didn't realize you were dating Hana. Skip said something that hinted at it now that I think about it, but, well ... I thought you guys were just friends. Which, still, I mean — I don't know how to word it. But I am sorry." His voice was genuine and soft.

"It's okay. I'm not out, and my dad didn't know about me and Hana. So it just ... wasn't talked about often. Skippy was probably used to that. When I visited New Paltz was one of the only times I could really be myself. I guess I forgot that other people kept my secret too."

"Were you guys together long?" he asked. Daisy pursed her lips at his question, and he backtracked quickly. "You don't have to talk about her if—"

"No, it's fine. I like talking about her. It's the best way to keep her around," Daisy said.

"I get that. It almost makes you wish ghosts were real when you lose someone you love."

Daisy snorted, and John gave her a bemused look.

"Sorry, I just — yeah. It'd be great if ghosts were real." She looked in the rearview mirror and saw Hana dramatically draped across the backseat. The song playing on the radio ended, and "Heaven is a Place on Earth" started playing.

Daisy laughed. "She loved this song. And it keeps playing on the radio. I didn't think it was that popular of a song. But it's, like, *everywhere* now."

"That's always how it is. Like you go to pick up your brand-new car thinking you're unique and then see them everywhere you go for the next week."

"Yeah. I guess little things are everywhere if you go looking for it," Daisy said. This wasn't true, of course, if you were looking for clues about who murdered your ex-girlfriend and framed it as a suicide.

"So, tell me about her. What would her back-of-the-book blurb be?"

Daisy laughed and looked at the backseat in the rearview mirror again. Hana met her gaze and smirked, not making a noise, as if John would hear her if she did.

"19-year-old lesbian philosophy major Hana Holm spends her free time reading books she's happy you've never heard of and cheating on her girlfriend," she said before she could stop herself. Hana's face pinched.

John let out a startled laugh. "Right for the throat, huh? What happened to not speaking ill of the dead?"

"I mean, it's not like she's here to hear it," Daisy said. Hana pouted in the backseat.

"That's really hard. I'm sorry you lost her so soon. It seemed like no one knew how much she was struggling."

"Yeah. It would've been easier if it was, like, a car crash or freak accident or anything else," Daisy said, dancing around the fact she believed this was actually a murder.

"I can't imagine. There was a kid a year younger than me in high school who killed himself, and the whole school was freaked out for, like, years. It's part of the reason I wanted to go to college outside of my hometown."

"Where are you from?"

"Babylon, down on Long Island. My parents really wanted me to go to Stony Brook since it's so close, but I knew I'd know kids from my high school if I went there," he explained.

"That's nice. I'm supposed to go to New Paltz, but it's just hard because of Hana."

"I can't even imagine. At least you can transfer if you hate it."

"That's true. I don't even know what I want to study, so I can always switch to somewhere else since I'm not going for a specific program."

"Yeah, picking a major is the worst," John said before launching into a story of how he ended up becoming a history major.

Once the topic wasn't so depressing, John was easy to talk to, and Daisy found herself laughing and joking more in that twenty-minute car ride than she had since Hana died. With the pressure of being at a party with strangers gone, John was funny and sweet, and she realized she was having fun. It felt foreign after so long of being miserable over Hana, and Daisy was so involved in their conversation that she lost track of their path until they were on her street.

"Well, it looks like we're here," he said a few seconds after the GPS announced it. Daisy grimaced at the thought of having to talk to her dad about who drove her home. Maybe she would get lucky, and he wouldn't notice that this wasn't Skippy's car.

"Thanks again for the ride. We should hang out sometime, this was fun," Daisy said. John smiled brightly at her and plucked his phone out of its holder, opening up his messages and handing it to her.

"Text yourself so you have my number and I have yours. That way we both have the power to reach out," he said with an easy smile. Daisy punched in her number and texted herself "hi!" before handing it back to him.

"Well, I'll text you or something. I swear I'm usually much more fun at parties," she joked.

"I guess we'll have to find out," he teased. "Have a good night."

Daisy climbed out of the car and walked to her front stoop before she turned and waved to John. He waved back before he drove away, and she watched his headlights disappear before she went inside.

She called out a quick hello to her dad on her way to her room. Hana was waiting for Daisy with her arms crossed.

"Skippy is nuts," Hana said simply.

"Yeah. No idea why you're friends with her," Daisy said. She put her bag down on the floor and jimmied open her broken nightstand drawer to take out the bottle of wine she stashed there. She needed another drink to deal with this right now. Hana picked up a stress ball off Daisy's desk and started throwing it up in the air and catching it.

"John seemed nice. I mean, he clearly wants to sleep with you, but he's only human," Hana said.

Daisy sighed and screwed the top off the wine, taking a long drink right from the bottle before rounding on Hana's ghost. "You don't get to be jealous. You're dead. I can't have you anymore, I need to move on." The words felt sour in her mouth, but she needed to say them.

"You don't have time to hook up with some rando that Skippy is clearly obsessed with. You need to be focused on catching who killed me," Hana demanded.

Daisy barely held in a scream. "You think I'm not trying? I went out with your stupid friends to find out their alibis. I got them. I'll cross them off the list. Just because my entire life doesn't revolve around you doesn't mean that I don't love you anymore."

"You still haven't read my journal, and you almost kissed someone else," Hana said.

Daisy set her bottle down and surged forward, catching the stress ball out of the air and throwing it across the room. It bounced off the wall and rolled behind her desk.

"You. Are. Dead. I *can't* kiss you anymore. And it's not like you didn't kiss other people while you were alive. While you were dating me. While you claimed to *love* me."

She hated how her voice broke when she spoke.

"That was different," Hana shot back. Daisy stepped away from Hana and picked up the wine bottle again, taking another large sip.

"I can't do this right now," Daisy said, tears pricking in her eyes. The ghost looked sympathetic, and Daisy wished she could hold Hana again.

"Get some sleep. Things will be better in the morning," the ghost said.

Daisy shook her head. "I doubt that. It's not like I'll wake up and you'll be alive again."

Hana gave Daisy a sad smile. Then she was gone and Daisy was, once again, all alone. She reached into the back of her closet, pulling out one of Hana's sweaters that still smelled like her perfume, and laid it next to her pillow. She hid the almost empty bottle of wine back in her nightstand drawer, changed into an oversized New Paltz T-shirt Hana had gotten her after she got her acceptance letter, and cried herself to sleep.

Chapter 10

Hana — age 18

8/24/18

Dear Diary,

Don't get me wrong, I'm so glad I'm out of Penfield. I was starting to really hate that everyone there knows one piece of my life and thinks they actually know me. They think I'm just the girl with the dead dad, or that one out lesbian, or Daisy Polo's best friend, or that girl they sat next to for a few months in a class. They don't know who I am now or who I want to be, and what's even worse is they don't even care to find out.

But New Paltz isn't quite what I thought it would be. I'm hoping that here people can actually get to know me, but it's been weird these first few days. Going from everyone knowing me to no one knowing me is a really weird change. As much as I resented everyone knowing my name in the cafeteria, there was a safety net in Penfield — there was always someone around that I could hang out with. Usually Daisy, but other people too. But here? No Daisy. No Jenna from third period who was always happy to chat. No one knows me.

I've never been alone before, not like this. I've been lonely, sure, but not actually alone. It doesn't help that my roommate doesn't seem to want to be friends with me. She only cares about joining the a capella group on campus. I almost resorted to watching Pitch Perfect *to get her attention earlier, but I'm not desperate enough yet.*

I'm getting dinner with Alexis from orientation and her roommate (whose name is Skippy???) in a few minutes so at least I'll have someone to eat with. I might've skipped lunch today because the thought of eating alone at the dining hall was too daunting. But I'll just eat extra for dinner to offset it.

I should go or I'll be late.

Sincerely,
Hana

. . . .

Stepping out of the oppressive August heat and into the dining hall was supposed to be a relief, but Hana was nervous to meet Skippy. She spotted Alexis across the hall and waved, and the other girl returned the gesture.

"Thanks for waiting for me," Hana said.

"Of course. This is my roommate, Skippy. Skippy, this is Hana. We were in orientation together. Hana did a great job in the lip-syncing competition."

Hana's cheeks heated up, and she laughed awkwardly. "I can pretend to know the words to awful pop songs like no one's business," Hana joked.

Skippy let out a snort. "They really choose the absolute worst music for them, don't they?"

"Yeah. I'm just glad they didn't record the whole thing. My girlfriend would have an absolute field day if she saw it," Hana said.

She waited for there to be a sidelong glance, an ounce of judgment on their faces, any sort of sign that they cared that she was dating a girl, but it never came. The other girls laughed, and the three of them grabbed food and settled at a table. The meal wasn't as awkward as Hana feared, and by the end she was no longer faking her comfort.

"I heard about a party happening on Monday if you want to come," Skippy said on their way out.

"I have an eight a.m. Tuesday morning," Alexis said, "so I'm out, but you should go Hana! It should be fun."

"Yeah, I'm down. Where is it?" Hana asked.

"It's at a house in town," Skippy said. "Apparently there's a huge underground music scene here. My brother is a senior, so he told me about it. Although he did say that I can't act like a freshman, whatever the hell that means." Skippy rolled her eyes.

Hana laughed. "I promise to act as un-freshman-like as possible. I guess I'll be leaving the lanyard at home, then?" she joked. Skippy laughed, and the girls exchanged numbers. Hana was looking forward to the next day for the first time. Maybe she had found someone that would help her feel like herself.

Skippy and Hana hung out the whole weekend, though Alexis ditched them most of the time for a boy she met in her dorm that she was obsessed with. By the time classes started on Monday, Hana considered Skippy a friend despite only knowing her for three days.

The first day of class was daunting, but it felt easier once Hana and Skippy realized they shared their first ever college class — Intro to Philosophy.

"I won't lie. I'm taking this class because I got it mixed up with psychology," Skippy admitted after their first class.

"A bit more Plato and less Freud," Hana teased.

"Yeah, that's how it seems. Are you still in for that house show tonight?" Skippy asked. A boy with floppy blonde curls tucked under a backwards hat wearing jean shorts and a jersey for a team Hana didn't recognize who was walking out of the same room rushed to fall in line with them.

"Did you say house show," he said.

"You have some very selective hearing there, huh?" Hana asked through a snort of laughter.

He shrugged. "I heard there's a good music scene, but I haven't found it yet. I'm a huge music buff," he admitted.

"Well, maybe I'll give you the address. What's your name?" Skippy asked.

He stuck out his hand to her to shake. "Aaron. He/him. And you guys?" Hana barely hid her smile at the fact that a guy who looked like he would fit in every frat stereotype introduced himself with his pronouns. Maybe New Paltz was what she wanted it to be.

"Skippy, she/her."

"Hana. Also she/her."

Aaron grinned at them.

"Cool! I'll bring drinks to the pregame if you let me come with you," Aaron said.

"That seems like a pretty fair trade," Skippy said with her own grin. She handed him her phone with Instagram opened up, and he followed himself.

"Once you follow back, I'll DM you when and where we're pregaming," Skippy said. He nodded, then looked at the room numbers on the walls.

"Well, I should be walking the other way to get to my next class, but nice to meet you guys!" he said before turning around and making his way hurriedly down the hall.

"When they said making friends at college was easy, I didn't think they meant it was *that* easy," Hana admitted.

Skippy laughed. "Who knows. This could be the start of a beautiful friendship."

And it was. Hanging out with Aaron was fun — he had great music taste, didn't try to hit on them, and brought his friend Victor with him. Victor was shy, but came out of their shell a lot more once Hana did a few shots and started talking about how much she loved her girlfriend.

"I just feel better being around queer people," they admitted on the walk to the party.

"It seems like you're in the right place, then," Skippy said. "I was on tinder earlier and there were, like, so many girls on there. So many more than there were in my hometown." Hana didn't even realize Skippy was queer. Maybe that's why they clicked so quickly.

"I can't wait for Daisy to meet you guys," Hana said. "She's literally so cool. She's not out so no one in our hometown really knows we're together, but we don't have to hide here." Hana reveled in the thought.

The house show was loud, hot, and sweaty, and Hana loved every minute. The lights in the basement were strung up over the "stage" area where a few sweaty guys were playing, and she couldn't understand the lyrics over the wail of the guitars and the brisk beats of the drums. The sound wasn't good, but the energy was electric, and Hana couldn't get enough.

After the party, things shifted. She started hanging out with her new friends every day, and college stopped feeling so lonely and terrifying. The weeks rolled together, full of late-night study sessions and bonding over the terrible dining hall food. She went out on Fridays, Saturdays, and sometimes Tuesdays since she didn't have Wednesday classes, and she hung out with Aaron, Skippy, Victor, and a girl named Chrissy she was paired with on a project in their philosophy class.

She half hated being back home for the long weekend at the start of October. She was trying to fit herself back into the person she was before she left for New Paltz, and it was like squeezing into a pair of jeans from middle school.

"It's going to be amazing when you visit," Hana said to Daisy when she was home. "You'll love New Paltz so much. I can't wait for you to get your acceptance too. We'll have so much fun together." Daisy smiled brightly back at her, and they made plans for all the things they would do the next fall.

By the time late October rolled around, Hana felt like she belonged in New Paltz. She still missed Daisy, but the moments were less like a spear to the heart and more like a finger pressed to a fading bruise.

She didn't call Daisy as much anymore, though they texted every day. Hana was so busy learning and growing that she found it hard to care about Daisy's high school drama. It felt inconsequential now. Daisy would feel the same when she came to New Paltz.

Hana was beginning to understand why so many people broke up with their partners once they started college, though she didn't plan on breaking up with Daisy. Once Daisy was away from Penfield, she would change too, but the waiting was taking a toll on Hana.

The night before Halloween her entire friend group went out dressed as cowboys. They glued their own rhinestones and feathers to cowboy hats, and they each chose a color to dress in. Hana thought they all looked beautiful and young and stupid and perfect. She chose to dress in all black. She was going to spend the night freezing in her high waisted jean shorts, crop top, and flannel, but it was worth it. She even found black cowboy boots only one size too big at the thrift store to complete her outfit.

"This show is going to be so fun," Chrissy said on the walk to the party. She was adorned in bright blue, and it made her usually gray-blue eyes look electric.

"Yeah, the bands are dressing and playing as other bands for the night," Aaron piped up.

"Sweet. What bands are playing, sunshine?" Victor asked, teasing Aaron for his choice of bright yellow for his costume. Aaron elbowed Victor, but the flush on his cheeks showed he didn't hate the nickname.

"I think, like, early 2000s stuff. Should be fun. Who has the rum tonight?" Aaron asked.

They had started a tradition of drinking rum right when they got to a party, and Hana loved that it felt like they were creating a pact between the five of them every time they went out. Friends at the start, friends till the end.

"I have it," Skippy said in a sing-song voice. Her older brother held no moral issues with underage drinking, so she was able to get him to pick up alcohol for the group whenever they wanted it.

"You're the best, Skip. Did you give Georgie our love?" Hana asked.

"Of course," Skippy said with a laugh.

"George is the only true ally," Victor said solemnly, and they burst into drunken giggles.

"Plus, he's hot," Aaron said. Skippy smacked his arm, and they all laughed so hard they had to stop to catch their breath.

A swell of love for her friends rose in Hana's chest. She would have them by her side for the rest of her life, and that night she could almost see their futures intertwining.

She could imagine all of them being in each other's weddings and raising their kids to call each other aunts and uncles. Hana didn't know who she would become, but she was sure of these people in a way she was never sure about anything in her life. She wondered if she had felt something similar when she met Daisy all those years ago.

The party was in full swing by the time they got there, but it was in between sets when they walked up. They fished their five dollar bills out of their pockets to hand to the person working the door and smiled when they got a small iridescent stamp on each of their hands. Hana was completely wrapped up in belonging, and after they took their communal shot of rum, she pulled Chrissy and Skippy to the basement to get a good spot for the next band.

When the music started, the three of them danced and screamed their hearts out to a song that was popular when they were kids while passing around the rum. Hana was pleasantly buzzed when she noticed a girl across the room eyeing her. She was dressed as an alien, and every time the girl looked over, her eyes raked down Hana's body like a palpable touch. Skippy and Chrissy floated away in the crowd, and Hana found herself drifting towards the girl.

"Our costumes kind of match," the girl said, half-yelling over the music.

"Cowboys and aliens? Are we supposed to be enemies?" Hana leaned in close to be heard over the band.

"Maybe. Want to go somewhere quieter?" she asked. Hana nodded and the girl gripped her hand before pulling her upstairs. She led Hana through the first floor to the deserted back porch, vacated once the band started. Hana shivered when the cool October air brushed her skin, and she pulled her flannel off her waist and around her shoulders. If the girl noticed that Hana was cold, she didn't comment on it.

"My name is Frida," she said, sitting down on the top step and stretching out her long, tan legs in front of her. She was tall with straight brown hair cropped in a sharp bob. Hana was immediately in awe of her and could feel herself getting pulled into her orbit.

"I'm Hana." Hana dropped down next to Frida.

"Cool name. You smoke?" she asked. Hana shook her head, but Frida took out a second cigarette anyways.

"It's as good a time as any to start," she teased, handing Hana the cigarette. Hana laughed at her boldness and watched as Frida lit a cigarette. The strong-smelling smoke immediately chased away the crisp, refreshing bite of the October air invading Hana's nose, and she fought not to make a face. Instead, all she thought about was how she wanted nothing more than to look like she knew what she was doing. Frida held up the second cigarette like a question hanging in the air.

Hana leaned forward and wrapped her lips around the yellow end, and when Frida flicked the lighter to life at the other end, Hana breathed in. The smoke was hot and cloudy and scratchy in her lungs, like she'd inhaled hot beach sand, but she resisted the need to cough.

She mimicked Frida's movements and took the cigarette out of her mouth to release the smoke. It was a relief, but she tried to be subtle as she gulped in the night air.

"Tell me about yourself, Hana who doesn't smoke," Frida said. She looked like a tableau of everything Hana was warned about in D.A.R.E., backlit by the flickering porch light and smiling at Hana.

Hana took another painful drag from the cigarette. "Not much to tell. I'm a philosophy major, I think. I'm from outside Rochester. I smoke now."

"Philosophy? Cool. That's a degree you get because you just love to learn. I like that."

"What about you? Frida who offers cigarettes to random girls at parties," Hana joked. Frida laughed.

"Only pretty girls," Frida said with a wink before adding, "I'm a women, gender, and sexuality studies and English double major. I'm a junior. I probably shouldn't smoke."

She leaned forward to count off each item, but she didn't lean back when she was done. Hana didn't know when she moved closer, but before she knew it Frida was kissing her.

It was electric, and messy, and an absolutely terrible idea. Hana didn't care, though — all she cared about was the thrill of the kiss and the older girl who thought she was interesting and pretty.

After a few more seconds Frida pulled back, took a drag of her cigarette, and tipped her head towards the stars dotting the clear night sky to exhale the smoke. Hana let her own cigarette keep burning untouched.

Even though it was cold out, Hana was flushed. She forgot all about Daisy and her small problems and the fact she was a few hundred miles away missing Hana. The box in her mind she once used to lock away her love for Daisy reopened with a sigh of relief as if all the time spent empty was a chore. Hana barely noticed the ways that Daisy was plucked from her mind.

"Man, I could really go for a joint right now. I live down the street if you want to come with me." Frida stood up and offered a hand towards Hana. The subtext of the invitation was clear, and there was no mistaking her intentions as just friendly. Hana smiled and took her hand.

"Sounds good," Hana said. Frida grinned and kept their fingers laced, tugging Hana up. They dropped their cigarettes into an ashtray on the edge of the deck and made their way around the side of the house towards the street.

"I should let my friends know I'm leaving," Hana said, glancing behind her.

Frida's eyes scanned Hana's body hungrily. "Okay. I can wait here unless you want to text them." Hana shivered, but it wasn't from the cold.

"Yeah, just let me text them," she muttered. She shot a quick message to their group chat letting them all know she was heading out, purposefully not saying that she was going home so that she wasn't exactly lying. She had a feeling that they would try to talk her out of this, and she had already made up her mind. She tucked her phone in her back pocket, reached for Frida's hand again, and let herself be pulled away from the party and into the night.

The house Frida lived in looked exactly the way Hana expected it to. The living room walls were covered in a range of different movie posters, and there were random odds and ends all over.

"I live with a DMP major," she said to explain the posters, which she pulled Hana past on the way up the stairs.

"Oh, yeah, that makes sense," Hana said, pretending to know what a DMP major was.

Frida laughed a little at her. "It stands for digital media production. This is me, though, no movie posters in sight." She gestured around the bedroom they had walked into. Hana nodded and sat on the edge of Frida's bed.

Frida's room was small. She didn't have a bed frame, and she turned on the LED strip lights covering the walls instead of the overhead light. They faded through the different colors of the rainbow, casting new shadows in the room every few seconds. There were a few piles of clothes next to the closet that Hana wasn't sure were clean or dirty and only one thing hung on the walls — a giant tapestry of Van Gogh's *The Scream*. Instead of nightside stands, there were piles of books in various states of distress being used to hold an alarm clock, phone charger, and a water bottle covered in stickers. Hana's eyes raked over the books, trying to find a title she recognized.

"I only buy used books for my lit classes. Then I never want to read any of them again, so they end up as furniture," Frida explained when she noticed Hana looking. Frida walked over to her dresser, the only real piece of furniture in the room, and started playing a Fleetwood Mac record. She turned and closed the distance between them before placing her hand on the side of Hana's jaw with her thumb resting on her chin. Hana looked up at her with a smile.

"You're really beautiful, you know," Frida said. It wasn't a question, more of a statement, as if Hana was supposed to know that she was beautiful, and Frida was just reminding her. It was the same tone Hana used when her roommate almost walked out of the room without her key. It was a tone that was casual and spoke of Frida's honest belief in Hana's beauty.

"You're not too bad yourself," she teased, placing a hand on Frida's waist. Frida smiled, and then they were kissing again.

The rest of the night was creating a new pile of clothes on the floor, kissing, and trying to stifle their moans after Frida revealed how thin the walls were. Frida didn't ask why it was so easy for Hana to stay quiet.

Hana fell asleep with the unfamiliar scent of the other girl wrapped around her and woke up the next morning to sunlight streaming in through a thin gap between the blackout curtains. She got up, and Frida barely stirred.

Hana fished her phone out of the pocket of her shorts and winced at all the waiting notifications. She had a handful of messages from the group chat — everyone was confused and told her to text when she got home if she didn't crash immediately. She shot off a text saying that she was all good and would tell them about it over their usual hangover breakfast.

Then she started reading all the messages from Daisy.

• • • •

Daisy

I miss you. Remember Halloween last year?

When your mom agreed for god knows what reason to work the overnight shift at the ER?

Getting to hand out candy to kids was so fun. It was like we were playing house

And we broke into your mom's supply of red wine. Which, for the record, still tastes bad

Anyways I may be drunk at Anna Richards' party but I love you and I miss you and I hope you're having fun cowgirl

Text me when you're home safe I love you angel

• • • •

The weight of what Hana had done crashed into her with the force of a tidal wave, and she wasn't sure if the nausea in her stomach was from what she drank last night or the onset of guilt.

What was she thinking? How could she hurt Daisy? She cheated on the girl who was there for her and held her after she found out her dad was dead. The girl that bought Hana her favorite candy when she was sad and drunk texted her how much she loved her. She needed to get out of there before the guilt sent her into a spiral that she was certain Frida wouldn't want to comfort her through.

After she was dressed, she leaned over the bed and gave Frida a small shake.

"Frida? Hey, I've got to head out. Last night was fun," Hana said. Daisy was the only person she had slept with before this, so she didn't know what she was supposed to do.

"Yeah, it was cool. Leave your number or something. We can do this again," Frida mumbled, still half asleep.

Hana froze. If she kept this to herself, the truth could never hurt Daisy. She could tell her friends that she went to Frida's house to smoke and slept on her couch because she was too high to walk home alone. It would be all too easy to separate her worlds and write different stories to appease both sides.

She never needed to keep anything important from Daisy before, but she was in college to learn, right?

Even though she shouldn't, she wrote her phone number on a piece of paper she found on the ground and placed it on the pillow she'd slept on. She nearly tumbled while slipping on her oversized boots before setting off downstairs, her cowboy hat clutched in her hand and her flannel wrapped tightly around herself for the walk back to campus.

Maybe if she hadn't left her phone number, she could have forgotten what she did, but when Frida texted her the next day, she responded. And when Frida texted her just before midnight on

Thursday, Hana went over to her house and did it again. It happened almost a dozen times before Hana admitted to herself that she needed to stop or tell Daisy.

She would fix her mess, but first she needed one last memory to wrap things up neatly. Just one more time, she told herself, then she would be done with this and stop chasing the thrill she got from Frida.

Hana watched the last of the leaves fall from the tree outside Frida's window and told her she just wanted to be friends from now on. Frida agreed easily and didn't ask questions.

Chapter 11

Daisy — July 2019

THE DAY AFTER THE PARTY, Daisy got a text from Skippy with a terse apology. She went with Aaron's original excuse, though she added the new detail that she often started getting mean when she drank whiskey, and she apparently did a few shots of Jim Beam before she spotted Daisy with John.

Daisy accepted her halfhearted apology and went on with her life. She wouldn't see Skippy for a little while, and there were more pressing things to worry about in the meantime. She needed to figure out how to respond to John's texts and if Hana was murdered. And if she was, Daisy needed to catch the killer.

She crossed Hana's friends' names off her suspect list after adding a note with their alibis. It was time to read Hana's journal. First, though, she had to how to quell the queasy feeling that popped up every time she thought about reading the words Hana hid from her eyes while she was alive.

The easiest way, she figured out while trudging through a breakfast with her father where she expertly hid her slight hangover, was to try not to think about it. She would take the ghost's words as the truth and believe that Hana wanted her to read the journal. Anything that would keep her mind occupied so she didn't have to face the horrible truth.

Opening Hana's journal took more effort than she thought. It was just an ordinary composition notebook with no lock, not even an elastic holding it shut. But Daisy was struck with the thought that once she read the journal, there would be that much less to learn about Hana. Daisy thought she would spend her entire life learning new things about Hana, but there were a finite number of her secrets left in the world now.

She took a deep breath and read the first journal entry.

· · · ·

3/7/19

Dear Diary,

Today is that magical first day of fake spring. I know it's probably going to snow again next week, but right now it feels so nice. A moment of warm sun after a hellish winter. Maybe things will be okay after all. Shit, I have to meet Chrissy, we're going to study on the quad (aka sit next to our open books and gossip and tan).

Sincerely,

Hana

· · · ·

Daisy wasn't sure why she thought that every one of Hana's journal entries would be something groundbreaking and revolutionary, but the innocuous first entry gave her more confidence to keep reading the rest.

But as Daisy read on, she noticed that a lot of the pages were ripped out, some entries cut in half or missing entirely. Hana didn't journal every day, so it was hard to tell how many were missing, but there were at least 15 pages ripped out of the notebook, which was a lot considering the fact that Hana only filled half of the notebook before she died. When Daisy flipped through the empty pages, a piece of paper with a key taped to it fell out from between the pages, and she picked it up hesitantly.

Hana's ghost appeared, a smile on her face. "Finally! You found it. I knew you would."

"What is it?"

"Read it and see."

Daisy followed the ghost's instructions and unfolded the note.

. . . .

Dear Daisy (or whoever else finds this),

I think I'm in too deep. I've been looking into my dad's death, and someone is onto me. I don't know anymore if Jake Hansen was working completely on his own when he shot my dad. I know there were witnesses and everything, so, yes, Jake killed him, but I don't think that was all.

I'm scared that something is going to happen to me, and I'll take this investigation and everything I've uncovered to the grave. So this note is my safety net and also a goodbye if it comes to that. I really hope it doesn't come to that. I don't know what there is after death, if it's the eternal glory of heaven like we've been promised, or if it's nothing. I know I'm not supposed to dwell on that, so I try not to, but I'm not particularly good at doing what I'm supposed to. I can't decide if I would prefer for the afterlife to be perfect or nothingness. Knowing the way this world works, I'm sure it will fall somewhere in between.

If anything happens to me, I don't want to leave without a final word. So just in case, this is my goodbye. Because if dying young is my fate, if it's part of God's plan, I can't stop it, but I've always been determined to have the last word.

Mom — I'm sorry I didn't try harder since Dad died. He really was the glue of this family. I know you're trying to fill that void with Dennis, but really, please stop. He's not the man you think he is.

Will — Sorry I broke that promise.

Daisy — I don't think you want everyone reading what I have to say to you. Remember that place from your list? Your letter is there. Please know you were always my best friend even when I treated you worse than you deserved.

Until we meet again in whatever dreams come after this,
Hana

. . . .

Daisy stared at the note in disbelief, tears rolling down her face. It was true. All of it was true. Hana had been murdered. She didn't kill herself. Her ghost was looking at Daisy expectantly, but before either of them could say anything, Daisy's phone started ringing.

She reached for it in a daze, still comprehending what she'd read. When she saw it was Will calling her, she swore at herself. She knew he was going to call around this time, but she was so wrapped up in reading Hana's journal that she didn't notice it was creeping towards the time for their weekly call.

"Hi Daisy!"

"Hey, Will. How's Barcelona?"

"It's amazing. You would love it here," Will said before launching into a story about the highlights of his week. He was keeping her and Henry updated in their family group chat, but it wasn't the same as actually talking about what he was doing. Daisy laid down while he talked, throwing in a comment here and there while he excitedly went on.

"If you did all that in a week, I can't imagine how much more fun you're going to have while you're there," she said.

"Yeah, they're definitely keeping us busy. I'm just glad we have a late start tomorrow because a bunch of us are going out to some bars tonight. Being above the legal drinking age here is awesome. But enough about me, how has your week been?"

"It's ... well, it's been fine."

"Just fine?"

"Hana's friends came and visited for a memorial thing since they couldn't make the funeral."

"Oh."

"And they're all nice, but ... they're *Hana's* friends, you know?" Daisy stared up at the ceiling, finding shapes in the popcorn texture like she'd been doing since she was a kid.

"Yeah, I get that. Are you ... are you okay?

"As okay as I have been. I think things will be easier once I leave for school."

"Yeah, getting out of Penfield will help," Will said. "And I know we talked about only doing this one phone call a week, but you know that if you ever need me—"

"I can call, I know. I know you'll always be there for me," Daisy said.

Will sighed. "I'll be home before you know it. And you know, Fairfield isn't all that far from New Paltz. Less than two hours, and I can visit any time."

"That'll be nice," Daisy said.

"Yeah, and I—" Will cut off as someone called his name.

"I'll let you go. Have fun tonight, but not too much fun," Daisy teased.

"Alright *dad*, I'll keep that in mind. I love you."

"Love you too. Bye," Daisy said. She hung up and dropped her phone on the pillow next to her. Hana's ghost appeared, lying on her side next to Daisy and facing her.

"How's Will?" Hana asked.

"He loves Barcelona."

"Great. Now that we covered that, thoughts on the note?"

"You really do have a one track mind," Daisy grumbled, sitting up and reaching for the note again. She reread it, but nothing had changed in the few minutes since she'd first read it. She still didn't understand it.

"What do you mean, the place from the list?" She looked up at the ghost.

"I don't know. I wrote this the day I died, so it's fuzzy. Do you have any ideas?"

"No. I mean, what list are you even talking about? Do you have anything I can go off of?"

Hana took the note out of Daisy's hands and read it before handing it back. "I must've thought it was something you could figure out. So ... figure it out."

"Wow. So helpful," Daisy snarked.

"I'm doing the best I can with what I've got. It feels like I'm losing more memories every time I come back. It's ... I don't know how much longer I'll even be coherent. Things are different now, time is different. It feels like I've been dead for years."

"It's barely been a month."

"I *know* that," Hana snapped. "But it's different for me. I'm not supposed to be in this in between. It's not a place where souls are supposed to stay for a long time."

"I'll get you out of there. But ... if I solve your murder, I'll never see you again?"

"Yeah. I'll be gone. To whatever is next."

"Oh." Daisy didn't particularly like Hana's ghost showing up, but the thought of losing her again made Daisy feel hollow.

"Yeah. So chop chop before I start forgetting more stuff." Hana clapped to emphasize her point. "Where do you think your note is?"

"I'm not sure. Maybe I'll go get more of your journals and see if you mention anything in there."

"I guess that works. Just don't procrastinate like you did with reading this journal. I'll see you later," Hana said before disappearing again.

Daisy picked her phone back up before she could second guess herself and called Noriko.

"Hello?" Noriko said. She sounded tired — the warmth and life of her usual voice dimmed when Hana died, and through the small speakers on Daisy's phone it sounded like it was entirely gone. She hoped it was just the call quality.

"Hi Mrs. Holm," Daisy said, unsure if she should dive right into asking to come over.

"Oh, hi Daisy! How are you doing?"

"I'm okay! The job is going well, and I'm getting excited to leave for school," Daisy listed off, knowing that was what Noriko cared about.

"That's great, I'm so glad to hear that. Is anything wrong? Or is there anything I can help you with?"

"Actually, yeah, there was a book of Hana's that I wanted to read. Is it okay if I come over later and grab it?"

"Of course. I leave for work around six, can you come before then?"

"Oh, maybe I can come by tomorrow then. I was about to meet up with a friend to go dorm shopping," Daisy lied.

"Oh, that's so exciting! You know what, you know where the spare key is. Why don't you just let yourself in?"

"Oh, thanks, Mrs. Holm, that would be perfect."

"Great. Well, I won't keep you. Have fun picking out dorm stuff, and you know ..." Noriko hesitated. "All of Hana's dorm stuff is still packed up in the basement. You're more than welcome to take whatever you want from it."

"Oh, thank you," Daisy said. She didn't know why it felt like such a surprise that Hana's things were in her basement, waiting for a return trip to New Paltz that would never happen, but it left Daisy a little breathless.

They said their goodbyes, and Daisy swallowed thickly in an attempt not to cry.

Just in case her dad spoke with Noriko, Daisy decided to leave the house. She gave him the same excuse she had given Noriko and spent the next few hours just driving around, killing time by trying to think about what Hana was talking about. Daisy loved making lists, and she wished Hana had been a little less vague in her letter. She got fast food for dinner and sat in the parking lot, scrolling through years of summer and winter bucket lists, yearly resolutions, goals, and even to do lists to figure out what Hana was talking about. Daisy had a long list of possible places Hana could be referring to, and she diligently noted each one down with plans to go through the list later to see which one Hana was most likely referring to.

She drove to the Holm's house and arrived at six fifteen, not wanting to accidentally run into Noriko if she was running late. Daisy went into the backyard and grabbed the spare key from the loose brick in the pool area, which Hana chose as a hiding spot when they were younger. It gave Daisy a sense of relief to know that even with Hana gone, Noriko hadn't moved the spare to one of the more convenient spots she tried to talk Hana into using.

Daisy went in through the back door and slid off her shoes, taking in the quiet. She walked towards the front of the house where the staircase was, taking in all the small changes. At first, she didn't understand how Noriko could wipe away so many traces of Hana and Mark, but all at once it clicked.

If Hana's shoes were left in the closet, if her coats were on the matching wooden hangers, or if her keys and water bottle were on the credenza by the door, it would almost be like she was just out for a minute. With her things in their place in her home, it would seem as if she was coming back, and the constant realization that she wasn't would hit every minute of every day that Noriko spent in her home. Framed photos that once told the story of a happy family were now a tale of Noriko's loss.

Daisy walked around the rest of the floor to see how Noriko had scrubbed Hana away. Most of the changes were subtle. Hana's favorite books were gone from the shelves. The gaming console that Hana rarely used was removed from under the living room TV. The door to the office was still locked the way it was the day of Mark Holm's funeral five years earlier. Hana had tried the handle when they got back to the Holm house after the funeral luncheon, and when she found it locked, she sat on the floor outside of the room and cried. Daisy thought it probably looked like a time capsule the way most of Hana's room did, another room Noriko left to rot so she wouldn't have to think about her loss.

Daisy was compelled to look in the office, so she reached her hand along the top of the door frame to look for the key that should be there. Hana told her about it once when they were drunk, how she found the key's hiding place but never used it. But Daisy didn't feel the key where it should've been, and she remembered the one taped to Hana's note. She pulled it out of her bag and hastily shoved it into the lock, and when she twisted it the door opened with a soft *click*.

Daisy opened the door, expecting to see a room untouched for the last 3 years, but it was obvious that someone had been in there recently. Someone who knew that Noriko wouldn't be checking in here by the looks of it — the once tidy office from Daisy's childhood memories was a complete mess. There were papers and markers strewn across the desk and folders piled on the floor next to the plush rolling chair. The books on the shelves were all slightly out of place, like someone looked through all of them before tucking them back in their spots. The only person who worked this way was Hana. But what would she have wanted in this room? What was she looking through old paperwork and case notes for?

Daisy looked through the papers on the desk, but when she moved them a puff of dust flew into the air and sent her into a coughing fit. The wound of losing Hana was still so fresh that she forgot that even if Hana had been working in here, the office would still have at least a month's worth of disuse coating it.

Daisy sat down at the desk and flipped through the files, which looked to be documentation of Jake Hansen's threats against Mark Holm over the years. Hana annotated one of them, the last one Mark ever received, which came just a few weeks before Hansen murdered him. The threat itself was rambling and nonsensical, but Hana's notes brought a clarity Daisy wasn't sure she would've found on her own.

This letter is a mishmash of all of the others. Entire phrases and paragraphs borrowed and reused — he never did this before. It was also over two years since his last letter. What changed? Why did he snap when he did? Was he paid to kill dad?

Daisy didn't know what to think of Hana's annotation, but she gathered all the letters anyways, tucking the entire pile into a manila folder hidden beneath them. She looked in the drawers of the desk, but there was nothing but old office supplies there, so she picked up the office key and folder of death threats before venturing back into the hall and locking the office door behind her.

Daisy made her way up to Hana's room, unsure of where exactly Hana would hide her old journals. Hana loved keeping secrets, clearly, and Daisy was sure Hana would've found an interesting hiding spot. She stood in the middle of Hana's room, pointedly ignoring her bed, and looked around. A copy of *The Lightning Thief* on the bookshelf caught her attention — Hana and Daisy were obsessed with the Percy Jackson series they were in middle school, and Daisy picked it up to stare at the well-worn cover. She flipped through the pages and swore she could smell the cheap body spray she used to wear in seventh grade when something behind it caught her attention.

Instead of the dark wood of the back of the shelf, a sliver of a notebook cover was visible in the gap between books. Daisy pulled off all the books on the shelf, carefully stacking them in the order they were in on the shelf. Her efforts revealed years worth of Hana's journals hidden behind the books, and Daisy collected all of them, shoving them into a reusable grocery bag she found in the closet. She carefully placed all the books back on the shelf, but she took *The Lightning Thief* with her. If Noriko asked, she could claim this is what she came for.

"Man, we loved that book. Remember when we used to read it out loud to each other?" Hana's ghost asked, appearing next to Daisy. Daisy startled and dropped the book, but Hana caught it easily.

"Shit, you scared me."

"Sorry, should I have led with 'boo?'"

Daisy glared. "Hello would work too."

"Well, hello. Find anything good?"

"All your journals — nice hiding spot — and also the files in your dad's study," Daisy said, gathering all her things to leave Hana's room.

"The files ... right, yeah! The letters, right?" Hana asked.

Daisy gave her a perplexed look. "Yeah. Are you ... what else have you forgotten?"

"Nothing much. Get home safe. I'll be back later." Hana disappeared before Daisy could ask more questions. It was kind of perfect that Hana could now make a dramatic exit whenever she wanted.

When Daisy got back home, she dumped all of the journals on her bed. Before she started reading the rest of the journals, she cracked open her own notebook to write down everything she learned from the Holm house.

• • • •

- Noriko got rid of all the traces of Hana
  - It's like Hana was never there

• • • •

Daisy paused after writing that last line before crossing it out. It wasn't really relevant to Hana's murder.

• • • •

- Noriko got rid of all the traces of Hana
  - It's like Hana was never there

- The key on Hana's letter was for her father's office, which she was working out of

- Hana annotated death threats against her father

- Hana thought someone might've paid Jake Hansen to kill her father

· · · ·

Daisy figured that she wasn't going to have anything else of importance to add and flipped to a fresh page to write down notes about the journals. She grabbed a pad of sticky notes from her desk, opened the first journal, and jotted down the dates of the first and last entries before sticking the note to the front. Once she was done, she ordered them from the oldest, all the way back from when Hana was starting sixth grade, to the newest, whose last entry was days before Hana died. There was at least one page ripped out after that one, though, so Daisy wasn't sure when Hana's actual last entry was.

Henry called Daisy for dinner, and she was glad for the excuse to avoid reading Hana's journals once again. Soon she would be brave, but for now she let herself be a coward for another night.

Chapter 12

Hana — age 19

11/20/18

Dear Diary,

I'm dreading seeing Daisy again. How can I face her without immediately spilling everything I did? I mean, I cheated on her. I cheated on her twelve *times. And I just ended things with Frida on Saturday. Even though I told myself I would do it all last week, I just kept going back to her. But that's over now.*

On top of seeing Daisy again, I also am going home again. And on the one hand I hate it and I'm so glad I left for college, but I'm kind of looking forward to it. At school I can be whoever I want, but I also want everyone to see me as the person I want to be, not always who I am. I painted a picture of myself that's more vivid than I intended, and sometimes it's hard to shine as bright as people think I can. But at home I can be a burning sunset or a muted orange and people still know me.

Well, I still have another two hours of this train ride (if we're on time) to contemplate how much I fucked up the best thing in my life. I think I'll take a nap to avoid thinking about it.

Sincerely,

Hana

• • • •

"It's so good to see you, sweetheart," Noriko said when she picked Hana up from the train station. "I know the trip is a long one, but I'm glad that you're back to combat my empty nester syndrome."

Hana had never thought of her mother as having a scent before, but as she was crushed to the chest of the woman that raised her, Noriko smelled like home. Tears pricked in Hana's eyes, and for a minute she considered telling Noriko everything. About the way she loved Daisy and how she betrayed her and the guilt consuming her and how overwhelming life was when she didn't know who she was meant to be, just that it wasn't who she was now.

The station was crowded with people coming back to Rochester for the holiday, and Hana spotted a few reunions going on while they walked outside to Noriko's car. A middle-aged man who looked disgruntled during the entire trip now smiled and held two small children vying for his attention on either hip. It made Hana's heart ache, and she hurried after her mother a little faster than before.

Noriko had managed to arrive early enough to get a close parking spot, which Hana was grateful for as the November night bit at her ungloved hands. Noriko opened the back door for Hana's duffel bag with a wide conspiratorial smile, and before Hana could question the look, Daisy popped her head out.

Her smile was bright enough to light up the dreary parking lot, and Hana wanted to cry. Instead, she smiled and let Daisy envelop her in a hug. A black hole opened in Hana's chest, sucking in all of the stability she'd gotten from seeing her mother and crushing her into herself. How should she act around someone that she loved and hurt so badly? How did she hide the destruction Daisy knew nothing about?

"I'll put your stuff in the trunk," Noriko said with a smile.

"I missed you," Daisy said, still hugging Hana. Hana clung to her as if holding Daisy tight enough would wash away the sins Hana had committed against her. If she loved Daisy enough now, maybe it would make up for the fact that she did something that would destroy Daisy when she found out. *If* she ever found out.

"It's weird to be back in Rochester," Hana murmured, climbing into the backseat after Daisy. She felt like they were kids again on their way to soccer practice or swim lessons, giggling and talking quietly in the backseat while Noriko pretended not to hear anything they said. The black hole pulled more insistently.

"I bet," Daisy said. "Thanksgiving should be fun, though. I'm glad you guys are coming over again this year. It's always a better day when you guys come over."

Hana remembered the first year that the Polo family came over for Thanksgiving, the year after her mom's adopted parents both passed away within two months of each other. Hana and her parents used to go to their house every Thanksgiving, and most years it was the only time Hana saw the people who raised her mother. That first year Noriko was meticulous about the house being impeccably decorated and all the meals being properly prepared, obsessed with the idea of hosting the perfect Thanksgiving to avoid having to go to the large Holm family event Hana's paternal great aunt and uncle hosted. The year that Mark died they went to the Polo house instead because Noriko didn't really have the energy to cook or clean, even though it was nine months later. Hana survived the year after her father's death with microwave meals and boxed mac and cheese, but she never mentioned it to anyone. Noriko did the best she could.

Dennis showed up at the Polo's house that year, too, and Hana tried not to be upset about it. He'd gotten divorced shortly before Mark died, and even though she knew it made sense that he wouldn't spend the holiday with his ex-wife's family like he used to, it still felt wrong to have him in Daisy's house. He didn't have any excuse to miss the party that his family hosted, unlike Noriko and Hana, who were always on the outskirts of Holm events even before Mark died.

Something about having him talking with her mom when her dad wasn't around anymore felt wrong in a way she couldn't explain. It made her angry and territorial and annoyed that he thought that his pain over a divorce he probably initiated could be as painful as losing her dad to a lunatic with a gun. She ignored the fact that he lost his brother and instead picked a fight with Daisy the way she always did when she was upset about her dad that year. Daisy reacted the same way she always did — like a wounded animal that rolled over to prevent further damage. Hana didn't even have the heart to really fight that day, and they made up before dessert was served.

"As long as you got me a vegetarian option instead of turkey, I'm excited," Hana teased, speaking loud enough to clue Noriko in that she was also a part of the conversation.

"Don't worry," Noriko said. "We got your weird non-meat holiday roast thing. It seems like the least appetizing thing I've ever seen, but whatever makes you happy. Can you really eat well at school without meat? You look too skinny." Hana laughed, even though she knew she had lost weight unintentionally that semester. Sometimes the only vegetarian option at the dining hall was fries, and Hana could only eat so many before the grease made her feel sick.

"I am not. You just haven't seen me. Only a few months and you forgot all about what I looked like, Mom? Harsh," Hana joked. Noriko rolled her eyes and Daisy giggled, earning a sidelong glance and a smile from Hana. Her phone buzzed, and she looked down at it to see a text from Daisy, who was asking Noriko an innocuous question about the route they were taking.

· · · ·

Daisy

I wish I could kiss you rn

Not touching you is driving me insane

Hana

Ask my mom if you can sleep over and you won't have to
keep your hands off me

• • • •

Daisy glanced at her phone and swallowed thickly. Hana held back a smirk.

"Mrs. Holm, is it cool if I stay over tonight? I'd just be in the way at my house. Plus, I think Hana has probably forgotten what it's like to sleep in a room alone," Daisy joked. Hana tried not to look startled at the sentence, forgetting for a second that Daisy was talking about having a roommate.

"Of course, Daisy. You know you're always welcome at our house. Do you need to grab anything from your house?"

"No, I think I have one of everything at your house anyways."

"Yeah, you can borrow some clothes from me to sleep in," Hana said. Daisy smiled at her, and Noriko's eyes flicked between them in the rearview mirror.

"Alright. No drinking tonight, though. I don't feel like dealing with hungover teenagers on Thanksgiving," Noriko said.

Daisy looked startled, but Hana just laughed. "Mom, I'm only 19. I have never touched alcohol once in my life. Whatever are you talking about?"

Daisy gave her a tight smile, and Hana realized she had never told Daisy about how much Hana and Noriko's relationship had improved now that they didn't live together. Once Hana was far enough away to be her own person and miss her mom, she found that she understood Noriko a lot better. She saw her mom as a person who was heartbroken and hardworking and not just as someone Hana could constantly take and take and take from. It was an odd realization, but one that colored the way she was looking at her mother now.

Hana wondered what it was like when her mom went to college. Did she pull all nighters and survive on snacks and laugh too loud with friends in the library the way Hana did? Noriko went to a local state school so she could be close to her parents if they needed help around the house. She was an only child, adopted when her parents were in their late thirties. She used to feel a responsibility to take care of them as they got older, but once she married Mark, she could afford to hire an at home caretaker for them and didn't have to visit as often.

When did Noriko start to feel disconnected from her parents? Did the years of driving them to doctors appointments and using her nursing degree to care for them create resentment Noriko couldn't move past? Did they drift apart when she went away for school and she started feeling the way Hana did now? Did Noriko feel like she held an ocean of knowledge of the world in the palm of her hand and the life she used to live at home was nothing more than a glass of water after a nightmare?

When they got back to the Holm home, Hana breathed in deeply. An essential oil diffuser going in the living room made the entire floor smell like lemon and cinnamon and *home*.

"I made up some cookies for tomorrow, but I think there are enough for you girls to take a few," Noriko said while they took off their coats and shoes. It reminded Hana of when they were eight and nine years old and tried to come inside covered in dirt after playing outside for too long. Noriko bribed them with freshly baked chocolate chip cookies to persuade them to hose themselves down outside so they wouldn't track dirt through the house, and it worked like a charm. Hana blinked back tears at the sudden memory, but she hid it by turning to hang her coat in the closet.

"Thanks, Mrs. Holm. You're the best," Daisy said.

"Yeah, thanks, Mom." If anyone else noticed how thick Hana's voice was, they didn't comment.

Daisy carried their glasses of milk and chocolate chip cookies so Hana could bring up her bags, and they retreated to Hana's room. Once the door closed, Daisy set down the food quickly and practically launched herself at Hana, kissing her before Hana could even drop her bags. Hana was struck by the lightning of the moment, by her own desire to get Daisy closer and lose herself in the girl she loved, and she forgot her guilt for a minute. When she remembered and pulled away.

Daisy pressed her forehead to Hana's and smiled. "Hi," she murmured, her voice raspy.

"Hi," Hana replied with a small smile. She pecked Daisy's lips before flicking her eyes to the bed.

"Want to listen to some music?" Daisy asked, knowing what Hana was thinking. Daisy's ability to read Hana used to be a gift, a symptom of their connection and love for each other, but now it felt like a fatal diagnosis. Still, Hana put on the indie band that she was obsessed with lately while Daisy watched her with hungry eyes.

Being with Daisy was familiar, easy. They knew what they liked from years of loving each other, and Hana couldn't help comparing everything that Daisy did to what Frida had done. Daisy knew just where to kiss her neck, while Frida was always a bit too far to the left. Maybe Frida learned the placement from someone she loved once as well. Daisy smelled different and tasted different and was all soft edges where Frida had been rough. Daisy rushed with her in a way Frida never did because Frida never worried about them getting caught.

Seeing Daisy again proved to Hana once and for all that ending things with Frida was the right decision, and being with her at all in the first place was a colossal mistake. She couldn't lose this, couldn't lose the way that Daisy looked up at her like she was some kind of God-sent revelation.

Afterwards, they ate their cookies and put on pajamas and fell back into bed completely wrapped in one another.

"I missed you so much," Daisy said, her voice small and vulnerable in the quiet of Hana's room.

"I missed you, too. It's so different not having you so close anymore," Hana said.

"Well, I applied to New Paltz. If I get in, we'll be together again, and it'll just be across campus instead of across the state."

Hana's heart clenched at the thought. What if Daisy came to New Paltz only to find out what Hana had really been doing? What if she met the person Hana was turning into and hated her?

"When do you find out?" Hana asked, holding in her more poisonous questions.

"I think they start sending stuff out in, like, January. You'll know as soon as I do, though. You know I tell you everything," Daisy said. She was being honest. Daisy never lied to her about anything. Then again, Daisy never did anything that she would ever have to lie to Hana about.

"I love you, Daisy Polo," Hana murmured. Daisy smiled against her chest where her face was pressed, and Hana barely stopped herself from tearing up. If Daisy found her out of place declaration weird, she didn't say anything about it.

"I love you too, Hana Holm. Good night." Daisy pressed a kiss to Hana's collarbone before going quiet.

Daisy loved Hana. Hana had known that since the first time they kissed, but she never quite understood how just that feeling was enough for Daisy. She didn't need to be constantly reminded that Hana loved her. She didn't need to show it off. She didn't need anything to love Hana.

When Daisy said she loved Hana, she said it the way she would any other basic truth. Bird calls sound like songs. The sun rises in the east. Daisy loves Hana. That kind of devotion was a comfort to Hana before Frida, but now the sure, strong love that she used to be drunk on was hitting her liver. She didn't deserve to be loved the way Daisy loved her, but she was too selfish to walk away. It was easier not to deal with the headache of telling the truth.

"I can feel you thinking too hard," Daisy murmured. Hana startled. She thought Daisy was already asleep. Daisy tucked her chin over Hana's shoulder and turned to look at Hana, her green eyes shining through the dark like a beacon.

"You're the best thing that's ever happened to me," Hana murmured. It was true and she didn't deserve it.

"And I'll still be the best in the morning. Go to sleep," Daisy teased. Hana kissed the top of Daisy's head instead of answering and finally forced herself to fall asleep.

The next morning Daisy left after they ate the breakfast Noriko made for them, and Hana waved from the doorway while Henry drove her away.

"Hana, can I talk to you for a sec?" Noriko called from the kitchen, drawing Hana back inside. Hana walked into the kitchen and stared at the controlled chaos Noriko had created.

"What's up?" Hana asked.

"You two are dating, aren't you?" Noriko asked.

Hana gaped at her mother. "Um, I—"

"Honey, best friends don't look at each other like that. I wasn't born yesterday," Noriko said, rolling out a pie crust like this was a casual conversation.

"I, well, yes, we are, but, I — are you going to tell Daisy's dad?" Hana asked, immediately worrying how Daisy would feel about the revelation even though it felt like a relief that Hana didn't have to hide this from Noriko anymore. Hana may not want to hide their relationship, but she would never want anyone to out Daisy before she was ready.

"No, I won't do that to either of you, but I don't want you to feel like you have to keep hiding in your own home. I know you're away at college, and you're entering adulthood. Besides, you could be doing much worse while you're away if there isn't a girl like that waiting for you at home," Noriko said. Hana's face crumpled, all of her guilt and self hatred coming to the surface, and she started crying. Noriko set down her rolling pin and rushed over to pull her daughter into her arms.

"I cheated on her," Hana sobbed, "and I can't tell her because she'll hate me. I've ruined everything because I can't have anything good without messing it up."

Noriko made shushing noises and held Hana until she cried herself out. When she was done, Noriko pulled back and brushed Hana's hair off her wet face.

"I know you know what you did was wrong, you don't need me to tell you that. But you can't keep this inside," Noriko said.

"But I can't tell her. It would destroy everything," Hana said.

"Well, then you need to think long and hard about the fact that you hurt Daisy and decide whether the truth is what she needs. You're an adult now. You should learn the price of honesty and the weight of keeping secrets."

Hana nodded, and Noriko gave her a small, sad smile.

"Your father and I kept secrets from each other. Ones that will never be revealed now. But even if he was lying to me about some things, it didn't matter. I trusted him and I loved him and nothing he could have done would have stopped that. There is power in silence, and we both knew that. We would tell each other if it was important enough. If Daisy is the right one for you, you can do that. You know her better than I do. I won't tell you what to do other than think about it."

Hana was shocked. The thought of her parents, who loved each other more than she'd ever seen two people love each other, hiding secrets from each other felt like something she was never supposed to know.

"What's something you never told him?" Hana asked. She needed to think, and she was still wrapping her head around her mother's advice.

"I never told him that I almost dated Dennis first," Noriko revealed. "Years before your father and I were together, Dennis and I went on a date. He was at a dinner party that I went to back when I first got my degree and started working at the hospital. He asked me out to dinner, and I thought he was charming until he asked where I was *really* from. Things were different back then, but I still knew I could never be with a man that thought he could speak to me that way. When I met your father, I didn't even put it together that they were brothers until I met the family. I told him I met Dennis before, but he never knew anything beyond that. He didn't need to because it never mattered. One date with Dennis didn't change the way I loved your father, so it didn't matter. He never asked, and I never cared to tell him."

"Oh," was all Hana said. There was nothing else to say to an admission like that.

"Yes. And, of course, your uncle got better with time, but your father was always the one for me, right up to the day he died."

"What about now?"

Noriko crossed her arms over her chest. "What do you mean, 'now?'"

"Is he still the only one for you?" Hana asked.

Noriko dropped her gaze to her overpriced slippers. "No, he's not. I'll never love someone the way I loved your father, but I'm sure I'll love again," Noriko admitted. Hana nodded like it was new information, but it wasn't a surprise. This was an awfully big house that her mother lived in all alone while Hana was gone. How could she fault her mother for trying to fill the rooms with life again? Still, a pinch of anger sizzled in her chest

"That's ... Will you tell me? If you meet someone?" Hana asked.

"I will. Once it's ... really something. You don't have to hear about every date," Noriko said. Hana wrinkled her nose at the thought.

Noriko laughed. "Yes, exactly. Now, I need help with the pies. I'll even let you put on whatever music you want, but do consider my poor ears won't you?" Hana rolled her eyes at her mother's teasing, and the seriousness of the moment leached away like autumn melting into winter.

By the time they got to the Polo's house that afternoon, Hana was still turning her conversation with Noriko over in her head. She tried to push it to the back of her mind, but all it did was expose new parts of the idea she needed to consider.

They went through the usual niceties, the game of their parents pretending to be annoyed that they were drinking wine, and the small talk about life Hana expected. Things were going smoothly until the doorbell rang. Hana didn't know anyone else was coming, but her mother sprang to her feet and smoothed down her dress with a bright smile.

"Oh, that'll be your uncle," Noriko said, going with Henry to greet Dennis. Hana finished the rest of her wine in one pull.

"Hey everyone," Dennis said when he walked into the room. The others gave generic greetings in response, but Hana couldn't get herself to do it. She wanted to be happy to see him, but the only thing she felt was annoyed. He didn't belong here, not like the rest of them did.

"How was your drive?" Noriko asked. Hana couldn't stand the stupid small talk they would make for the rest of the night. She was trying to come up with a good excuse to leave when she noticed the way that her uncle and mother were standing. His hand hovered over her waist, and she was angled fully towards him like she was holding back from touching him.

Earlier, Hana hadn't thought twice about why the lie Noriko gave as an example was about her uncle, but now it became clear. This was something Noriko was thinking about all the time. This little lie was sitting in her brain and weighing down all her thoughts. Noriko needed to tell herself she made the right choice because there was no longer the option to correct her mistakes.

"We're going to watch the dog show," Daisy declared, standing and pulling Hana along with her towards the living room.

Will followed after them, laughing. "Daisy, why are we watching this? You just get upset about all the dogs that don't win." He sighed.

"It's better than listening to them talk about the drive from one side of the town to the other. Besides, I've grown this year. I know they're all winners, and I definitely won't get mad," Daisy said matter-of-factly.

"I'm holding you to that," Will said.

Daisy rolled her eyes and threw the TV remote to him. "I'm going to go grab the wine. Why don't you get to the right channel?" Daisy turned and walked out of the room.

Once Daisy was out of earshot, Will turned to face Hana. "I know something is up with you. I don't know what, but just ... don't hurt her."

"You already gave me the shovel talk, like, as soon as you found out we were dating," Hana said. The joke fell flat.

"I'm serious, Hana. You know I love you and you're one of my best friends, but ..."

"But I'm not your sister?" Hana finished.

Will grimaced at her words. "I just — Daisy is so naive. I don't think she could handle you breaking her heart."

"You don't have to worry about her, Will. I'll always take good care of her. You know that," Hana said. Saying the lie was like licking the sticky glue on the inside of an envelope. Sharp and sweet with a side of hesitance so you wouldn't cut your tongue on the paper.

"I know, I just have to say it. So how's college? Is your mom still pushing for you to transfer to an ivy?"

"Yeah, as per usual. She started leaving pamphlets around about Harvard and Yale's philosophy departments. I think there was even one from NYU. She must really be desperate since she's always said that isn't a *real* ivy league school." Will laughed, and Hana tried not to notice the tightness to his smile.

Will was attending Fairfield for something business related, and he was on a full scholarship for lacrosse, which was the only way he could attend the school. He didn't have a trust fund he could use to pay for college and college-related expenses like Hana. One of the reasons she was so excited to go to New Paltz when she first discovered it, aside from knowing it would piss her mom off, was the fact that Daisy could go too. It was a state school, and the cheapest state school in New York on top of that, and back then she saw herself as the right person for Daisy. Now she knew if things didn't work out between them, she wouldn't be able to go a day without seeing Daisy somewhere on campus. She wished she could convince Daisy to go somewhere else without revealing why.

Daisy came back into the room and immediately held up her phone to take a picture. Hana gave a bright smile and threw up a peace sign, Will laughed, and Daisy smiled at the picture.

"That's gonna look great on my wall."

Daisy's walls were plastered with printed out pictures of anything and everything Daisy found interesting, which meant there were a lot of pictures of Hana up there already. She counted once before she left for college and saw her face up there fifty-seven times. She wondered how many more times she appeared by now.

"You're lucky you've got such a good-looking brother. Otherwise your walls would be devastating to look at since there's so much of Hana's face," Will joked, and Daisy blushed and rolled her eyes. Hana threw a pillow across the couch at him, and it devolved into a pillow war for a few minutes until the adults came in and told them that if they wanted to be treated like adults responsible enough to drink, they would have to act like it.

Hana let herself be happy, and sitting on the couch she realized she couldn't lose this by telling Daisy about Frida. She vowed that if a day came when she was strong enough to survive losing Daisy, she would tell her.

Chapter 13

Daisy — July 2019

DAISY ONLY LET HERSELF procrastinate reading the rest of Hana's journals for a few days before finally settling in to read them on Tuesday afternoon. She had never been nosy before because she always trusted Hana, and she was scared of how these journals would show Hana was undeserving of that trust.

She started with the oldest journals, the ones from middle school, but Daisy only read a few pages of the first before realizing there wasn't going to be anything relevant in there. If Hana referenced an old event Daisy could always go back.

The only entry she sought out was from the day Hana came out to Daisy. That was the day Daisy realized it was possible to like girls *and* boys after Hana explained the LGBTQ+ spectrum over ice cream, and she always wondered if Hana noticed the change. She never asked about it when Hana was alive, so instead she turned to the words that thirteen-year-old Hana left behind.

• • • •

8/17/14

Dear Diary,

Well, I did it. I successfully came out to Daisy yesterday. It went well, she seemed cool about it, but I think I have a new problem. I think I might have feelings for her. I mean I know I'm a lesbian, but I've never had any sort of real crush before. And Daisy is straight, otherwise she probably would've said something. Right? I don't know. This is the worst. This is so cliche. Isn't the whole reason people are nervous about being friends with lesbians is because they think they'll have a crush on

them? I'll just have to get over it. I'm just going to not think about it as hard as possible until it goes away.
   Sincerely,
   Hana

. . . .

The fact Hana had written this while Daisy was also realizing the way she felt towards Hana was more than friends made her heart ache. Hana really was the love of Daisy's life, even now a little over month after her death.

Daisy was sitting on the floor surrounded by the journals, and Hana appeared curled against the wall with her knees pulled into her chest. Daisy picked up the journal Hana started the day she went away to college, and the ghost sighed.

"I'm sorry in advance," Hana murmured.

"About what?" Daisy asked.

"I ... I wasn't good to you," she said.

"I know you cheated on me. You already told me," Daisy snapped.

Hana sighed and ran a hand through her thick black hair. "I didn't tell you everything though," she said apologetically. "I lied about a lot and ... well, I never lied to myself the way I lied to you. I'm sorry about what you're going to read, but ... there are other things. You can't skip that one." Daisy nodded resolutely and cracked open the purple composition notebook that ranged from August 2018 to December 2018.

Hana was right. Hearing how lonely Hana was and how much she missed home hurt to read since she'd never actually told Daisy any of this when she was alive. Her sympathy for Hana evaporated when she got to the day after Hana met Frida.

Daisy always assumed that Hana got drunk at a party, made a mistake, and cheated on Daisy in a fit-of-passion, one-night-stand hookup. Finding out that it was a weeks-long affair made her sick to her stomach, and she calmly closed the journal and put it back in the stack next to her bed.

"What are you doing?" Hana asked.

"I can't do this right now. I can't do this at all — just, why? So many lies, and for what?"

"I got to that. I wrote it in there, you just have to—"

"I don't have to do anything," Daisy shot back. "For all I know you're not even real."

"We're back to this shit again? For god's sake I thought you were *smart*," Hana snapped.

Daisy reared back from the ghostly figure and shook her head. "That's rich to hear from the person who told me the truth about cheating only to not clarify how many times they cheated. Absolutely rich."

"I mean, you never asked, so—"

Daisy scoffed. "Oh, so it's my fault that even when you told me the truth you were still hiding things?"

"Look, I get that I messed up, but you not investigating my murder because you're, I don't know, jealous, is—"

"I'm not *jealous*," Daisy said harshly. "I'm upset because the person I loved lied to me by omission for months and then lied to my *face* about the lie by omission."

"Just, come on, keep—"

"I can't keep centering my entire life around someone who is gone and not coming back. This isn't a breakup. This isn't something where we might make up. Does it even matter how you died if the fact of the matter is that you did?"

Daisy couldn't take a full breath, couldn't expand her lungs past the ache in her chest.

Hana stared at her in disbelief, her mouth opening and closing a few times before she finally spoke. "Of course it matters. The truth matters. I'm trapped in this limbo where I'm losing my mind, and my mom still thinks—" Hana cut herself off with a sharp intake of breath and a shake of her head.

"Don't look at me like I'm a belligerent child. For the love of God, it's past the time to stop looking down on me," Daisy spat out.

"Then start acting like a grown up," Hana snapped back. Daisy flinched back at her words, and Hana winced.

"Look," Daisy said coldly. "I'll pick it back up when I'm not feeling like I want to vomit, alright?" She was giving in to Hana like she always did.

Hana nodded in agreement. "Yeah, maybe a nap or something? I think if you get some rest that would be good for you, right?"

Daisy rolled her eyes and picked up her phone. "Oh, I'm not napping. I'm texting John back."

"Seriously?" Hana looked at Daisy like she was a toddler throwing a fit.

Daisy pointedly did not look at Hana as she opened an unread text she got from John earlier in the day. "Yes, seriously. He's cute and he's nice to me and I need something ... uncomplicated to think about."

. . . .

John
Hi! Are you busy today?

Daisy
No, want to do something?

John
Yeah! Have you ever been to the water tanks at Cobbs Hill?

. . . .

John's message sparked something in Daisy's brain, and she tore through her things until she found Hana's letter again. *The place from the list.* Of course — Hana was talking about her senior year bucket list, and the place was the water tanks where they tagged their initials that winter. How could she forget?

. . . .

Daisy
I have but I'm still down to go!

John
Cool! Meet you there in an hour?

Daisy
Sounds good, see you soon!

. . . .

"John seems…"

"Now it's your turn to not be jealous," Daisy snapped. Hana gave Daisy a last appraising look and disappeared.

Daisy got ready quickly, throwing on a pair of jean shorts and a flowy green peasant top with flowers embroidered along the neckline. She twisted her hair into a messy french braid, dabbed on a few swipes of mascara, and hesitated before applying a coat of the lip gloss she'd taken from Hana's room. She threw it in her bag on the way out and walked confidently down the stairs so her dad wouldn't think she was doing anything suspicious.

Daisy lied to her father, telling him she was going to hang out with someone from high school, and Henry didn't question it. It was much better than the courtroom level interrogation she would face if he knew she was hanging out with a boy.

Daisy sang along to the radio loudly and rolled down all the windows so she could feel the balmy July air. Even though she'd spent every morning that week at the camp's outdoor pool, she still felt like she was losing out on summer before now. Maybe it was the fact that for every morning she spent outside with the sun and the songs and the routine monotony of day camp, she also spent an entire afternoon in her room wrapped in her duvet sleeping to procrastinate investigating her dead ex-girlfriend's death. Maybe it was the fact that the only time she'd hung out with people her age outside of work this summer was the memorial and party with Hana's friends. Maybe it felt like it was really summer now because she was doing something that was stupid and fun in a normal, teenage way.

She got to the park early and waited for John in the shady clearing between the road and the path's entrance. She convinced herself it didn't make sense to walk to the tanks and look for whatever Hana left for her alone when John would be here any minute. She worried that the graffiti she and Hana spray painted the previous December would be gone, but she tried not to worry about that yet.

"Daisy! Hey, what's up?" John called from the edge of the clearing, pulling Daisy out of her spiral. When he got to her, he pulled her into a hug, and Daisy sank into it. Everything about him was so different from Hana, and it made it easier not to lose herself in thoughts of the ghost following Daisy.

"Hey! This was a good idea. I haven't seen the water tanks in forever. I always like seeing what changed."

"Honestly I don't remember what used to be up half of the time, but it's always nice to see what's here." John laughed at his own forgetfulness. Daisy asked about his day while they started on the short path to the water tanks.

The tanks were two giant cylinders placed directly on the ground at the top of a hill in Cobbs Hill park, and though they were once an unknown secret, they were slowly becoming a more well known destination among people who loved Rochester. The trail to find them was short, but most people that visited the park stayed on the paved path around the reservoir, so the area around the water tanks was never very crowded. Daisy didn't know when people had started tagging the tanks, but all the easy-to-reach areas were covered in layers of different designs and names and disruptive, messy scribbles. The insides of the tanks used to be mostly graffiti-free, but someone had removed the welded-on doors a few years earlier, and now the insides were covered too.

Daisy let John lead the way, and he chose to walk around the tank that didn't have Daisy and Hana's graffiti on it. She was only half listening to what he had to say, instead scanning the area to see if anything looked out of place, if there was any indication of where Hana had hidden something for her.

"So how did you find out about this place?" John asked.

"My brother told me about them a few years ago," Daisy lied. She wasn't about to tell John that her ex-girlfriend introduced her to the place. Will had mentioned the tanks before, but it was in passing, and Hana was the one who actually brought Daisy here.

"Nice, does he live around here?"

"No, he goes to Fairfield. He's in Barcelona right now for a summer class," Daisy said. They were now circling the tank with her graffiti, and she was barely listening as they neared the spot.

"Oh, that's cool. Are you guys close?"

She and Hana's graffiti was still there, and the memory of the night they put it up knocked the wind out of Daisy. She didn't realize how hard it would hit her to see the evidence of their relationship there in streaky, dripping spray paint spelling out "D + H for" because they had been interrupted while Daisy was writing "forever." Daisy took her eyes off the graffiti when she realized John was waiting for her to respond.

"Yeah, he's the best."

"That's nice. I've always wished I had a sibling, but it's just me."

"I don't know what I'd do without him." Daisy was glad for the distraction from thoughts of Hana. "Our mom died when we were little, and there's something about having a sibling going through it together that's different from my dad comforting me, you know?"

"Yeah, that makes sense. I'm sorry about your mom," John said. It was almost an afterthought, and Daisy shrugged it off as she scanned the ground around the tank, trying to find any evidence of what Hana might have hidden for her. She was starting to doubt this was the right place at all.

"Thanks. I was really young when she died, so I don't remember much about her," Daisy said. She didn't add that her grief now was compounded by the death of her mother, Hana's father, and Hana herself, each loss piling on top of each other like logs on a fire, raging higher every time.

"That's tough. My grandpa died a few years ago, which sucked even though he was old, and yeah I'm just putting my foot in my mouth so I'll shut up," John said.

Daisy laughed and knocked her shoulder into his. "You're fine, don't worry about it. I'll let you know if you mess up too badly."

"Sounds like a good deal."

They kept talking and did another lap around the tanks, but Daisy didn't see anything out of place in any way. If John noticed the fact that she was paying more attention to the ground and the woods around them than the tanks, he didn't mention it. They made their way back to the trail and then to the parking lot, and Daisy stopped at the driver's side door of her car, not sure what would come next. After her first date with Hana, they ended up at Daisy's house cuddling and watching movies. She didn't think that would happen now.

"Are you busy tonight?" John asked. "My friend is having some people over if you wanted to come and hang, and maybe we could grab food or something before." Daisy smiled. John made it so easy to be around him. He was uncomplicated and kind and undoubtedly into Daisy.

"I don't have any plans, so that sounds good," Daisy said. They hashed out the details of meeting at John's house and went their separate ways.

Once Daisy was alone in her car, she took a shaky breath as it hit her that her lead was wrong. She was so sure earlier that the water tanks would be where Hana left something for her, but she was wrong, and she hated herself for it. Seeing their graffiti again hurt her too, and she let herself be upset for a minute before starting the drive to John's house.

John told her to just come in when she got there, and when she hesitantly stepped through the front door an entire group of people greeted her, including John.

He sprang to his feet and came over to say hi. "Everyone is nosy as hell and came down to say hi, but no worries if you don't want to hang out with everyone."

"It's okay. I like people."

"Great! Then you'll like everyone except Chris," a girl called from the group, which made them all burst out laughing.

"Well, hi everyone and Chris," Daisy said, causing another round of laughter.

John's friends were nice, though Daisy kept getting lost at the references of inside jokes and past events. They ordered pizza and ate it while playing a drinking game to prepare for the party.

At eight p.m. exactly, one of John's roommates, Todd, stood up and clapped his hands. "It's time to go! As the self-elected party tsar of the summer, we have to leave now or we'll never make it out," he announced. They all got up and started moving, making their way towards the door. John took Daisy's hand while they walked the few blocks to the party, and she let him. It was easy to forget about all the things bothering her when she was with him.

"John! My man!" a voice called as soon as they walked through a wooden gate into a backyard draped with twinkling lights and filled with people.

"Kyle! My dude!" John responded. Kyle smiled at John but quickly turned his gaze to John holding Daisy's hand.

"And who is this?" Kyle asked.

"This is Daisy, she's friends with Skippy," John responded.

"I think calling Skippy my friend may be a stretch if I'm being honest," Daisy joked.

"Oh shit, are you the one she was blowing up at last week?" Kyle asked.

"Yep, that was me. She was in angry drunk mode."

"That makes sense," Kyle said. "Anyways, you guys wanna smoke? I was just about to head up to my room with a few people."

Daisy looked to John, who was already nodding, and she loved being folded into the party so effortlessly. Hana always expected Daisy to just go with the flow and figure things out, but here it felt like they were slowing down to help her catch up.

Unlike John's house, this house was clearly new to being used as college housing. It was taken care of over the years, and the beautiful details were well-preserved, like intricate carvings on the window trim and a sparkling chandelier in the once-dining room, which now just looked like a glorified beer pong arena complete with a tarp covering the hardwood flooring under the folding table.

"Isn't this place cool?" John asked.

"Yeah, how did you end up here?" Daisy asked.

"Jackie's dad bought the house to start renting out," Kyle said, "so we're the first college tenants of it. No way any of the rest of us could afford such a nice place without him giving us a deal, so it's awesome. More money to spend on the fun stuff." Kyle led them upstairs. His room felt haphazard with high ceilings and crown molding contrasting comically with the Tarantino movie posters and cheap psychedelic tapestry.

"Cool room," Daisy said even though she kind of hated it.

"Thanks. My girlfriend helped me pick out the tapestry. She's got a real eye for it, don't you, babe?" he asked a girl rolling a joint on his bed.

"I like to think so. He needed something to balance the overwhelmingly male energy of the Pulp Fiction poster," she joked. Daisy laughed, and when John sat down in a bean bag chair, she settled on the ground next to it.

"Shit, do you want the chair?" John shifted to stand back up. "I didn't mean to make you sit on the ground, that was a dick—"

"It's fine. I would've said something if I cared," Daisy said with a smile. He looked relieved and relaxed.

Kyle's girlfriend lit the joint, took a long drag, and passed it to John before speaking again. "So Daisy, what are you doing around here? School?" she asked, draping herself over Kyle.

"I'm from Penfield, but I'm going to New Paltz," Daisy said with a smile.

"No shit? I've heard cool things about it there. Good music scene, right?" Kyle asked.

"I don't know yet, I'm starting in the fall," Daisy replied. She took the joint when it was passed to her and took a hit, trying her hardest to look like she knew what she was doing.

"Oh man, are we corrupting you? Blink twice if you need help," Kyle joked. His girlfriend huffed out a laugh and looked away. Daisy wondered what she did wrong so quickly to make the other girl dislike her already.

"Nope, thoroughly corrupted already. But thanks for the check."

John smiled at her when he handed the joint back to the couple sitting on the bed.

Two girls pushed open the door. "Damn you started without us, Kyle. Rude," the first one said. Her hair was cut into a short pixie, and her clothes were boxy and looked purposefully mismatched. The other girl wore a hyper feminine hot pink babydoll dress, elaborate makeup, and layered jewelry. Daisy immediately knew that the two girls weren't straight — it was obvious they didn't consider the male gaze at all while getting dressed.

"Cool dress," Daisy said before Kyle could defend himself to the girls.

They looked down at Daisy and smiled. "Thanks! Who're you?" the second girl asked.

"I'm Daisy, I'm here with John."

"Sweet. I'm Jackie," the masc girl replied. "This is my girlfriend, Nina. Nice to meet you." Daisy smiled brightly, glad to be proven right.

"Alright, now that we're all introduced — are you going to smoke or just complain about being excluded," Kyle's girlfriend teased, holding out the joint to Jackie.

"Yeah yeah yeah. Why aren't we playing music? Is it really a smoke sesh without good music?" Jackie asked.

"Oh yeah," Kyle said. "I was supposed to do that. I literally had the app opened and got distracted. I got this." A second later, music started playing through the Bluetooth speaker on top of Kyle's dresser.

Daisy nodded her head along to it. "I feel like I know this song and I have no idea why."

"It's Skip's favorite band, maybe you heard it around her?" John asked, dancing around mentioning Hana.

"Oh yeah. Hana definitely played it for me at some point," Daisy said dismissively, taking the joint when it was offered to her. John gave her a tight smile at the mention of Hana, but luckily the others in the room didn't seem to notice the slight tension between them.

"You know, it's a great night for a swim," Nina said. Kyle, his girlfriend, and Jackie all groaned.

"What? Why are we groaning?" John asked.

"Nina has been campaigning to get us to break into the pool down the block for weeks," Kyle's girlfriend groaned.

"I'm just saying there's no cars in the driveway tonight," Nina argued, "and there weren't any last night either. I think they're on vacation, and I believe that a pool like that deserves to have someone swimming in it."

"Who the hell has a pool in downtown Rochester?" Daisy asked.

"Exactly! That's what I'm saying!" Nina said, gesturing emphatically.

"What's the worst thing that can happen? We get arrested?" Daisy asked. Everyone looked at her like she was crazy.

"Yes. That's clearly the worst thing that could happen," Jackie said.

The conversation pivoted back and forth, everyone arguing while Daisy watched. She only chimed in to add that her dad was a defense attorney, but other than that she let the friends argue about things. By the time the joint was gone, the group decided they were going to take the risk.

"So how are we doing this?" Kyle asked.

"Sneak out the front, don't come back if we start getting chased unless you're sure no one is behind you?" Nina proposed immediately.

"You really have thought of it all, haven't you, babe?" Jackie said fondly. The way she looked at Nina made Daisy's heart ache, and she averted her gaze quickly. Her head felt like a whisp of smoke, all her thoughts only visible for a moment, but if she tried to grab them, they faded away to nothing. It was like forgetting, but without the pain of remembering. She didn't know if the remembering would hurt even worse tomorrow, but even that foreboding thought drifted away as soon as it came to her.

"Alright, let's go before you guys chicken out." Nina leaped to her feet.

"You're actually good with this, right?" John asked quietly.

"Yeah, it'll be fun." Daisy smiled wide in hopes that John would believe her.

"You're really something, you know that?" John said with wonder in his voice while he helped Daisy up off the floor.

"So I've been told," Daisy teased. She walked with a slight swing in her hips, the way she saw cool girls walk in movies. She wondered if the impact was the same, but she couldn't look back to find out. That would shatter the cool girl illusion.

Everyone was laughing and shushing each other on their walk. When they got to the house, Nina walked through the unlocked pool gate like she belonged there, and the rest followed. There were no cameras or alarms around the dark, empty house, and Daisy couldn't believe how lucky they were. There were automatic lights embedded in the pool walls, and the pool glowed like a cerulean entrance to another world.

"Alright, let's do it," Nina said before pulling her shirt over her head.

"What?" Daisy asked, suddenly unsure of what she'd gotten herself into.

"Just down to your underwear," Nina added when she saw Daisy's hesitation. "If we have to run, you have dry clothes. Less noticeable."

"Alright." John kicked off his shoes before unbuttoning his jeans and sliding them down his legs to reveal black boxers. He grabbed his shirt by the back of his collar and tugged it over his head, revealing his slightly soft stomach and the trail of hair leading from his chest down to the band of his underwear. He pulled off his socks, and

Daisy realized that while she was watching John undress, the rest of the group was already stripped down. She quickly followed everyone else's lead, and she tried her hardest not to cover herself with her hands. She was used to wearing a tank top and shorts over a one piece at work, and her dad refused to let her buy a bikini since she couldn't wear them to work. She was distracted from her insecurity when Nina and Jackie splashed into the pool.

"C'mon, let's do it." John extended his hand out to Daisy. She smiled and the pair ran and jumped into the pool with their hands entwined.

"What are we even doing?" Daisy laughed when she resurfaced.

"Being dumb college kids?" Kyle replied from across the pool. Daisy giggled at his answer and floated onto her back, staring up at the inky blackness of the starless sky and trying to find a star past the city's light pollution.

"Nina, this is great," Jackie said with a sincerity that made Daisy ache. "You're a genius and all of us should be eternally grateful to you."

Daisy sank underwater to escape their love and remembered when she would spend Saturday swim lessons growing up trying to find out how long she could hold her breath. She pushed until she was laying on the floor of the pool and opened her eyes, squinting against the burn of chlorine and watching as the lights on the side of the pool lit up the others and distorted them into unsteady, waving figures. They were splashing each other, and the water was choppy and hard to see through with patches of white foam cutting through the clear blue. Daisy wished she could stay down there staring up at the uncertain shapes of the world above her forever — at least down here nothing pretended to be solid or to know itself. Underwater was the truth of the world: everything was always changing and shifting and nothing was immovable.

Her lungs were starting to burn when John kicked underwater to her and grabbed her around the biceps, hauling her to the surface with a smile on his face.

"Fifty-seven seconds," Daisy gasped out with a laugh.

"Oh?" John replied, still holding Daisy under one of her biceps and using his free hand to brush pieces of hair that were loose from her braid out of her face.

"I held my breath for fifty-seven seconds. You can compliment me now, I know you're impressed," she said, still breathless.

"I'm very impressed," he said, suddenly very close.

Daisy closed her eyes and let herself be kissed under the starless sky and the jostle of the water surrounded by the laughter of people she didn't know before this night and might not know after this night.

She tried not to think of Hana, but since she only ever kissed Hana before, she found herself tracking the differences between Hana and John. John tasted like whiskey and chlorine, his hands were so much bigger than Hana's were, and he held her tighter than Hana ever could. Every time she compared him to Hana, she tried to recenter on the boy kissing her. He had on some masculine evergreen body spray, one that reminded her of the scent Will wore in high school that Hana hated. Daisy tried to reel back from the memories of Hana, but they swam in front of her and pushed against her chest like they could distance her from John.

Daisy pulled back, still breathing a little heavily from being underwater and the kiss. Their foreheads were pressed together, and John let out a small chuckle. Daisy smiled in response and gave him a quick peck before putting her hands on his shoulders and pressing him underwater before darting away. He came up a second later, spluttering and laughing and trying to chase after Daisy.

They spent the next twenty minutes playing chicken and splashing each other, and then they decided they were done pushing their luck and got out of the pool. They had just finished getting dressed and putting on their shoes when a man slammed open a window next door and leaned out.

"Hey! You kids shouldn't be in there!" the man yelled.

"Run!" Nina shrieked, clutching Jackie's hand and pulling her forward. They all grabbed their clothes and took off running, laughing the whole way. John held Daisy's hand and pulled her along, and when Daisy looked back after they turned a corner, she realized no one was following them.

"No one is following us!" Daisy whisper yelled. They all cheered in quiet voices, and John picked up Daisy and spun her around while she laughed.

When they got back to Jackie and Kyle's house, they rejoined the party in the yard and regaled everyone with their daring adventure and near-miss escape. Daisy couldn't remember the last time she felt so carefree, the last time she felt like she was about to embark on a life that stretched out miles and miles ahead of her.

"Glad you came out?" John asked her. Daisy thought of the journals tucked away in her closet and smiled in spite of them.

She smiled at him. "Yeah, I am."

Chapter 14

Hana — age 19

12/24/18

Dear diary,

I went to see Dad today. Mom was working tonight, so I just went on my own. I don't think she cares that we went the last two years. Maybe she forgot. Or maybe she's sleeping with Uncle Dennis and feels weird about going to see her late husband's grave. Could go either way.

There was someone else at dad's grave today though. Jake Hansen's sister. Her name is Lindsay. She told me that none of it ever made any sense to her. I guess Jake was finally over it. He got some minor charge for public intoxication the year before he died and had to do court mandated AA and really turned his life around. But then suddenly he went and killed my dad. Then he killed himself. Lindsay said he was drunk when he died. What changed? What made him fall off the wagon? She kept saying it just doesn't make sense, and she said that she found out he put aside $10k for his funeral and for their mom. She doesn't know where he got the money, how he saved that much, especially if he relapsed. All I can think is that someone paid him to kill my dad and then he couldn't face the guilt. It sounds crazy — I know it does — but I can't stop thinking about it.

I owe it to my dad to look into it. It can't hurt, right?

Sincerely,

Hana

· · · ·

Hana lay on the floor of her living room the morning of December twenty-sixth looking up at the small tree Noriko insisted was good enough for the two of them. When her father was still alive, they would get a fifteen-foot tree special-ordered from a farm an hour away, and Noriko would spend hours decorating it perfectly. They would have a smaller tree in the den where they all would hang all the nostalgic ornaments together, but since her dad died, it became their only tree. It still felt unnatural, even during this third Christmas without her dad.

Noriko used to go all out with decorations so that when the extended Holm family would come over for Christmas dinner, she would get compliments and all the wives would fawn over her table arrangements and the elegance of the fake snow on the mantle. It was the only time Noriko was really treated like part of the family.

Now another Holm relative hosted the meal every year, and Noriko and Hana didn't attend. Noriko said she would go if Hana wanted to, but in all honesty, Hana didn't like any of her distant relatives and the subtle backhanded comments they would make about her "lifestyle." She saw her grandparents as rarely as possible after her dad died — they liked to make comments about her not living up to the Holm name, and she liked to dream up scenarios where she called them out for being bigots. It was better to keep some distance.

Since her dad died, Christmas dinner consisted of pasta and frozen garlic bread, which they would eat in their pajamas while watching cheesy movies like *White Christmas* and the claymation version of *Rudolph*. This year, though, Hana's uncle had joined them, and they ate a more fitting Christmas dinner, and the movies came afterwards. They dressed casually this year, barely a step above pajamas, but Hana was still irritated by the change in the fragile routine she and her mother established. The two of them were trying to heal and continue their lives, and Dennis was just a reminder of the empty space her dad had left. She spent most of Christmas dinner fantasizing about life if Dennis had died that day instead of her father.

If her father were still here, he would ask her if she liked her presents, especially the new clothes from Noriko, and her mother would smile indulgently at him. He would insist that they say grace over their food, though he didn't do it for every meal. He would ask Hana about school and Noriko about the patients she was working with, and he would care about their responses. He would mention how lucky he was to have his favorite girls with him, and Hana would pretend to be embarrassed and annoyed, and Noriko would blush like a schoolgirl.

Dennis had stayed over as well because the three polished off a few bottles of wine, and he claimed he was too drunk to drive. Hana didn't really believe him, but she had been too buzzed the night before to put up a fight. But now it was almost time for breakfast, and he was still here, expecting to be fed instead of leaving like he was meant to. Like he was *supposed* to.

Breakfast was awkward, and Hana ate as quickly as she could before excusing herself by saying she had some reading to do for one of her spring classes.

She walked down the hall towards the stairs, but at the last minute she walked past them to her father's office. She tried the door and found it still locked, so she jumped up until she knocked the key off the top of the door frame.

When she unlocked the door, she almost expected the knob to stick, but the door opened easily. It wasn't that Hana wasn't allowed in the study. It just felt wrong going in without her father. Noriko had locked the door the day after Mark died, claiming she didn't want anyone to have access to any of his old files, and Hana couldn't think of a single time either of them had gone in there since. It felt taboo for them, like Noriko flirting with her late husband's brother or not buying the big Christmas tree.

When Hana pushed the door open, dust danced in the thin strip of light streaming through a gap in the curtains. No one, not even their housekeeper, had come into this room after Noriko locked it, not even when Hana found the key on top of the doorframe a few years earlier. On the desk there was an empty whiskey glass, a stack of files, and one open folder. The strip of the folder that was exposed to light was bleached almost white, though the rest of the desk was seemingly unbothered.

Hana closed the door behind her and took a seat at the desk, blowing on the layer of dust coating the dark, shiny wood. It kicked into the air, and Hana covered her mouth to stifle the sound of her cough before she looked at the open folder on the desk.

It was a file of death threats against her father, all from Jake Hansen. Laid out in black ink, partially redacted by the sun, were detailed reasons why her father was a terrible human being that Hansen wanted to kill. She didn't know who was reading them in here, if her own father was reviewing threats against him or if someone was looking into things after his death.

Hana had been shielded from a lot of the media circus surrounding Hugh Stanley Stewart, an all-around terrible person her father had represented when Hana was ten. When he was arrested for killing Courtney Brennan, Jake Hansen's girlfriend, Mark Holm defended him, citing a lack of concrete evidence. When Stewart walked free and went on to kill another woman, Jennifer Hiller, Mark refused to represent him again, and the next lawyer he acquired couldn't get him off again.

Reading through Jake Hansen's letters, Hana understood some of his rage. The mere idea that someone else might have been involved in her father's death was sending her into a spiral, so if she knew exactly who was responsible for letting her father's killer walk free, she would probably be violent too.

She read through the letters quickly, trying not to flinch at the violent things Hansen was describing that he wanted to do to Hana's father. When she got to the last letter she paused, reading it over again and trying to figure out why it felt so different from the others.

The first two dozen letters were detailed, angry, and clear about why Mark deserved the things Hansen wanted to do to him. A dozen of them were written the year after Stewart went free, and another dozen were written during his trial and conviction for killing Hiller. The last letter was dated January 15th, 2016 — just over a month before Hansen killed her father, and the tone wasn't the same as the others. She was rereading it when one of the lines stood out — "I want you to feel the same pain Courtney did. I want you to know what it feels like to have your stomach carved open." It was gruesome, but that wasn't what made it stand out. He said the same exact thing in one of the earlier letters. Hana spread out all the older letters and started scanning them, realizing that a majority of Hansen's final threat was repeated from older letters, Frankensteined together until it read like something new. The grammar was corrected in a few places too, like whoever wrote it couldn't help but fix the mistakes. The only new part of the letter referenced Noriko, even though in the earlier letters, he focused all his rage on just Mark, never bringing his family into it.

Unless Hansen went through a transformation in the two years between his last two letters to Mark, he didn't write this letter. Hana wasn't sure who would have been able to fake it, who could've been angry enough at her father to write this letter and scare him. They would need access to all these letters and the ability to get it to Mark in a way that would lead people to believe Hansen wrote it.

Hana didn't realize how hard she was shaking until she tried to pick up a pen to make a note on the final letter. The first few words she wrote came out shaky and unsure before she was able to calm herself enough to finish the note, but it took a lot of effort to get the sentences out. She dropped the pen back on the desk when she was done and rose onto unsteady feet to make her way out of the study.

She locked the door behind her and dropped the key in her pocket — if she tried to put it back, she would definitely draw her mom and uncle's attention. She couldn't deal with that right now.

Hana was only one step up the stairs, the study key burning a hole in her pocket, when her mother and uncle came from the kitchen. Dennis' overnight bag was slung on his shoulder, and they were laughing at something Noriko said. Hana tried to keep the angry look off her face.

"Hana! Good timing, your uncle is just about to head out," Noriko said.

"Bye, Uncle Dennis. See you later," Hana said, continuing up the stairs. Noriko apologized to Dennis, but Hana made no move to turn back or say a better goodbye.

She was barely able to hide the key to the study in a drawer of her vanity when her mom appeared.

"What's the matter with you?" Noriko asked.

"Hi Mom, thanks so much for knocking. Sure, you can come in my room," Hana snarked back.

Noriko crossed her arms and stared down Hana. "Sorry, I thought we were being rude today. I was just following your example."

"Have you ever read the threats Jake Hansen sent dad?" Hana asked. Noriko's face shifted, going from disapproval to surprise to the barest hint of soul deep pain before landing on a resigned expression.

"I have."

"Why didn't dad represent Hugh Stewart for his second case?"

"I ... why are you asking me this?"

"I always think of him more during the holidays. So now I'm thinking about this."

Noriko studied Hana, as if she was waiting for her to crumble, to take back her question and say she didn't want to know. But Hana was growing up, and the more she saw her mother as a person and not just a mother, the more she had to wonder about her father. Noriko eventually sighed and came to sit next to her daughter.

"Stewart came from a wealthy family. For his first trial, they hired your father's firm. Your father … he usually didn't take murder cases. But this one — well, no other attorney had the bandwidth for it, and Landon told Mark that if he did well on the case Landon would make him a partner."

"And the second case?"

"Working the case for Stewart was … hard on your dad. He knew that Stewart was guilty. But the prosecution's case was flimsy at best. Mark believed in a fair trial, and everything they had was circumstantial. Stewart was found not guilty, and your father made partner and tried his best to forget about all of it. But he swore to me and to everyone at the firm that he would never do a murder trial again. When Jennifer Hiller was found dead … He was beside himself for months. When the Stewarts tried to hire him for their case, he told them to go to hell. They went with Marchino & Yega instead, and Yega didn't have as easy of a case as Mark did. Your dad regretted getting Stewart off every day until he died."

"What do you think made Hansen finally kill Dad?"

"I don't know. I've asked myself the same question a million times. He was unstable. The best I can guess is he was working himself up to killing Mark for a long time, and something small finally made him snap. I wish I had the answers, but I don't."

"Maybe it's best we don't know," Hana said.

Noriko patted Hana's thigh and stood to leave the room, but she turned back in the door frame to say one last thing to Hana. "I know the holidays are hard. And I'm sorry that I didn't tell you ahead of time that things would be different this year, but there's no need to take it out on your uncle." Noriko closed the door before Hana could respond.

Hana fell back onto her bed and tried to slow her racing thoughts, but it was useless. She picked up her phone and saw a text from Daisy.

. . . .

Daisy

Still want to hang out today?

Hana

Absolutely. What are you thinking?

Daisy

Something out of the house. A walk maybe?

Hana

Cobbs Hill? We can tag the water tanks and cross "do something mildly illegal" off your senior year bucket list?

Daisy

You had me at mildly illegal. I can drive. Pick you up in 20?

Hana

Sounds good, see you then!

. . . .

Hana got dressed quickly before heading downstairs with a messenger bag slung over her shoulder. Her mother didn't say anything when Hana first passed her, but after she went into the garage and came back in, Noriko eyed her wearily.

"Seeing Daisy?" she asked.

"Yeah, we're gonna go do something. Not sure what exactly," Hana replied. The lie came as easy as breathing. She put on her shoes and hoped her mother wouldn't ask too many questions.

"Okay. Will you be home for dinner?" Noriko asked.

"Probably. See you." Hana headed out the door before Noriko could say anything else. She had to wait out in the cold for a few minutes, but it was worth it to avoid awkward small talk with her mother.

"So what has you feeling so rebellious?" Daisy asked once the car door closed behind Hana. For a minute, Hana considered telling Daisy the truth — that Noriko knew they were dating, that someone else had written the last threat Jake Hansen made against her father, that Noriko and Dennis were becoming more than family — but she didn't. She took a deep breath and decided on a half-truth instead.

"Just ... holidays, you know?"

It wasn't untrue, and Daisy didn't need the burden of Hana's problems. She was too happy and carefree and innocently naive to deal with the intricacies of the world Hana was facing.

"Yeah, I get it," Daisy responded. "My dad still cries every Christmas because he misses my mom, and I remember the first Christmas after she died, we didn't even get a tree. The only reason we did any celebrating at all was because my grandparents picked up Will and I."

Sometimes Hana forgot Daisy had lost her mom since she died before Hana met the Polos. They always seemed complete with just the three of them, and she wondered how different things would have been if Mrs. Polo was still around.

"Yeah. So clearly the only way to deal with this is to ignore my feelings and do something vaguely illegal," Hana said.

Daisy laughed and reached over to squeeze Hana's hand before returning it to the wheel. "Something vaguely illegal is definitely the answer."

"So how was your Christmas? Did you and Will manage to get drunk before your dad noticed?" Hana asked, quick to turn the conversation away from her problems. The rest of the short car ride was spent talking about Daisy and Will's Christmas antics, which Hana only half listened to. Anxiety was creeping in her chest and making her feel twitchy, and she needed to get moving and do something before all of her anxiety latched onto the truth and dragged it out into the light. As soon as Daisy put the car in park on the curved road around the reservoir, Hana was already up and out of the car.

"Feeling antsy?" Daisy asked.

"Just very excited to finally break out the spray paint," Hana joked, swinging the bag at her side. Daisy smiled and scanned the park before holding her hand out for Hana to take. Daisy's paranoia hurt Hana, but she ignored it like always. That was the price of loving Daisy, and Hana was willing to pay it.

The day was cloudy, making it feel like it was much later than early afternoon, and the trail was empty as they walked, only the echo of their steps around them. The path was muddy, but not yet frozen like it should've been that time of year.

"It's kind of eerie, isn't it?" Daisy said as they walked up the final uphill stretch.

"It's because the forest is so quiet in the winter," Hana responded. They got to the end of the path and stared up at the water tanks, and Daisy leaned into Hana's side.

"Where do we want to write something?" Daisy asked.

"What do we want to cover up is the real question," Hana said.

Daisy was silent for a moment, staring at the graffiti as they circled one tank and then the other. "It's kind of sad, isn't it? To be making art that you know will be covered up?"

"I don't know, I think it's kind of exciting."

"Oh?"

Hana stopped in front of a picture of a girl painted entirely in shades of blue. "To know that what you make will be changed by someone new is kind of exciting. You get to have your impact and other people get to decide if it should stay or not."

Daisy smiled at her. "You're so weird sometimes. I love that about you."

Hana laughed and reached into her bag to take out the can of spray paint. She shook it, and the clink of the ball rattling around in the can echoed through the silence around them.

"What should we write?" Hana asked. Daisy shrugged and took the can out of Hana's hand, shaking it a few more times before drawing a small, sloppy daisy next to the girl's face. She held it for too long in a few spots, and the spray paint dripped down the cold metal.

"Oops," Daisy said, watching the drops of paint race each other to the frost-covered ground and run out of momentum halfway there.

"Well, at least it'll get covered up eventually," Hana said with a smile. Daisy laughed at that before standing on her tip toes, placing her left hand on Hana's shoulder to balance before writing "D+H" above the blue girl's head. It was just high enough that it would be inconvenient to reach, and Hana watched the concentration of Daisy's face while she tried to keep the paint flowing steadily.

"There. That should stay for a while," Daisy said triumphantly. Hana smiled at the girl she loved, and her heart clenched, overwhelmed by guilt. She wished she could go back in time and grab the version of herself from that stupid Halloween party by the shoulders, shaking her until some semblance of sense was knocked into her thick skull. Daisy was still admiring her handiwork, and before Hana could say anything, Daisy leaned back up to start writing "forever" under their names. Hana took a step back, knocking a rock down the hill behind her, and when it crashed into another rock, she gasped.

"Shit, was that someone else? We should go," Hana whispered.

"Oh God, um, okay, what do we do with the paint?"

"Give me it." Hana grabbed it out of Daisy's hand, popped the top back on, and threw it in her bag. There was silence again, but Hana still ushered Daisy back to the main path before leading her back to the car. When they reached it, Daisy let out a laugh of relief and Hana joined in.

"So what did the graffiti end up saying before we were interrupted?" Hana asked.

"Just 'D+H for,'" Daisy responded.

"Fitting. Our time on the earth is indeterminable after all," Hana said sagely. Daisy laughed at her serious tone, and Hana smirked back.

"You're ridiculous," Daisy said. Hana laughed a little, but it felt forced.

She didn't know how much time she would have with Daisy or with anyone. Maybe Daisy would wise up and leave her, or maybe she would finally be brave enough to let Daisy go. Maybe one of them would die the next day in a terrible accident, like Hana's father and Daisy's mother. There was no knowing, only the unfinished sentence clinging to the side of the water tank, waiting to be completed or covered over and over and over again.

Chapter 15

Daisy — August 2019

DAISY SLEPT OVER AT John's after the party, and even though she had to show up to work exhausted the next day, she didn't regret it for one minute. She fell into an easy rhythm with John that was completely different from her relationship with Hana. The rush of a simple, meaningless crush was all-consuming, and Daisy let herself get wrapped up in it. She became friends with all of John's friends, and the rest of July and start of August slipped away with more parties, dates, mornings lifeguarding at camp, and a few awkward dinners with Noriko, Dennis, and her dad where Daisy tried her hardest not to look at the empty seats at the table.

When she kept coming up short on finding Hana's note, she let the investigation fall to the wayside. She hated arguing with Hana's ghost every time she showed up, but it was better than having nothing left of the girl she loved other than the all-consuming grief that crashed into her at random intervals. Hana stopped showing up to argue and instead just lingered in the corners at parties, watching Daisy with mournful eyes that Daisy was becoming very good at avoiding.

She woke up the third weekend in August and realized she didn't remember the last time she had cleaned or even tidied her room. It felt like she spent every spare moment with John, and she neglected the basic upkeep of her life in the meantime.

John was out of town the night before because he was visiting his grandparents in Syracuse, and Daisy drank herself to sleep to avoid Hana's ghost lingering in her doorway, inching the door open to let in the hall light her dad always left on.

It was raining out, and Daisy took advantage of her sudden burst of inspiration by deep cleaning her room and listening to cheesy music she used to love in middle school. She was almost done getting everything organized when she came across Hana's journals.

After she read the truth about Hana's affair, she'd tucked them under her bed where she wouldn't have to see them ever again. She realized that in her need to get away from them after she read the entries about Frida, she never actually finished reading Hana's second to last journal.

Daisy settled down on the ground next to her bed, picked up the journal, and thumbed through until she found the entries from after Thanksgiving. She skimmed them, noting that Hana was more stressed about her finals than she let on, and it wasn't until Daisy got to the final two entries, dated December twenty-fourth and twenty-seventh, that she really read them.

This was when Hana started looking into her father's death and when she made that note on Jake Hansen's death threat in her father's study. She must have forgotten to tear out the pages in this notebook when she was taking out the ones from her last journal. Daisy was glad Hana forgot to tear this out.

• • • •

12/27/18

Dear Diary,

I think something is up with how my dad died. Something about Jake Hansen's last death threat feels off, like he didn't write it. But if he didn't, who did? And how does the person who wrote this note relate to my father's death? I mean, I know Jake Hansen pulled the trigger. I know he's the one who <u>actually</u> killed my dad. There were witnesses who saw him running from the scene. But what if it wasn't his idea? What if someone else put him up to it? Gave him the idea? And what if that person made sure Hansen could never rat them out?

I know it's insane to think that someone else is involved in my dad's death. It seemed cut and dry. But I have a feeling that I'm right, and I have to investigate this. Either I'll get proven wrong or I won't, but if I never look into things I'll always wonder. And I can't stand not knowing something important.

Sincerely,

Hana

P.S. — Daisy and I tagged the water tanks yesterday. I love her so much. I wish I could be the person she deserves, and I wish I could stop doing things that will hurt her when she finds out about them.

• • • •

A wave of grief crashed over Daisy, and she gasped at the feeling of it invading her senses, permeating everything around her. She wished she could go back to this version of Hana and hold her and tell her none of this was worth it. Finding out the truth would never bring back Mark Holm, and searching for it took away Hana too. If that version of Hana could see this version of Daisy, would she think twice about her investigation? Who would mourn Daisy if she met the same fate as Hana?

Daisy flinched when her phone rang, and she didn't even look at it before answering and putting it to her ear.

"Hello?"

"Daisy!" John greeted her. "I'm on my way back from my grandparents' house, and I just got off the phone with Todd, so I thought I'd call instead of text. What are your thoughts on a beach day?" he asked.

Daisy looked out her window at the gray skies and light rain still falling. "But it's raining out?"

"So? We'd get wet anyways, we're at the beach. Plus, no crowds."

"But what about our stuff?"

"Jackie offered to drive all of us in that van she just got, so we can leave our dry stuff in her car."

Jackie had decided she wanted to spend the year converting a sprinter van into a tiny home so she could travel the country for a while after she graduated in the spring.

"I ... okay," Daisy agreed. "Yeah. I mean, as long as there aren't thunderstorms, why not? I'm in."

"Amazing. Meet at my place in an hour?"

"See you then," Daisy said before hanging up. She needed the distraction, and nothing said distraction like hanging out in the rain with the boy she was having a summer fling with.

Daisy took one last look at Hana's journal entry before putting it back in the pile on her floor and getting ready.

She skipped makeup, figuring the rain would just take it off anyways, and put on a black one piece with a flowing flowered sundress over the top. She clipped on her favorite necklace that she wore almost every day — a gold locket with a daisy on the front that had belonged to her mother — and braided her hair before throwing a beach towel in a tote bag to bring with her. She went downstairs and was slipping on a pair of sandals when her dad cleared his throat from the living room.

"Heading out?" Henry asked.

"Yeah, just hanging out with some friends," Daisy called back, slipping on her rain jacket and hoping Henry wouldn't ask any more questions.

"Okay, be safe out there. People forget how to drive when it rains like this," Henry responded dismissively. She took her easy escape and ran to the car, already partially soaked by the time she got in it. She wasn't sure how good of an idea this excursion was, but she needed to forget for the night, this one last night. In the morning, she would start looking again at all the places Hana possibly left her note, try to look more into Mark Holm's death, and stop using John as a distraction from her real life. But for tonight, she was committed to being a normal, irresponsible eighteen-year-old.

"Great weather for a beach day," Hana said, appearing in the passenger seat. She hadn't really spoken to Daisy for the past week, and she was startled by Hana's appearance.

"It'll be fun," Daisy said, flipping on her car radio and putting in an old Miley Cyrus CD she thrifted a week earlier with John.

"It will be, sure. Who doesn't love sitting in the rain and ignoring their problems?"

"Hana, I swear to you that tomorrow I will start retracing my steps and rechecking the evidence I have, but as of right now I have nothing to go on. Until I find your note, all I have are dead ends."

"You leave for New Paltz on Thursday. If you don't solve this by then—"

"I know," Daisy interrupted, "but it's not like one afternoon of acting like a teenager without a tragic backstory is going to ruin an investigation with no new leads."

"Fine." Hana paused before adding in a soft voice, "You look beautiful. You should have fun." The ghost disappeared, and Daisy turned up the volume on her stereo, trying to drown out the gentleness of Hana's departing words with cheesy pop music and the flick of her windshield wipers.

She parked right in front of the house, and John was sitting on the porch when she arrived. As soon as she stepped out of the car, his eyes were fixed on her.

"Are you ready for a beach day?" he asked, grinning at her like a little kid, all joy and no embarrassment. Daisy smiled and gave him a quick peck on the lips. John would never be right for her, but she would pretend like he could be for just a little longer.

"Absolutely. Had to make sure I packed the sunscreen," Daisy teased. He put his arm around her shoulders and walked her into the house where everyone was getting their things together.

"Hey, are Jackie and Nina almost here?" John asked. Todd gestured to the street where Jackie's sprinter van was pulling up.

"Who's ready for the beach?" Kyle called, flinging open the door to the backseat and revealing a few rows of bench seating. Jackie had just gotten the used van a few days earlier, so she hadn't taken out the seats yet. John, Daisy, Todd, and John's other roommate, Gabe, all made a dash through the rain to the van. John, Daisy, and Todd ended up stuck in the way back with John in the middle, a position he volunteered for even though Daisy was smaller than him and probably should've taken the seat.

John's body was warm against her side, and she shivered at the contact. He mistook it for her being cold and draped an arm around her shoulder, pulling her closer with a grin. Daisy smiled back and leaned into his side. Although she'd slept over in his bed after nights out quite a few times, they hadn't slept together yet. He understood that she was younger and fresh out of a long-term relationship with someone who had died, so he never pressured her, but she could tell he wanted her.

"How was Saint Martin?" John asked Jackie and Nina once everyone was settled into the van and they were on their way to the beach. She stayed tucked into John's side while Jackie and Nina started detailing the epic highs of their ten-day vacation. Daisy laughed and asked questions at the right time and teased John just the right amount.

She fit here, she knew she did, despite being younger than everyone else, despite all of them knowing each other better. She could rebuild the person she was around these people. She could burn away the version of herself that Hana loved and be reborn as the kind of girl that went almost skinny dipping in strangers' pools and knew how to take a shot without wincing and didn't talk about her dead ex-girlfriend. She wanted to be that girl so badly, but sitting there surrounded by the near strangers she called her friends, she was never going to be that girl.

Daisy couldn't leave behind who she was and become someone entirely new, someone unaffected by her past life. She couldn't burn away what once was; she had to build layer upon layer upon layer of herself, like Rome rising over the centuries. No matter how many times she tried to burn her old self away, the sediment of the ashes would still be left behind. Maybe it was time to put the fire out, but she would let herself have one more night of dancing in the flames before she returned to the reality of who she was.

When they pulled into the parking lot for Charlotte Beach on Lake Ontario, it was almost entirely empty — no one else was crazy enough to show up at the beach on a rainy Saturday afternoon. Most people would go to a movie, or bowling, or just stay home, but not John and his friends.

They all climbed out of the van and immediately stripped down to their swimsuits. It was one of the hot, rainy days that only comes in the heat of August. The rain was warm against Daisy's exposed skin, and she settled into the girl she was trying to be like an actor walking onstage.

John and Todd carried a cooler Nina had brought down to the beach with them, and Jackie grabbed a bag that she wouldn't reveal the contents of before they made their way to the deserted boardwalk in their swimsuits and sandals.

"It's kind of eerie. I don't think I've ever seen it this empty in the summer," Todd said.

"Yeah, it's like we stepped into another world." Jackie casually slung her arm over Nina's shoulder as they walked. Daisy ignored the pang in her chest watching the two girls together, instead turning back to look at John, who was already watching her. She smiled at him and forced herself to be present in this moment, not in the past or the future, just for this one last day.

When they got to the beach, they all took a beer out of the cooler and cracked them open, but before they started drinking, Todd cleared his throat.

"To the final weekend of the summer," he said, raising his Genesee beer can in the air. The rest of the group followed suit then took their first sips, and Daisy drained half of hers in one go. John tugged on Daisy's arm once she stopped drinking and nodded towards the open stretch of beach.

"Want to take a walk?" he asked. Daisy nodded and they went on their way, hand in hand.

"This summer has been fun," John said once they were out of earshot of his friends.

"Yeah. It's definitely not what I expected it to be," Daisy said.

John winced. "I know we don't talk about it, but I am really sorry about Hana. I know losing people can be hard." Daisy wanted to scoff at him that he didn't know anything about loss, that the death of his ninety-three-year-old grandpa a few years earlier may have been sad, but it wasn't like losing Hana. John didn't know what it was like to lose someone who still had their whole life ahead of them, to watch as the light of an entire future blinked out.

"Yeah," Daisy said instead. "Thanks for giving me something fun to look forward to all summer. I'm pretty sure that if I didn't have you guys, I would've just slept any time I wasn't working."

Although John wasn't right for her, and he would never understand why he wasn't right for her, she did appreciate him. When she was with John, things were simple. It was just flirting and drinking games and parties at places she would probably never visit again after this summer.

"Well, I'm glad we could be here for you. And I know you're going away to school in a few days, but I was thinking—" John was cut off by Daisy's startled shriek, and they both wheeled around to see Todd ten feet behind them holding a super soaker. Daisy had never been so happy to be blasted with freezing cold water from a water gun before in her life.

"Come on, love birds, it's time for war!" Todd shouted, hitting John square in the chest before taking off back to the cooler where Nina had emptied her bag containing a multitude of water guns. John ran after Todd, and Daisy drained the rest of her beer before heading back towards them.

They spent the next hour running around shooting each other with water guns and developing a drinking game around it. By the time they finally tired themselves out, everyone aside from Jackie was drunk and giggling. They swam in the lake for a little while, rough housing and playing chicken. But after a few hours, Nina shivered so hard her teeth knocked together and Jackie called it.

"Who wants to head out?" Jackie said. "I'm pretty sure I have the ingredients for Irish coffee at my place if we want to warm up and keep the party going."

"As the party master—" Todd started.

"I thought you were the tsar?" Kyle interjected. Kyle's girlfriend, who Daisy discovered was named Emily a week after they met, laughed.

"As the party *tsar*," Todd said, "I declare that the party is now moving to Jackie and Kyle's place. After we get pizza." Gabe cheered and lifted up the cooler over his head.

"Put that down like a normal human. A hospital trip will ruin the vibe," Nina chided. Gabe rolled his eyes but relented, and the group gathered their things and made their way back to the car, where they all wrapped themselves in towels before climbing in.

The car ride was pure chaos. Nina put on the playlist they'd been building at all the pregame and hang-outs for the past month, and everyone sang along to their favorites on the drive. There was at least one person singing at all times, several conversations happening across the van, often with people speaking over each other, and Jackie issuing threats of continually higher severity the more annoying everyone became. They stopped for pizza on the way back to the house, and they were politely asked to leave after the third time Gabe laughed so hard he fell out of his chair.

By the time they got back to John's place, Daisy's cheeks hurt from laughing so hard, and she could almost forget why she would be leaving these people behind so soon.

"Go get changed. We'll wait here," Jackie said when she pulled up to the curb. They climbed out and headed back into the house, gripping their towels and clothes in their hands. The boys raced each other to the house, with Daisy nominated as the referee.

"I think ... I think Todd won," Daisy declared. Todd was several feet ahead of the other two, but the losers still groaned.

"I think we might need to review the tape," Gabe joked.

"I don't know. I think Daisy has a good eye." John winked at Daisy.

Todd and Gabe made gagging noises, and John retaliated by throwing Daisy over his shoulder and running upstairs with her while she shrieked with laughter. Once they got upstairs, he put her down gently and grinned at her.

"Want me to give you a minute to change before we go?" John asked.

"What if we don't go?" Daisy asked, her eyes flicking down John's body before going back up to meet his gaze.

"I'm good with that too." John said before crossing over to his door and yelling out, "You guys go without us, we're staying back." He closed the door quickly, shutting out the sound of Todd and Gabe's responses.

Daisy threw her towel in a spot where it was least likely to get something else wet, and when she looked up, John was there, pulling her into him for a kiss. He seemed unhurried, like he wanted to take his time, but Daisy didn't want that. With time came space to think, and Daisy wanted nothing more than to not think on this last night when she let herself act her age.

Gabe and Todd left a few minutes later, and Daisy could tell John understood this was different, that they were going to have sex. She also knew that if he was really thinking, he would start his conversation from the beach again, but he was too tired and happy and drunk to remember reason, and Daisy was too much of a coward to end things without this one last goodbye. This was Daisy's last act of defiance as the girl she could never really be before she went back to who she was. She tried to weave goodbye in their kisses, tried to trace apologies into his skin where she held him, tried to give explanations in her movements, but she didn't think John understood any of it.

Afterwards, he smiled at her and brushed her hair back from her face to kiss her forehead. It felt too intimate, too real, and she wished she was sober enough to drive so she could leave right then. She'd already made her decision and said her goodbyes, and now she felt like Cinderella standing in the middle of the ball and letting everyone watch as her finery changed back into maid's clothes. It was a good thing John was blinded to who she was, otherwise, he might notice her illusion fading in front of his half-shut, tired eyes.

Chapter 16

Hana — age 19

2/14/19

Dear Diary,

I kind of accidentally tricked my friends into helping me with my dad's case. Which sounds worse than it actually is, but hear me out —

I wrote a short story for my creative writing workshop that's based on my dad's death. I switched around the genders and jobs and changed the names and ages a little bit and wrote myself out entirely, but it's similar enough that my friend's input was helpful. Because right now I'm just lost trying to figure out what the right next thing to do would be.

The story is about a young married woman named Jennifer (aka dad), her younger sister Jess (aka Dennis), and Jennifer's husband, Brett (aka Mom). Instead of a shooting, it's a mugging gone wrong, and the mugger died in a hit and run the day after he killed Jennifer. And of course, Jess and Brett started dating, but I changed it to a little over a year after Jennifer died.

Victor is obsessed with true crime, so I knew they would for sure have an opinion, but I wasn't expecting everyone else to get so into it too. Skippy even drew out a whole murder board in the study room we were in, which I took a picture of and put in my investigation notes.

We went over possible motives and I'll kind of summarize things here:

1. *Maybe Jess was already in love with Brett, and she hired the mugger to kill Jennifer then killed the mugger to get rid of the witness to her crime. Jess also got more control of the family business when Jennifer died, so money is also a motive. And control also means power, which means Jess would have the*

trifecta of money, sex, and power fueling her.

2. *Brett killed Jennifer because <u>he</u> was in love with Jess and wanted her, but didn't want to divorce Jennifer. If there was a prenup, this would also make more sense. So the "hired the mugger then murdered the mugger" theory works here too. So maybe money, maybe sex, not really power.*

3. *Both Brett and Jess worked together to kill Jennifer, then waited a year to get together so it wouldn't seem so obvious they killed her. Money, sex, power trifecta once again.*

I decided to write the story all three ways and see which feels more right. I think once I'm home for the semester I might have my mom and Dennis each read the version where their parallel character committed the murder since they're my two main suspects. Maybe if I pay enough attention to their reactions, I'll be able to figure out if they're guilty or not.

Shit, I have to go call Daisy. Even though I'm seeing her tomorrow, we're still Facetiming for Valentine's Day. I'm kind of dreading her coming to visit. I'm so worried we'll run into Frida (or one of Frida's friends), and they'll somehow tell her that I slept with Frida. My friends that I'm here with every day haven't even figured it out, so I don't know why I'm so worried. Maybe because Daisy knows me better than all of them combined. I wish I hadn't done any of it in the first place.

Sincerely,

Hana

· · · ·

Hana was excited to see her girlfriend to celebrate Valentine's Day, even if it was the fifteenth, but she acted differently in New Paltz than she did in Rochester, and she wasn't sure how Daisy would feel about the change. Plus, the idea of Daisy discovering how Hana had betrayed her was hanging over her head.

"When is she getting here?" Chrissy asked on the walk from their last class of the day back to their dorm.

"In like an hour. Daisy's February break is next week, so she convinced her dad to let her skip today," Hana replied.

"That's so nice. I'm excited to finally meet her in person and not just on the other side of a call while you're drunk," Chrissy teased. Hana laughed.

"Hey, I talk to her sober sometimes when you're around. Not often, but like … at least once or twice since you moved in."

Chrissy threw her head back and laughed, and Hana couldn't help but smile.

"So do you and Trevor have any plans for the weekend?" Hana asked.

"Yeah, his roommate went home for the weekend so we're having a night in tomorrow. But we made sure we're free for that Valentine's Day house show tonight."

"But you're staying at Trevor's tonight, right?" Hana asked. Chrissy laughed again, unconcerned by letting her joy be too loud, and Hana loved it. Chrissy's laugh was usually how Hana found her when they got separated at parties.

"Yes, no worries, no sock on the door required," Chrissy teased.

"It's so weird that I finally need to kick you out of the room."

"I know. Are you excited to show her all that New Paltz has to offer to convince her to go here?"

"Well, she seems pretty convinced she's going here even though she's waiting for some other letters to come in."

"So are you more worried that she'll decide to come here or that she might not?" Chrissy asked. Hana was startled at how Chrissy cut straight to the question Hana had danced around for the past month and a half since Daisy got her acceptance letter.

"I … I want her to go here. Of course I do," Hana argued.

Chrissy raised her hands in defense. "I'm not the one you need to convince." She didn't push Hana to respond, and a comfortable silence settled between them for the rest of the walk back to their dorm. She always knew when to leave Hana alone.

Some days, Hana wanted Daisy to go somewhere else so that the younger girl could learn that there was a much better match for her out there. Hana wasn't right for Daisy, and she deserved better, but Hana was still too selfish to let her go. Hana loved the comfort of Daisy, the way that Daisy knew everything about her — what Hana loved and hated and how she mourned and loved and rejoiced. Hana could never care for and love Daisy the way she deserved.

Still, she walked back to her dorm and tidied while Chrissy gathered her things for a weekend at her boyfriend's. After Chrissy left, Hana kept cleaning to keep herself distracted

Once things were practically spotless, she sat at her desk and looked at the photos of herself and Daisy she had taped to the wall. The photos covered all the years she knew Daisy, starting from the first day they met when they were kids with toothy smiles and girly dresses shining in the camera flash. Those same smiles appeared in the selfie they took in front of their unfinished graffiti when they went back to see it a few days after they put it up, and Hana wished she could love Daisy right.

She opened the top drawer of her desk where she was amassing all her information on her father's death to make sure things were hidden properly. She didn't want to tell Daisy about her investigation. If she slipped up, something bad could happen to her or, even worse, Daisy. She didn't want Daisy killed like her father, in some tragic accident that was easy enough to sweep under the rug.

Hana slammed the drawer shut when her phone buzzed with a text from Daisy telling Hana that she had parked. Hana took a deep breath before she made her way out to find her girlfriend.

When she got downstairs and opened the door, Daisy was already halfway up the path to the dorm. She looked like she wanted to run to Hana, but the ice and snow scattered across the walkway kept her from doing so. Hana only put on slippers before coming down, so she stood in the doorway waiting until Daisy stepped over the threshold.

"Hi, baby," Hana said, letting the door close and pulling Daisy into her arms. Daisy's duffel bag poked into Hana's side, but she didn't move away. Daisy pressed a kiss to the top of Hana's head, and it felt like home.

"I missed you," Daisy murmured.

"I missed you, too. Ready to finally see my dorm in person?" Hana asked, pulling away and taking Daisy's bag.

"Of course," Daisy said. They held hands and walked silently through the twists and turns up to Hana's room.

"So, this is it," Hana said when she swiped them into her dorm room. Daisy looked around, her eyes skipping over Chrissy's half of the room and settling on Hana's.

"Oh, you brough this print with you?" Daisy asked, smiling and pointing at a print of two hands, disjointed and disconnected from themselves and the body they were meant to belong to. Hana was riveted by it when she first saw it on the artist's Instagram, and Daisy bought it for her for her birthday a few years earlier along with a thrifted gold frame. It was the only actually framed thing hanging on Hana's wall.

"I did," she smiled at Daisy and toed out of her shoes, hanging her coat on a hook on the back of her door. "So, what do you think?"

Daisy had seen Hana's dorm in pictures, videos, and FaceTimes, but it was different seeing it in person. Hana didn't realize how much she cared about Daisy's opinion of her dorm until she stood there with the snow from her boots melting onto the dirty linoleum floors.

She wanted Daisy to like the way that Hana lived now that she could be herself.

"It's nicer than I expected from the way you talk about it. Where's Chrissy?" Daisy asked. Hana helped Daisy out of her coat and hung it up.

"She's at her boyfriend's. We won't see her until dinner," Hana revealed.

"Why Miss Holm, that seems presumptuous of you. All alone with no chaperone? The whole town will think I'm a ruined woman," Daisy teased before stepping out of her shoes and hopping up onto Hana's bed. Daisy just finished studying *Pride and Prejudice* in AP Lit, and she had picked up the habit of occasionally speaking like she was in an Austen romance. Hana stepped forward to stand between Daisy's legs dangling off the side of the bed and leaned up to put her lips an inch away from Daisy's.

"Well, if they're already thinking it, we may as well give some credence to their gossip," Hana said, their lips ghosting against each other while she spoke. The angle was awkward and not right, but she couldn't find it in herself to care.

There was no need to hide here. No fear that one of their parents would come home, no fear that their time was limited or that their space would be encroached upon. This was Hana's room, and she'd already guaranteed that the only person who *could* walk in wouldn't.

Hana took her time, something they rarely could do before, and she used the opportunity to show Daisy how much she loved her. As good as Hana could be with poetry and intricate metaphors, she never could quite get across with words just what Daisy meant to her. So many of the most profound things Hana felt were never translatable or explainable.

Afterwards, she laid her head on Daisy's chest, closed her eyes, and matched her breath with the rise and fall.

"Wow, that was ... wow," Daisy murmured.

"What do you think my women, gender, and sexuality minor is teaching me?" Hana joked. Daisy laughed and kissed the top of Hana's head.

"I'll definitely have to sign up for that next year," Daisy said.

"Yeah, just as soon as you commit." Hana traced shapes into the soft skin of Daisy's side, avoiding looking in her eyes.

"I did commit," Daisy breathed, excitement clear in her voice.

"You did?" Hana turned to smile at Daisy. She wasn't entirely sure how she felt, but she knew Daisy wanted her to be happy.

"I was waiting until I saw you in person to tell you. I was going to tell you as soon as I got here, but you're kind of distracting," she laughed.

"That's amazing. Where else did you get in?" Hana asked, sitting up and reaching for her sweater, which was hanging on one of her bedposts.

"I got into U of R, and my dad really wanted me to go there, but I don't want to stay that close to home," Daisy said.

"Didn't you apply to places in the city too?" Hana asked.

Daisy sat up and climbed off the bed to get redressed in her discarded clothes. "Yeah, but I didn't hear back, and then I realized I didn't care where else I got in. I want to come here."

"Well, I suppose we have all weekend for you to figure out if you made a mistake," Hana joked, pressing a kiss to Daisy's shoulder when she got up to get dressed too.

"If you love it here, I'll love it here," Daisy said. Hana winced, but luckily Daisy wasn't looking at her. She was searching through her bag for her phone, and when she found it, she picked it up and sighed.

"I told my dad I got here and then put it on do not disturb. It turns out that he called ... three times. I'm gonna call him back before he reports me missing or something," Daisy said. "Should I go in the hall, or ...?"

"No, you can stay here. I've got to run to the bathroom anyways. I'll text my group chat about when we're going for dinner, too." Hana gave Daisy a peck on the cheek before going into the hall. She texted her friends while she walked, hoping they were ready to eat soon.

· · · ·

Hana

When are we doing dinner? I'm starving

Chrissy

See I thought you would've eaten plenty by now

Skippy

Ooh is Daisy here already?

Hana

I'm gonna transfer

Victor

Do it you won't

Aaron

I want to eat soon!

Skippy

Aaron, you sweet summer child, we're trying to make fun of Hana. Can you stop thinking about food

Hana

A n y w a y s

dinner in 15?

Victor

Yeah I'm down. What do you think the odds are they have good vegan options today

Skippy

Bad odds broski

Victor

Guess Newpz wants me to starve :/

Hana

they want US to starve

anyways see y'all in 15 for hopefully edible food but more likely just fries

Aaron

Can't wait to finally meet Daisy!

· · · ·

After she freshened up, Hana went back to her room, and Daisy smiled and pressed her finger to her lips. She was still talking to Henry, though she didn't appear to be paying much attention to him.

"Yeah, Dad. I'll keep you updated. It's pretty cold out tonight, so ... I think we're just staying in and watching movies or something. We'll go into town tomorrow ... Yes, I'll be leaving first thing Monday. We've already gone over this. We're about to go get dinner, so I'll text you later, okay? ... Yeah, I love you, too. Bye." Daisy hung up with an exasperated, over dramatic sigh, and Hana couldn't help but laugh. "It's like he forgot that we already talked about when I was coming home. He has the memory of a goldfish, I swear," Daisy groaned.

"Maybe he'll goldfish-forget that you're gone and call every 15 minutes asking where you are."

"Don't say that. Don't even think it, it'll come true."

Hana laughed and put her hands up in surrender. "Okay, no manifesting that. Anyways, we should walk over to the dining hall. The wind tunnel under the SUB always makes me walk a little slower. Gotta make sure I don't blow away."

"The SUB?" Daisy asked.

"Student Union Building."

"Oh. Well, good thing I'm here to anchor you down then, huh?" Daisy said with a smile. Hana smiled back, and warmth flooded her chest as she looked at the girl she loved. She leaned forward and gave Daisy a quick kiss, and she could feel Daisy's smile before she pulled away.

"What was that for?" Daisy asked.

"'Cause I can," Hana responded. Daisy blushed and leaned down to give Hana another kiss, this one lasting a few seconds before Hana pulled away with a laugh.

"If you start that we'll never get to dinner, and I'll never hear the end of it from my friends," Hana said.

Daisy laughed. "I'm going to run to the bathroom so I look less ... like this. Save you the teasing," Daisy said, all-but skipping out of the dorm.

Hana used the time Daisy was gone to make her bed and find where her hat, gloves, and scarf were hiding. She was fully bundled up when Daisy got back, and Daisy quickly dressed in her own layers to brave the cold.

"I'm excited to finally meet your friends in person," Daisy said on their way out of the building.

"They're excited to meet you, too, but be prepared for some sex jokes. Also, remember that I think Aaron has a crush on Victor, and I want your opinion as a new set of eyes," Hana said.

"I thought Aaron was the straight one?" Daisy asked. She looped her arm through the crook of Hana's elbow, and it filled Hana's chest with warmth. It was refreshing to see how Daisy acted when she wasn't afraid of being outed.

"He is, but also it's New Paltz, and I don't think anyone is actually straight here," Hana joked. Daisy laughed, and it was a pure kind of joy Hana missed when she was away. Daisy was never this happy when Hana was three-hundred miles away from her.

"I love that. I'm so excited to come here," Daisy said, smiling down at Hana. Hana smiled back, but she hated that Daisy seemed so sure that she wanted to come here just because Hana was here.

Hana pointed out little landmarks while they walked across the campus, and Daisy smiled and asked questions about things on campus that Hana barely noticed anymore, like the oranges rolled onto the ice of the pond and the skateboard tracks through the slush on the sidewalks.

Dinner went better than Hana imagined it would. Her friends were welcoming but were clearly trying not to scare Daisy off.

"Where are we pregaming tonight?" Aaron asked when they were all done and getting ready to venture back to the dorms.

"We can use our room, right Chrissy?" Hana asked.

"Yeah, definitely. The party is at that big house next to the Gulf Station, so it's like a five-minute walk from Shango," Chrissy said.

"Sweet. What are we drinking?" Victor asked.

"I found a shady liquor store that takes my fake ID," Daisy revealed, "so I brought a bottle of vodka, but just a warning it's very cheap and probably tastes like rubbing alcohol."

"Oh, I like you, Daisy. When Skippy's boyfriend visited, all he brought was a fragile male ego. This is awesome," Victor joked. Skippy rolled her eyes and pushed Victor's shoulder lightly. Hana watched Aaron's eyes stick to the spot where they touched and almost laughed to herself.

"That's why he's my *ex*-boyfriend, my dearest Victor. Daisy seems like a lot more ... not-an-asshole than him," she said.

"I love that glowing compliment. A lot more of not-an-asshole. Can I get that on a t-shirt?" Daisy laughed, and everyone else joined in.

The others discussed what mixers they should bring, and Hana chimed in with her and Daisy's preferences before the group went their separate ways for an hour or two to get ready.

Daisy and Chrissy were much more fashion minded than Hana, and the pair were a whirlwind getting ready — judging clothes, sharing makeup, and even convincing Hana to dress to the Valentine's Day theme of the party they were going to that night.

They got ready while listening to Chrissy's pre-game playlist, one full of pop music by up-and-coming artists Hana never heard of before this year along with a handful of the eighties pop songs Hana loved, and Daisy was in her element. She loved the music, she loved making fun of Hana's dramatic faces as she tried to get her to wear something outlandish, and she loved being able to openly love Hana. Daisy didn't have the uncertainty Hana faced when she first came to college — there was no need to figure out who her friends were or how to fit into a new group of people, and she was flourishing after just a few hours.

"Can I do your makeup?" Daisy asked Hana once Hana was dressed in the red pants and white t-shirt the other girls coaxed her into.

"Yeah, sure," Hana replied.

"Ooh, can you use your girlfriend-privilege to make her wear glitter? I'm lucky if I can convince her to do eyeliner," Chrissy said.

"Absolutely. Have you ever seen the makeup I did for her junior prom?" Daisy asked. Hana groaned and mentally prepared for a makeup look that she would likely smudge before they got to the party.

When everyone else showed up, they broke out Daisy's vodka and paired it with lemonade Victor brought.

"To Valentine's Day being over," Skippy toasted.

"To discount candy," Hana added, and they all cheered and drank.

They spent the next hour drinking and joking before finally bundling up to head out. Hana and Daisy walked with their arms linked together on the walk to the party, laughing and openly flirting with each other in a way they were never able to back home.

"It's always super dark at this house, but they have some cool mood lighting that's fun for pictures," Hana said on their walk to the party.

"Yeah, this is just a little thing that Stella's hosting," Aaron said. "She lives in the house with, like, four or five other people. She's a sophomore in my drawing class, and she's pretty cool." Stella clearly had a crush on Aaron, but Hana didn't think Aaron had noticed Stella's interest.

"I hope it's not crazy crowded like it was for the last house show here. That was insane," Skippy said while they climbed the porch steps.

"One way to find out." Victor pushed the door open to a sudden wall of noise and humidity and drunk bodies filling every available space.

"Wow, this is … wow," Daisy said.

"Not quite like the movies, huh?" Hana asked. Daisy nodded, following everyone else as they stripped out of their winter accessories and piled them in a random bedroom Aaron claimed was Stella's.

"You guys made it! Hi!" Stella exclaimed when they walked into the kitchen. She was holding a "world's #1 dad" mug filled with something neon pink, and her cheeks were flushed.

"Thanks for inviting us. It looks like you've got a good turnout," Aaron said.

"Yeah, my roommates invited some people, too. Some of them are in the basement jamming if you want to go down there. Also, grab whatever drinks you want. We have some mulled wine and some Very Valentine's Jungle Juice," Stella said.

"Oh, cool. Want to grab a cup then head down there, Daisy?" Hana asked. Daisy nodded, and they poured themselves drinks into pink plastic cups, but before any of them could start drinking, Skippy pulled out a small bottle of rum.

"Is this the tradition I keep hearing about?" Daisy asked with a smile. Skippy nodded and held out the bottle to Hana, and she took a swig before passing it to Daisy. Daisy tried not to make a face, but Hana knew her too well. She squeezed her hand and pulled her towards the basement.

"How long before Victor and Aaron get together, do you think?" Hana asked Skippy and Daisy when they got into the basement.

"What? Isn't Aaron straight?" Skippy asked. Skippy was someone who was sure of herself every day of her life, and Hana didn't feel she had the capacity to explain that some people don't come out of the womb understanding that they're queer and instead took a little while to adjust to it.

"Just some food for thought," Hana conceded, "What do you think of your first college party, Day?"

"Well, this tastes too good. So right now, I'm a little worried," Daisy joked.

"Oh yeah, you're right. I give the party an hour before a fight breaks out," Hana teased.

"My money is on Victor versus Stella," Daisy said.

Hana laughed. "Man, I love you." Daisy blushed.

Skippy made a gagging noise. "Can you save some of the sweetness for when I'm not around? I already had to deal with all the cute couples on Instagram yesterday." She took a hearty sip of her drink.

"Of course. Very sorry for the strain to your heart," Daisy teased. Hana smiled at her girlfriend, but when she scanned the party to see if she knew anyone her stomach dropped.

Frida was across the room playing bass in the jam session. Hana's heart started pounding, and she wanted nothing more than to leave right then. Why did she think she could control the collision of her worlds without any casualties?

"They sound pretty good," Daisy said.

"Yeah, let's go listen," Skippy said.

"I don't know. It's kind of loud for me," Hana said. Skippy shrugged and went over to listen anyways, and Daisy looked at Hana.

"Everything okay?" Daisy asked.

"Yeah, it's just ... a lot down here."

"Want to go back upstairs?"

"Yeah, let's go."

When they walked back upstairs, Hana made a beeline for the punch and refilled her glass along with Daisy's.

"You okay?" Daisy was probably confused by Hana's quick turn in mood, and Hana wished she could explain without ruining everything.

"Yeah, it was just overstimulating down there," Hana said. Daisy accepted the lie with a nod.

They managed to snag an armchair in the living room as someone got up, and Hana sat on Daisy's lap in the dim glow of the clearly thrifted floor lamps around the room.

"Hana! Hey!" one of Hana's classmates said, turning to face them from her seat perched on the side of the coffee table.

"Hey! Daisy, this is Bev, she's in my creative writing class. Bev, this is my girlfriend, Daisy. She's visiting this weekend," Hana said.

"Oh, sweet! Welcome to New Paltz, dude. Your girlfriend is a great writer. She's writing this cool murder mystery story for our class," Bev said. Daisy wrapped an arm around Hana's waist, like she wanted everyone to know that Hana was hers, and Hana leaned into the touch.

She didn't want Daisy to know about the story or her investigation, but it was too late to tell Bev to keep quiet.

"Oh, really? Has my love of Sherlock Holmes and Agatha Christie finally rubbed off on you?" Daisy teased.

"No, I still hate them. I had to one up them," Hana joked.

"I mean, it's a classic story. I love that you left it so open ended because, like, not every case gets solved," Bev said.

"Honestly I wrote the ending, but it was too long for class."

"Ooh, so who did it?" Bev asked.

"I don't know," Hana admitted. "I wrote it both ways."

"That's so cool," Bev breathed.

"I want to read it," Daisy said.

Hana took a large sip of her drink. "Maybe later. I still have some edits to make."

"I'll hold you to it." Daisy squeezed her waist tighter for a second, interpreting Hana's dismissive comment as a promise.

"How's your story going?" Hana asked Bev, hoping to change the subject.

Bev heaved a sigh and launched into the tale of her writer's block, and Hana wished they could leave the party right now without Daisy worrying.

When there was a lull in the conversation, Hana pulled Daisy's arm off her waist. "I'll be right back. I'm just going to run to the bathroom upstairs." Daisy nodded at her before curling her legs up under herself to continue her conversation with Bev.

Daisy looked like she belonged there, perched on the beat-up second-hand armchair. The dim lights made the fly-aways from her hair glow like strands of spun gold, and the glitter on her cheeks sparkled with every little movement she made. She was so bright that it felt like the rest of the room was all shadow, all out of focus next to her. Hana turned away, unable to face the sun of her first love knowing that she'd already ruined everything.

When she came back downstairs, Daisy was wrapped up in another conversation, this one with Stella and one of her housemates.

"Hey, what's up?" Hana asked.

"We're just talking about that house show house from last semester that was on Manheim," the housemate said. "It sucks that everyone in the house moved. I bet the landlord is a dick or something."

He was leaning into Daisy with a wide smile and overly attentive gaze, and Hana wanted to hit him. She sat herself back on Daisy's lap, and Daisy pressed an absentminded kiss to Hana's head while the conversation went on. The housemate leaned away, and Hana started playing with Daisy's fingers, trying not be subtle about her possessiveness.

"You guys are cute," Stella said. "How long have you been together?"

"Three years. This was our first Valentine's Day apart, actually," Hana said. Stella's housemate suddenly spotted a friend across the room and left the conversation.

"Oh wow, that's wild. How did you guys meet?" Stella asked. Her face was soft, unknowing, like she hadn't seen the predatory stance of her housemate. Hana didn't want to start a fight, so she let herself and Daisy fall into a conversation about how their lives had been intertwining and weaving around each other for over a decade. Stella eventually was pulled away to deal with a spill somewhere, and Hana leaned back into Daisy.

"So, you made some friends?" Hana asked.

"Yeah. Thanks for the save. I didn't realize he was hitting on me at first, and then I kind of froze up," Daisy said.

"Happens to the best of us." Hana turned to face Daisy and fished the flask out of her pocket to take a sip.

"I suppose I could've just mentioned my girlfriend was in the bathroom."

Hana took a gulp of cheap vodka and tried not to wince. "When you spend so long hiding it's easy to forget when you don't have to anymore."

Daisy grabbed the flask and took a small sip, grimacing at the taste. "I don't know how I'm going to go home and go back to hiding, though. It was like Schrödinger's closet before. I didn't know what it was like to be out, so I didn't know to really miss it."

"Do you think you'll come out now?" Hana asked. Despite Hana asking so many times for Daisy to come out, the idea of her doing it now for Hana without knowing how Hana betrayed her made Hana's chest ache.

Daisy sighed. "I'm too drunk for life altering choices right now."

Hana couldn't express her newfound hesitation without explaining to Daisy why she felt that way, so she stuck to her usual line of thinking. "There's always something."

"Don't start, Hana. I missed you, just ... please. Not now."

"It's always the wrong time to talk." Hana took back the flask and drank again.

"We can talk tomorrow, when we're not drunk and in some stranger's living room."

"I'm sure if you wanted, that guy would love for you to not be a stranger," Hana said even though she knew she was being unfair.

"Hana, please," Daisy begged. Hana wanted to keep pushing, she wanted to make Daisy hate her so she would leave, but there was no point. Daisy would love her no matter how hard she tried to be unlovable.

"Sorry, you're right. I didn't sleep well last night. I'm just being moody."

"Okay. I love you."

"I love you too," Hana murmured, kissing Daisy chastely. Hana wished that loving her would be enough.

Chapter 17

Daisy — August 2019

DAISY'S HEAD STARTED pounding when her alarm went off.

"Oh man, turn that off," John muttered.

They had fallen asleep early the night before to the sound of rain pattering against John's window after splitting a bottle of wine.

"I have to get up. My dad wants me home for a brunch thing," Daisy muttered, crawling over John to get out of the bed. She felt sore and tired, and she groaned when she stood up.

"I want to sleep all day. Come back to bed," John muttered, reaching for her. Daisy took a deep breath, knowing that she didn't want to see John again after today.

"Listen, John, I ... You know, I'm leaving for college in a few days, and I think maybe—" Daisy cut off when John sat bolt upright.

"Are you — are we breaking up?"

"Were we ever really dating?"

"I mean, we never talked about it, but I thought that maybe we ... would at some point. I tried to say something yesterday, but with the water fight and everything ... I just didn't get a chance."

"Look, I'm sorry if you thought this was more than—"

"A rebound?" John asked. Daisy winced and started looking for her clothes to buy herself time. She didn't know what to say, but whatever it would be she didn't really want to be doing it in a pair of John's boxers and one of his shirts. She cursed herself for forgetting to bring a change of clothes the night before when she remembered that all she had to change into was a swimsuit and a sun dress.

"I guess. If that's what you want to call it," she said, walking out of his room to change in the bathroom. She folded the borrowed clothes before going back to him. When she handed him the pile, he took it from her hands and tossed it carelessly towards a pile of presumably dirty clothes.

"So that's it?" he asked.

Daisy nodded. "I just ... I'm not ready for anything after Hana. I didn't realize it before, and I'm sorry things ended up like this."

He scoffed and looked down to try to hide the tears in his eyes. "Are you?" he asked incredulously. Daisy didn't know how to respond, so she just walked out of his room and left his house as quickly as she could.

It was a beautiful morning, and there were more people out enjoying the morning than Daisy would've liked. She hoped she didn't look like she was on a walk of shame, but she was sure she did. When she climbed in her car, she put on the radio and tried not to cry. If she went home now, she could sleep for an hour before her dad insisted they leave for brunch at the Holm's house.

She flipped between radio stations, and every song made her think of something she wanted to forget. Love songs and breakup songs and hopeful songs and hopeless songs all cascaded over her until she finally shut off the radio and started her drive in silence. All her emotions and relationships were tied up into each other, and she didn't know how to unwind them. It was all too much and not enough, and she realized she was using John as a placeholder, as if being with him was like being with Hana. As if going to parties with him was anything like that weekend in New Paltz, anything like having a love that she would so desperately want to talk to once she was gone that she would see her ghost.

"So, you finally dumped him?" Hana asked, appearing suddenly.

Daisy barely stopped herself from jerking the wheel. "Yes. Congratulations, I still miss you so much that I can't move on even though you're never coming back."

"I know it's not the same, but you have to find out who killed me or else you'll never get over me. I'll always hang over your head like this," Hana said, desperate.

"I get it. I'm trying."

"Is that what the kids are calling it these days?" Hana intoned drily.

"I'm going to the water tanks again today, starting over and retracing all the places you might've hidden the note."

"That's a good start. If it's not there, then what?" Hana asked.

"Then — I don't know what then. I'm trying to figure out who killed you, but there's only so much I can do right now. I don't know enough, and everything is a dead end. You hid your tracks too well."

"I left enough clues. You can figure it out. You just have to read into things."

"I'm trying, okay?" Daisy shouted.

Hana's ghost was silent for a beat, and when she spoke again it was soft and quiet.

"I know you are. I'm sorry, Daisy. Have fun with my mom," Hana murmured before disappearing once again.

Daisy should go home, but she decided not to nap before brunch and took a detour to the water tanks instead. She worried that their graffiti would be gone since the month before when she visited with John, but she was also overwhelmed with the sudden need to know.

The park was quiet since it was early on a Sunday morning, and Daisy easily avoided the few people walking around the reservoir across from the trail head. She hiked the trail to the tanks quickly but wound slowly around the curve towards the spot where their graffiti was.

When she discovered that it was still there, she gave the painted words a watery smile.

It hadn't changed much in the past month. Her dripping daisy drawing was gone, covered by a new piece of art, and she was glad she had written their initials so high up. The new piece of art below it was a pastoral scene of a river flowing between some reeds, and Daisy stood staring at the small details for the next ten minutes before she snapped herself out of it. The sun was starting to peek over the trees, and she needed to get home soon. Her dad still somehow believed her lies about spending time with her high school friends, and she wanted to keep up the ruse even though she wouldn't be going out again before leaving for New Paltz.

She poked around the outside of the tower more, using a stick to dig at any spots that looked like they could hide a note, but there was nothing there. No matter how much Daisy thought this was the right place, she was wrong.

When she got home, she was relieved to hear her father singing in the shower. She rushed to her bathroom, afraid of what would happen if Henry somehow saw the way she looked right now.

She used her time in the shower to scrub all evidence of the person she was with John from her body. She wiped away the lightness of being unknown from her shoulders, the gentleness from the way he held her hands from her fingertips, and the last lingering taste of him from her lips. She felt like it was the day after Halloween, and she was rinsing away the remnants of an elaborate costume down the drain, colors swirling until the water ran clear and she was left with just herself again.

When she started drying off, her skin was tinged pink from the heat of the water and the pressure of her scrubbing, and the tough shell she'd developed since Hana's death was gone. She was raw and exposed and out for blood. She would find out who did this to Hana — she was done putting it off and distracting herself from what she needed to do.

She got ready for brunch quickly, and she realized she felt like herself for the first time since Hana had broken up with her. She skipped the more complex makeup she learned to do that summer to impress Jackie and Nina and picked clothes for the experience of wearing them rather than for the experience of other people seeing her in them. She was freer than she felt since she visited Hana in New Paltz, and the freedom felt dangerous, like she was going to forget to hold her tongue when she was supposed to. She needed to remember to be smart. Then again, Hana was always smart, and she still ended up dead.

"Daisy! We have to leave in a minute if we don't want to be late," Henry called.

"Sorry, all ready to go," Daisy said, coming downstairs to see her father already waiting by the door.

"Great! We'll be right on time," Henry said, and Daisy left the last remnants of who she was with John behind to go to Hana's old home.

Noriko was happy to see them when they knocked on the door, as she always was. "Hi you two! Come on in, I just finished the pancake batter." She stepped aside to let them in. "How're you doing, Daisy? Are you still enjoying working at the camp?" she asked.

"Yeah, it's nice to spend time outside and enjoy the sun. Plus, the kids can be pretty funny," Daisy said. The thin layer of joy Noriko had covering her face would fade away in an instant if Daisy even thought to reveal how her summer was really going.

"And she's almost ready to leave for school. She's got her whole dorm picked out and packed up," Henry said. Daisy plastered on a smile, thinking of the random dorm materials she ordered online so Henry would stop nagging her. She couldn't even remember what color the sheets were that she would be sleeping on for the upcoming year.

"What an exciting time. Have you decided on a major yet?" Noriko asked as they walked towards the kitchen. Daisy opened her mouth to speak, but Henry beat her to it.

"She's thinking about teaching. Daisy would make a great elementary school teacher with her always-happy energy, wouldn't she?" Henry asked. Daisy smiled tightly, thinking of all the not-child-friendly things she'd done in the past twenty-four hours alone.

"Yes, I can see that. New Paltz has a great program for that. I was always telling Hana whenever she stopped that philosophy nonsense, she should switch over to teaching," Noriko said. A quiet settled over them, and Daisy turned away to get plates and glasses out of the cupboard.

"Oh, thank you, Daisy. Want to go set the table?" Noriko asked. Daisy nodded and balanced what she could in her arms while walking into the dining room.

"Daisy, don't forget about Dennis!" Henry called.

"Oh, I didn't know he was coming," Daisy said, returning to the kitchen to get more dishes. In the brief moment she was out of the room, Henry had taken over the stove and started on the pancakes.

"Yes, he's just running a little late," Noriko said. "Here, why don't you bring the coffee to the table? I'll follow you with the cream and sugar."

"Make sure there's enough in there. Daisy loves her coffee sweet," Henry said.

"No, I don't," Daisy muttered. At the kitchen table, she made her coffee with a small dash of cream and took a sip.

"Men always think they know best, don't they?" Noriko whispered conspiratorially.

Daisy smiled even though her chest ached from the maternal moment. She wished her own mother was still around so that Daisy could ask all her questions about growing up and losing Hana. Even though Noriko was always there for Daisy, she wasn't Daisy's mother and never would be.

The sound of the front door opening caught their attention, and Dennis' voice boomed down the hall a second later. "Hello! I'm here. Sorry I'm late."

"Hey, Dennis! Want to get in here and help?" Henry called back.

"Sure! Be right there." Dennis came into the dining room and kissed Noriko on the cheek, almost absentmindedly. Daisy wondered when they had started dating and if Hana knew before she died. Is that what Hana's letter meant? Was she warning her mother away from dating Dennis because she thought he was dangerous or because she didn't like the thought of her mother and uncle being together?

Brunch was uneventful. They didn't talk about anything important, and Daisy was on autopilot the whole time. Her mind kept drifting back to Hana and the investigation Daisy inherited after her death. Once they finished, Daisy and Henry helped carry things into the kitchen, where Dennis was already getting ready to hand wash dishes.

"Thanks, Daisy. Do you mind loading the dishwasher?" Dennis asked. Henry was already walking back to the dining room, so Daisy nodded.

"Are you excited to go away to college?" Dennis asked.

"Yeah, it'll be different for sure. It's going to be weird not living in Rochester," Daisy answered reflexively. Every adult in her life already asked her this.

"I bet. I suppose it's nice you know some people at school already, though, isn't it?" he asked. The weight of Daisy's grief fell against the front of her chest, urging her to rip her heart out and give it to him as a reply.

"It would've been better if Hana was there," she said. Dennis paused for a moment, and Daisy hated the way that when he started moving again, his movements were measured, careful, like he was trying not to spook a wild animal.

"I'm sure she would've just held you back. Noriko told me about you two."

Daisy nearly dropped the dish she was holding, and she dropped her voice to a whisper to respond, though she could barely hear her own voice over the pounding in her ears. "What? She said she wouldn't — You didn't tell—"

"Your father? No. I don't understand your ... lifestyle, but Noriko told me in no uncertain terms not to do that." He was still too casual, too calculated in how he answered, and though his response should've been reassuring, her heart was still pounding. She always knew that Hana and her uncle didn't get along, but something felt off. She loaded the last dish into the dishwasher and walked out of the kitchen without another word.

When Daisy got back to the dining room, Noriko mentioned again that if she wanted to grab any of Hana's dorm stuff, she was more than welcome to it. Noriko had moved it from the basement to Hana's room, and Daisy took the escape that she desperately wanted after her conversation with Dennis to look through Hana's things.

Hana's room was the same as it was last time she was in there, though now there was a large trunk next to the closet door. Daisy opened it and tried not to breathe too deeply, worried that Hana's perfume would be soaked into whatever was in the trunk, but it only smelled like Noriko's preferred laundry detergent. Daisy looked through the trunk, only taking a few pictures of her and Hana and the framed print she had given Hana as a gift a few years earlier before closing the trunk back up and sitting on top.

Daisy glanced around the room when her eyes caught on a plastic bag in the closet, one she wrote off repeatedly during her past trips that contained a pair of muddy boots. Daisy pulled it out of the closet and reopened the bag, staring at the boots as if they would solve a mystery.

They smelled musty, like they'd been put in the bag while they were still wet. Hana was messy, but she was never a slob. Normally she would've cleaned off these boots as soon as she could, and the fact they were left muddy was unusual. Daisy poked around in the bag and pulled out Hana's favorite pair of jean shorts from beneath the boots.

Hana wore this pair of faded jean shorts almost every day in the summer. Daisy hadn't wondered where they went, but now that she saw them here, caked in mud and forgotten on the floor of Hana's closet, she knew that Hana must have put this bag in her closet the day she died. Which meant that most likely wherever she hid Daisy's note was somewhere muddy.

It didn't rain the day Hana died, and the dirt paths around the water tanks had dried up before mid-June. Then, it clicked where Hana hid the note, and Daisy threw the bag back in the closet, grabbed what she was taking for her dorm, and rushed downstairs.

"Dad, can we go home?" Daisy called, not even leaving the foyer to go find him.

"Sure, just give me a minute," Henry responded. Daisy felt like an exposed wire, and if she stayed in the house she would explode.

"Okay, I'm going to wait outside. Bye Dennis! Bye Noriko, thank you for breakfast!" Daisy said, already out the door and heading towards her father's car. Henry came out a moment later, walking briskly and looking irritated. He got in the car and started it silently, and Daisy turned on the radio in hopes of diffusing the situation. Only one bar of "Heaven is a Place on Earth" played before Henry slammed his hand on the power button shut it off.

"What was that?" Henry asked.

Daisy tried to remember what she did that would have angered her father. "What are you talking about?"

"Just leaving like that? Barely a goodbye? Do you know how rude you were being?" Henry got louder with every word until he was nearly shouting, and Daisy flinched.

"It — it's just weird being in Hana's room. I just wanted to go home."

"There's still no need to be so rude. You think Noriko isn't suffering, living in the house where her daughter died?"

Daisy stared at her lap where she held the first photo she ever took with Hana. "That isn't what I was trying to do."

"Well, you'll be happy to know that she was worried she upset you. I spent the last minute calming her down before handing it off to Dennis to take you home."

Normally, Daisy would back down, but she was tired of her father dictating what she could and couldn't do at all times.

She was sick of pretending to be someone else so he wouldn't be upset. "Sorry, do you want me to just get over Hana dying? Do you expect any of this to be easy for me?"

Henry shook his head, taking a hand off the wheel to sharply wave Daisy off. "That's not what I—"

"Yes, it is. I'm sorry if I'm not grieving in a more acceptable way for you."

"Daisy, that isn't what I meant." Henry gripped the steering wheel, glaring at the street in front of them. "Stop twisting my words."

"I'm not a kid anymore!" Daisy shouted. "You can't distract me like you did when mom died. I have complex emotions now; grief isn't going to look the same as it did when I was four years old and didn't understand death. I'm going to grieve, and I'm going to hurt, and I'm not going to be pretty while I do it. I'm so sick of trying to be the person you convinced yourself I am, and I can't hide what I'm feeling and pretend like I am okay for you anymore!"

"I don't expect you to be okay, but you don't need to lash out at the people around you." Henry took a deep breath to calm himself. "I'm worried that you're taking Hana's death a little too hard, okay? Sorry for being worried about you."

"Yeah, right. You want to hear how I've really been grieving?" Daisy laughed harshly, and she spoke without thinking. "I've been going to college parties and getting drunk with a bunch of twenty-year-olds. There you go, no more blissful ignorance that your perfect daughter is so innocent!" Once Daisy finished shouting, silence filled the car, thick like syrup.

"Seriously? Have I taught you nothing about how to be responsible?" Henry asked, his voice calm but barely masking the anger he had a moment earlier.

"What does it matter if I'm responsible?" Daisy threw her hands in the air and let out a hysterical giggle. "Hana was responsible, and she's still dead. Mom was responsible, and that didn't stop some idiot drunk driver from killing her!"

"Daisy Grace Polo if you don't stop right now—"

Daisy turned to look at Henry, wanting to read every ounce of his reaction. "You'll what? Ground me? I leave for college in four days. What do you want me to do?"

"You're done with the car. You can take it to work and back until your brother gets home this week, and then he has to drive you," Henry shot back.

"That's a real punishment. A few days without a car after I already decided I was done with the parties? You really got me, dad," Daisy said. She might have been pushing too far, but she couldn't stop. She couldn't measure her tone when she was bleeding out with the weight of her grief and her panic at the thought of not being able to go to the water tanks right away to look for Hana's note.

"I know you're grieving, but you're putting yourself in dangerous situations. Is this what Hana would've wanted for you?" Henry asked. At his words, it was like the last shreds of Daisy's self-control snapped.

Daisy laughed, and it sounded cruel. "Hana would've hated this actually. Because I was in love with Hana, and she was in love with me, and we dated for three and a half years, and we broke up a week before she died. And she would've hated that someone else was making me happy, so you're right. Hana would've hated this, but Hana is dead, so her opinion doesn't really matter anymore, does it?"

It was like all of the air was sucked out of the car at once. Daisy regretted coming out like that, but she was oddly relieved at the same time.

"You can't be serious," Henry said. Luckily, they were back home. Daisy stared at the photos in her lap, her chest heaving. Was her mistake telling him in this way or telling him at all? Either way, there was no stopping this conversation now.

"We were in love, and I was going to New Paltz so we could finally be together without having to hide. Or that was the plan before she left me."

"I can't believe you lied to me all this time," Henry said. Daisy opened the door and the late August humidity rushed into the car, slinking like a python and wrapping around her just as tight.

"I can't believe you never noticed." She got out of the car and slammed the door behind her.

When she got inside, she locked herself in her room and blasted her angriest playlist loud enough to hide the sounds of her father in the house. She pulled out a bottle of wine and stared at it. It was too early to drink, but she didn't know what else to do. It wasn't like she could go back to the water tanks like she planned. She had no one to call, no one who would drive her there no questions asked. Her best friend was dead, and she broke up with a perfectly nice boy and lost all his friends in the process. She hadn't spoken to anyone from high school since the day of Hana's funeral, and for the first time Daisy realized how isolated and alone she really was.

Hana appeared in front of her. "Daisy, come on. Just lay down, take a breather. You're okay." Daisy hadn't realized she was crying until Hana spoke, but now that she noticed the tears in her eyes, she broke. Her sobs wracked her chest, coming deep and unfiltered in a way they never had before, not even when she found out Hana died.

The music served as a silencer for her grief, ensuring her dad wouldn't be able to hear her. These were the kind of tears that weren't meant to be seen by any other living being, though she was glad for Hana's ghost. She was a sign that this was real, that the hole in the middle of Daisy's chest wasn't always there, that she didn't imagine the love and the loss and the absolute devastation of knowing she made so many mistakes with Hana that she couldn't fix. She didn't open the bottle of wine, and she ended up sitting on the ground curled around it, clutching it like a lone rock keeping her from being swept downstream by the current. Hana's hand was a comforting weight on her back, anchoring her down so she didn't drift away.

Eventually, she fell asleep on the floor next to her bed surrounded by a sea of used tissues and woke up once the sun was already low in the sky. Her playlist was done, and her room was silent around her. Her body ached from laying on the ground, though she managed to clear away the signs of her breakdown.

When she opened her still-locked door, there was a bottle of water and a warm grilled cheese. She wondered if her dad had knocked, if that was what woke her up from her slumber. She took the food and closed the door, and she ate while staring blankly at the journals on the floor. She would have to reread them if she was wrong about the note being inside the water tank. She hoped that the reason she hadn't found the note yet was because she wasn't looking in the right places and not because Hana's murderer killed her and destroyed it before she had a chance to hide it. Daisy needed to hold onto the hope that Hana's last message for her was still out there.

Before work the next day, Henry was waiting for Daisy in the kitchen, a cup of coffee as a peace offering on the island across from him. Daisy picked it up and took a sip, barely hiding her wince at the sickly, chemical sweetness.

"I talked to your brother. He changed his flight, so he'll be getting in this afternoon around one. Can you pick him up after you get out of work?" Henry asked.

"Oh, uh, yeah. No problem," Daisy said. She took another large gulp of coffee and left the kitchen as quickly as possible to avoid having to talk to Henry more.

The worst part of all of this was that she didn't know what upset her dad about their conversation. Was it the fact she was partying with college kids without telling him? Was it the fact she dated Hana and never told him? Was it the fact that she dated Hana at all? Daisy wondered if Henry was upset that she hid something from him or that he never figured it out.

Daisy didn't have time to stop at the water tanks between the end of her final lifeguarding shift and when Will's flight was coming in. While she waited outside of the airport to pick him up, she was scribbling down notes on how she could reinvestigate her cold leads if Hana's note wasn't where she hoped it was. She was so lost in thought that she didn't notice how much time had passed until there was a knock at the passenger side window, and she startled before looking up to see Will.

"Hey, wanna pop the trunk?" he asked with a smile. Daisy squealed and got out of the car, shoving her notebook in her back pocket before running to the sidewalk to hug her brother.

"I can't believe you changed your flight," Daisy said, laughing and still hugging him. He held her tight for another few seconds before letting her go, and she went back to the driver's side to pop the trunk for him.

"Well, Dad made it sound like you're on the verge of a psychotic break, so I thought it might be a good idea," Will teased. He put his bags in the trunk, and Daisy took a few deep breaths while waiting for him to get in the car. They were going to talk about her fight with their dad, and she didn't want to.

"So, I heard you're a party girl lesbian now," Will said, casting aside any pretense. "Some big developments considering I was only gone for a month."

Daisy laughed and joined the stream of other cars leaving the Rochester airport. "I ... may have let years of pent-up aggression out on Dad in the span of a few minutes."

"On the bright side you're going away to school in a few days."

"Yeah. I guess I'll find out if absence makes the heart grow fonder," Daisy said. Even though it was supposed to be a joke, Will saw through her casual facade immediately. The silence hung between them, and she waited for him to ask her what happened. What had Henry told him? She didn't really want to know.

Will pulled down the passenger side visor to look at himself in the mirror, and Daisy saw his eyes flick to her face in the reflection. "So, you finally told Dad about Hana."

"Yeah, and it went about as well as I hoped." Daisy pointedly kept her eyes on the road, not wanting confirmation that her brother was upset with her.

Will flipped up the visor, and it snapped back into place with a thump against the roof of the car. "To be fair, you were using it as ammunition against him."

"It wasn't ammunition, he told me I was overreacting to losing her. I was making him understand why I wasn't overreacting," Daisy said.

Will flinched. "How come you didn't tell me about the college parties?"

Daisy shrugged, trying to act nonchalant even though she was sure Will was annoyed she didn't tell him. "I didn't want you to worry. I was fine."

"Were you? You, like, freaked out on dad on a random Sunday afternoon and came out after years of hiding it." His stare was burning a hole in the side of her face, but she still didn't want to turn to see the disappointment she was sure would be written across his face.

She gripped the steering wheel when they came to a red light, watching cars speed through the intersection instead of turning to Will. "I was meaning to do it soon anyways."

Will laughed shortly. "Sure, but you didn't plan to do it like *that*."

"You can't tell me how to come out. I love you and I respect your opinion, but you don't get to do that," Daisy said.

Will sighed. "Are you relieved?"

Daisy paused for a minute, trying to figure out the truthful answer to his question. "I'm not yet, but I think I will be."

"Okay. But still, the partying wasn't a good idea. What did I tell you before I left?" He sounded so much like their dad, her hackles rose again.

"You gave me hypocritical advice then peaced out to Barcelona after my best friend killed herself, so sorry that I didn't follow your instructions," she snapped.

"She was my best friend too," Will snapped back.

Daisy was silent for another long moment. "I wish I left things off better with her. She was my best friend, and the last time I saw her I was just ... so angry at her."

"I understand," Will said, all the fight draining from him. "The last thing I said to her ... it wasn't right." Daisy finally looked over at him, and he was staring straight ahead, looking haunted.

"Did you talk to her after we broke up? I thought — didn't you say you wouldn't talk to her?" Daisy asked.

"I — well, it's not —" Daisy looked at him sharply, and he changed direction immediately. "I just wanted to talk to her about what happened."

Daisy wished they weren't in the car so she could throttle him for keeping this from her. "When the hell did you talk to her, Will?"

"It ... maybe a few hours before? I don't know if ... I might've been the last one to see her alive," Will admitted.

Daisy was glad they were on a familiar road because the only thing that kept her from crashing the car in her shock was muscle memory.

"What did you talk about?" Daisy asked, almost a whisper.

"I'll tell you when we get home. Just focus on driving," Will said, sounding defeated.

Daisy never sped as fast as she did on the last few streets to their house, and for once Will didn't comment on her terrible driving.

Chapter 18

Hana — age 19

6/9/19

Dear Diary,

I think my investigation is going well. If I wasn't on to something, I probably wouldn't have gotten a threat on my car windshield this morning, right?

I'll tuck the note in the back of this journal, but the gist of it is that I should stop investigating or bad things will start happening to the people I care about. Which is why I have to break up with Daisy.

I'm going to tell her the truth about Frida, and I know she'll leave me. She should. And maybe someday, once this whole thing is over, I can win her back. I'm already trying to think of ways to soften the blow, but I don't know how to do this. I ended things with Frida, sure, but that was casual sex, not a years long relationship that came after a decade long friendship. This might kill me. Then again, if anything were to happen to Daisy because I'm looking into my dad's death, that would <u>definitely</u> kill me. So it's the lesser of two evils to push her away and hope that I'll be able to win her back eventually.

I have to do this for her. I have to keep her safe. That doesn't mean that it's going to hurt any less, though.

Sincerely,

Hana

• • • •

Hana stared at the note, searching once again for any detail that might reveal who wrote it, that might bring her one step closer to discovering who her father's killer was. But just like the last hundred times she'd read the note she found attached to her windshield wiper with a rubber band, nothing was distinctive. The note contained perfectly correct grammar, and it was typed on plain printer paper. She had a feeling it was written by the same person who faked Jake Hansen's last death threat, but that was more of a hunch than something she could prove. She was pulled out of her thoughts by a text from Daisy

. . . .

Daisy
George's?

Hana
Sure. Pick you up in 15?

Daisy
Perf, see you then <3

. . . .

"Good morning, Hana," Daisy said when she got in Hana's car, reaching across and squeezing Hana's hand over the wheel.

"Good morning, Lazy Daisy," Hana replied easily.

Daisy groaned and buckled herself in. "One day I'll get Will back for telling you that nickname. Today is not that day, but one day I might." Hana laughed a little bit too hard, and Daisy gave her a confused look. Hana abruptly changed the topic by asking about Daisy's classes before the younger girl could ask what was wrong.

Over the course of the drive, Hana noticed that Daisy's usual bubbly self was deflating, and she cursed herself for all the harm she was doing to Daisy's life. She wished she could just tell Daisy she needed space until she solved this case, but Daisy would need to know everything to leave Hana alone, and her safety was too important.

They pulled into the parking lot of George's, but before Hana could get out of the car, Daisy put a hand on her arm, holding her in place.

"What's wrong?" Daisy asked.

"What?" Hana asked, not expecting Daisy to be so blunt.

"Something is wrong. You made a face when I talked about New Paltz, and you've been quiet all morning. All week, really. You're always busy, but you won't tell me what you're busy with, and, well, I don't know."

"I ... Well, what do you think I'm doing? You sound awfully accusatory." Hana knew what she had to do, and she hated herself for it.

Daisy shrugged. "I don't know what to think."

"I know you have a theory. Let's hear it."

"Are you cheating on me?" Daisy asked quietly.

"No," Hana said.

Daisy looked relieved. "Oh, okay. That's — well, that's good. So, what—"

"But I did."

Daisy froze. Her bright green eyes locked onto Hana's and held them, trapping Hana in the accusatory pain.

"What?" Daisy said in disbelief, as if all of this was going to be a joke, like Hana was playing some sick prank that she would give up any minute.

"Last semester there was ... this girl at a party. And I went home with her," Hana said.

Daisy looked like she was going to throw up, and without another word she got out of the car. Hana swore under her breath and got out with her, pausing when Daisy just closed her door and leaned against it, her back to Hana.

"How could you do this to me?" Daisy asked.

"I didn't — it wasn't about *you*," Hana responded. Daisy whipped around to face Hana, and they stood on either side of the car, staring each other down. Hana couldn't remember Daisy ever looking so angry. Hana wasn't just pushing Daisy away for the summer — she was destroying everything they had. But she needed to do it, needed to twist the knife to cut all the threads of their life together. She needed Daisy to be safe.

"It wasn't about me? You slept with some other girl, and it wasn't about me? Was it all about you like everything always is?" Daisy asked, her voice just shy of a shout. She was breathing like she just swam an entire length of a pool underwater, and there were tears in her eyes.

"It was selfish. I know it was, but I was just so wrapped up in the—"

"Oh my god. Seriously? So wrapped up in the moment you forgot that you were supposed to be with me? That you forgot you loved me? Do you even love me, or was I just convenient until you found something better?" Daisy demanded, her eyes locking Hana in place with the full force of her fury. Hana flinched back. Daisy deserved to be loved better, but she also deserved to be let go better than this.

"Look, Daisy, can we just talk about this like adults? You don't need to—" Hana started, but Daisy cut Hana off with a humorless laugh.

"Sure, let's talk like adults. What was your tax return like this year?" Daisy snapped. She took out her phone and started texting someone, and Hana needed to try to salvage a small part of this so that maybe one day Daisy would understand.

Hana started walking around the car towards Daisy, but froze in place when Daisy leveled her with the meanest glare she'd ever seen. "She didn't mean anything."

Daisy laughed incredulously and threw up her hands, almost throwing her phone in the process. "Then why would you do it?"

"Just ... to see if I could." Hana took another step forward, and Daisy took one back.

"When was it?"

"Halloween."

Hana never knew Daisy to be violent, but she'd never seen the other girl look so angry before. Hana was regretting moving closer.

Daisy looked like she was doing mental calculations, and after a second, she said. "So ... Before thanksgiving?"

"Yeah." Hana swallowed thickly, but it felt like there was something pressing on her throat, making it impossible.

"You slept with someone else, and then you came to my house and played family with me? Are you kidding?"

Hana flinched. "I wish I was."

"Why wait until now to tell me this?" Daisy demanded.

"I think we should break up."

"No shit, Sherlock," Daisy snapped. Hana held in the familiar reply of *Fuck you, Watson* and instead let silence fall between them. Daisy turned her back to Hana again, and Hana saw on Daisy's phone screen that she was watching Will's location, the small blue dot getting closer to them by the second. When Daisy put her phone in her pocket and started walking across the parking lot towards its entrance, Hana followed her.

"I still—"

"Don't you dare," Daisy said harshly, whipping around to face Hana, "Don't say you love me, don't ask if we can be friends, just don't."

"Okay, just ... call when you want to talk." Hana stepped back as Will sped into the lot, screeching to a stop next to his sister.

"What is there to talk about? You've made all our decisions for us. You cheated on me, and you broke up with me. You did this.

You made your grave, now have fun trying to keep warm with the goddamn worms." Daisy got into Will's car and slammed the door shut.

Hana walked back to her car. She sat there for twenty minutes, staring blankly at her steering wheel, until a text from Chrissy jolted her out of her trance.

She drove home in silence, ignoring the text, and she was relieved no one else was there when she arrived. She felt like a ghost, like she wasn't real, like it was another person that just broke Daisy's heart. She thought it would be a relief to know that she didn't have to lie to Daisy anymore, but the truth felt worse. Hana hadn't just broken things, she had disintegrated them. There was no repairing this.

This was the only way, though. Daisy was stubborn, and she loved Hana too much to accept a breakup without a real, concrete reason. If Hana said she didn't love Daisy anymore, Daisy would be around more than ever trying to win back her affection. If Hana said she didn't see a future for them, Daisy would mold herself into exactly the type of girl she thought Hana wanted until they were together again. Daisy would change herself if she thought she was the problem, so the only way to leave Daisy was to reveal Hana's own flaws, her own inability to love the way Daisy deserved, even if they both hurt more this way.

Maybe someday Hana could try to make things right between them. Maybe Daisy could forgive her, could believe her if she promised never to do it again. If Hana caught the mastermind behind her father's investigation, Daisy would at least hear her out. But even if they were together again someday, this would always hang over them. Hana's deceit would never go away. After all, Daisy was right — Hana alone did this to them. She didn't really consider how it would feel for Daisy to be left, only how Hana would feel leaving her. She knew that Daisy's hurt would hurt her too, but she didn't know it would feel so sharp and brutal. She was too wrapped in the case, and she was forgetting the fact that her life was happening now, not on a dark street downtown on a cold February day years in the past.

Hana barely left her room for the next three days. She listened to the same album on repeat and hyper-focused on the case and only told Chrissy about the breakup. Their other friends didn't even know Hana cheated on Daisy, and she wasn't ready to admit it to them. Chrissy only knew because Hana broke down crying one night after a party where she saw Frida that April, and Chrissy was sworn to secrecy.

"Maybe I should've just broken up with her and not told her," Hana said on a video call with Chrissy on the third day of her self-imposed isolation.

"That would've been kind of a dick move, though. I mean you guys dated for, like, three and a half years. She deserved to know the truth about why you're breaking up."

"I mean, probably, but it just sucks because I miss her, and I love her still, and I feel like … like I made a mistake breaking up with her."

Chrissy sighed. "Well, you can't take it back, so there's no point in over analyzing it. You just have to move forward with things. Do you want to win her back?"

"I do, but … what if she's what's best for me, but I'm not what's best for her?"

"Do you really think you're the one who should decide what's best for her? She does have her own mind, you know."

"Yeah, she does," Hana said. "Maybe I'll, like, get her a sorry present. See if I can salvage our friendship. And maybe we'll get back together one day or maybe … not."

"It might be a good idea to give her some time to cool off. I mean … you did just kind of drop it on her that you cheated. And, like, in public."

"So, you think I did the wrong thing?"

"I — no, that's not—" Chrissy paused to collect her thoughts. "Look, here's the thing, I think you did the right thing telling her, but you didn't do it the best way you could've."

"Oh yeah? What's the right way to tell someone you cheated on them?"

"I mean the best way to do it is to not cheat on them in the first place," Chrissy snapped.

"Whatever. I'm already judging myself enough, I don't need your help. Bye."

Hana hung up before Chrissy could respond and spent the rest of the night staring at the threatening note and hoping she had made the right choice breaking Daisy's heart.

The next day was a Thursday, and she dreaded this day because it was when her uncle came over for dinner. Apparently, Noriko and Dennis began this new tradition while Hana was away for the semester, and she hated it with every fiber of her being.

Tonight, though, tonight Hana would make this meal matter. From what she was figuring out from investigating her father's death, there were a few possible scenarios that left him with two bullets in his body on that February afternoon.

Option one was that what the police claimed was true. Jake Hansen killed Mark Holm and then killed himself. Hana didn't think it was the whole truth anymore.

Option two was that Jake Hansen was hired to kill Mark Holm, but after the fact he had a change of heart and the guilt caused him to kill himself. This felt more possible, but there was still something off about Hansen's suicide that Hana couldn't put her finger on.

Option three was that Jake Hansen was hired to kill Mark Holm, and then whoever hired Hansen killed him to cover up their involvement. This was what Hana believed, in her soul, was the case, but she still didn't have enough actual evidence to support her hunch.

This dinner was the perfect opportunity for her to have her mother and uncle read the short story she had written that semester that mirrored her suspicions for her father's death. She printed out two copies, one ending where the spouse did it and one where the sibling did it, and left them up in her room to grab when an opening came up. Tonight, she would scare their guilt out into the open like her words were a hunting dog and their crimes were birds startled out of tall grass. She just needed to point and shoot.

"Hana! Your uncle is here," Noriko called a little after five. Hana walked down the stairs as casually as she could.

"Hello, Uncle Dennis," she said when she reached the bottom of the stairs.

"Hi, Hana. How's summer treating you?" Dennis asked, his voice light and jovial.

"It's been pretty good so far. I had the chance to finish a short story I worked on for class this semester," she responded. She wanted to pretend like she was innocent, docile, and non-threatening today, and she even got close to wearing one of the sun dresses that Noriko routinely snuck into her closet. Instead, she wore a flowing white lace top and a pair of light wash jean shorts. Her bare feet were quiet against the tile of the foyer, and her hair hung loosely around her face.

"I didn't know that. That's great, sweetheart," Noriko said, exchanging a surprised look with Dennis. It was unusual for Hana to offer insights about her life, especially with so little prodding.

"Do you guys want to read it after dinner?" Hana asked, still acting demure and non-threatening.

"Sure, that sounds great!" Dennis shared a look with Noriko that Hana chose to ignore, instead floating towards the kitchen and getting out dishes to set the table. She hoped that by acting the way her mother constantly told her to, she could get them both to relax so their reactions to her story would be genuine. If she seemed like the perfect daughter and niece, they would be caught off guard by the mirror of their crime in her story. She set the table without a word and pretended not to notice Noriko's pleased smile at the gesture.

"I think a Chardonnay will go best with this, don't you, Dennis?" Noriko asked from the dining room. It wasn't meant for Hana, but she still acted on the comment. Drunk actions were sober thoughts after all, and she wanted to get to the root of her uncle and mother's possible motives. Hana grabbed three glasses out of the China cabinet in the dining room and placed them at each of their seats. When Noriko returned with the wine, she didn't comment on Hana's glass, but of course Dennis did.

"I'm sure a glass of wine is nothing compared to what you've been up to down in New Paltz," he joked, watching Noriko pour all three of a glass.

"Yeah, I wasn't really drinking expensive chardonnay at house parties." Hana laughed. Noriko seemed confused again by the friendly interaction, so different from Hana's usual antagonistic demeanor when it came to her uncle.

"I remember when I came back after Freshman year and I had curfews again, it threw me off," Dennis said. "I was so used to doing what I wanted that I wasn't even breaking rules on purpose. It was just what I was used to."

Hana laughed, enjoying the quick flick of surprised eyebrows from both Noriko and Dennis at her enjoying a conversation with him. "Yeah, I don't have a curfew considering Mom usually works the night shift." Noriko gave her a tight smile in return.

"Having an understanding mother definitely helps the situation, I'm sure," Dennis smiled. Hana gave her own smile in return and began eating her food in small, measured bites, the way her mother always tried to get her to.

"How's the hospital been, Nori?" Dennis asked.

"Same as always. We had a pretty crazy night last night — you know how it gets leading up to full moons," Noriko joked. She delicately speared a small piece of her chicken onto her fork and brought it to her lips. Hana watched Dennis tracking the movement and hated the way his eyes traced the lines of her mother's fingers and the slim silhouette of her shell pink lips.

Hana managed to keep up her ruse for the entire dinner, simpering and smiling the way she was taught to but never had in the past. Dennis seemed to be enjoying the fact that Hana wasn't trying to fight him, but Noriko shot her frequent glances that told Hana her mother wasn't quite buying her full demeanor shift as easily.

"Do you guys still want to read my story?" Hana asked once they all finished eating.

"Yeah, that sounds great. Why don't you go grab it while we clean up?" Noriko asked. Usually, she would make Hana help clean when they had guests, but with how often Dennis was around, it seemed as though Noriko was starting to think of him as a resident of the house. Hana tried not to think too hard about it.

She went upstairs to grab her story, and when she came back down, she poured herself another glass of wine and knocked it back while eavesdropping on Dennis and Noriko.

"Maybe she's just finally growing up?" Dennis questioned.

"Maybe, but I don't know. She's been really quiet the past few days, and I think she might've gotten in a fight with Daisy or something. I can't really figure it out," Noriko worried. Hana bristled. She just wanted them to feel off their game, not to try to figure out why she was out of sorts.

"Well, you know how girls are," Dennis responded. "One of them probably borrowed a shirt or something and spilled a soda on it or something like that." Hana wanted to throttle her uncle for his stupid backwards thinking, but Noriko laughed at his comment like she agreed. Hana's dislike for her mother flared up.

"Yeah. Maybe it is her growing up and maturing. College can do that to kids sometimes," Noriko said.

Hana carefully set down her wine glass and walked back to the top of the stairs silently before loudly coming down them so they would know she was coming.

"Fresh off the presses!" she called, almost skipping into the kitchen.

"Great. Why don't you bring them to the living room?" Noriko said. She turned to Dennis. "I have that record you wanted to listen to, Dennis." Noriko gave him a soft smile. Hana hated the look, hated the softness, the familiarity of it. She hated even more that the expression was on her uncle's face as well, a face so similar to her father's it was like seeing a ghost for a second. She turned and walked to the living room, setting the stories down to pour herself the last of the bottle of wine.

"Don't go too fast, now, Hana. You might end up spilling a secret," Dennis teased.

Hana barked out a laugh. "It'll take more than a few glasses of wine for me to show my cards." Dennis gave a tight laugh back, and Hana loved that the softness he showed Noriko vanished, the hint of Mark's kindness disappearing with it.

"So, the story?" Noriko asked.

"Of course, here you go. I mean, you know I'm not a creative writing major, but my class liked it. My teacher too — I got an A."

"That's great, kid," Dennis said, and Hana barely stopped herself from bristling at his words. She handed Noriko and Dennis the story, picked up her journal from the coffee table, and settled back into an armchair. She doodled flowers in her notebook until she realized she was drawing daisies, and she flipped to a fresh page to write down any observations about the duo reading.

Dennis stayed largely impassive, and the only changes to his face were his eyebrows furrowing and a slight twitching of his lips on the page Hana thought contained a joke. Noriko's face, on the other hand, changed as she went through the story. She looked sad, nostalgic, confused, and, in the end, upset. She flipped the story shut a few seconds after the side of the record finished and the room lapsed into silence aside from the scratching of Hana's pen.

"What did you think?" Hana asked. Noriko and Dennis glanced at each other before answering.

"It was good. I liked how you led to the ending. It could've gone either way," Noriko said sagely.

"Yeah, that was good. I liked the jokes the detective made," Dennis said.

"Do you think it was realistic?" Hana pressed.

Dennis nodded. "Yeah, I think so. The story felt like it could really happen."

"Hmm, okay. And mom? Anything else you liked?"

"The husband seemed a little too adamant about being uninterested in the sister before his wife died. Maybe do something with him showing he wasn't interested before," she said, her tone measured and her words careful, but confusion coloring her words when she added, "I never understood why people would kill their spouses. Just get a divorce, you know? A divorce lawyer is much cheaper than a defense attorney." Hana nodded and jotted down a few more notes before standing and plucking the stories out of their laps.

"Thanks for reading. I think I'm going to go lay down," Hana said, heading upstairs. She sipped her wine and sat on her bed while watching the sun sink down out of the sky through her window. The colors burned and swirled together while she tried to figure out if her family members were actually instrumental in killing her father.

Chapter 19

Daisy — August 2019

"YOU THINK YOU WERE the last one to see her alive?"

Daisy and Will sat at their kitchen table, in the seats they'd claimed as children and never tried to switch around. Daisy had a glass of water gripped between her hands, and she fought to look up from its surface to look at Will, but he wouldn't meet her eyes. He was flushed, and he nervously picked at his cuticles. Daisy didn't notice in the car, but Will looked tired. More tired than he should be after a fun trip abroad, even if he was going out every night.

"I ... probably? I don't know. I saw her, and then I left, and then I ... I found out she was dead. I biked over there to talk to her, but I was home before you got back from your pre-calc final. I made us mac and cheese before you got home, remember?" he asked. Daisy knew exactly what meal he was talking about. She'd vomited it back up when her dad told her that Hana was dead.

"Why didn't you tell me?" Daisy asked, her voice a whisper. If she spoke any louder, she would start crying.

"Because I went there to talk about you, and I ... I wasn't nice to her. So I didn't say anything because what if ... what if it was me that pushed her over the edge?" Will asked, but there was something about the way he said it that let Daisy know he was holding something back. It was a tone she heard him use for their dad a million times, but never with her.

"What could you have possibly said that would make you think that?"

"I just — she didn't seem like herself, but I still ... There was something off about her. I thought she was just annoyed that I was calling her out, but I just got so mad at her that I didn't think about how she felt, just how I did."

"What did you say to her?" Daisy pressed.

"I'm sure you know that I gave her the shovel talk before. I mean, that's standard big brother stuff, right?" he asked. Daisy nodded. "I went there to tell her how bad she messed up, and I know that's probably stupid and misogynistic, but Hana was my friend, and I wanted to talk to her about it."

"Why would you do it when you were so mad?" Daisy asked.

"I didn't — I wasn't mad before I got there. I was upset with her, but I wanted answers. And I know you told me not to ask, but after how long I've known her, I thought that she owed that much. I wasn't angry when I got there."

"What made you get so mad?"

"She seemed so distracted. Like she just wanted me to leave, and she was so ... rude. I went there to talk to her, and she wasn't even giving me the time of day. You know how she could be so dismissive even if you were trying to tell her something important. I yelled at her, and she just ..." Will shook his head as if he was trying to shake the memory loose.

"Did she seem ... sad? Or depressed? Or upset?" Daisy asked. She needed to understand where Hana's head was at. Was she distracted because she had a lead in the case? Had she already hidden Daisy's letter? Did she accidentally say something about it that Will didn't understand?

"She seemed ... like she was in her own world. And she said ... Well, she said something about you that I know isn't true. Then I started yelling at her, and I ... I told her I would never forgive her for what she did to you. And then," he paused, swallowing hard against the tremble in his voice, "and then she killed herself. She's gone, and I ... I have a hand in it. I will always have her blood on my hands." He sounded broken open and raw. Daisy didn't know he was so guilty about Hana's death.

"It wasn't your fault that she ... that she died," Daisy said. She contemplated telling him about the investigation, but something held her back. She was starting to understand why Hana kept her out of this before.

"You don't know that," he said bitterly, wiping at his eyes when he thought she wasn't looking.

"I guess you're right. Hana took the truth to the grave with her."

"Yeah. Look, I'm tired, so I'm going to go take a nap. I'll see you whenever Dad gets home and decides we have to have that family meeting," Will said.

"I ... yeah, of course. We can talk more later."

Daisy waited until she couldn't hear Will rustling around in his room anymore before she moved. She grabbed her rain boots out of the front closet and Will's car keys off the hook before quietly locking the door behind her. She didn't let herself worry about the excuses she would have to make to Henry and Will later, she just needed to focus on finding whatever Hana left for her. Hana's ghost was already waiting in the passenger seat when Daisy got in the car, and Daisy sighed.

"This feels like a good move," Hana said.

"This better be real. *You* better be real. If not, I ... if you killed yourself because the investigation was a dead end or something, I ... I'll—"

"You'll what?" Hana's ghost goaded.

"I don't know! It's not like I can blow up my life any more than I already have!" Daisy exploded.

Hana's face became somber. "I'm sorry. But I didn't kill myself, I promise."

"So glad that a potential figment of my imagination isn't lying to me, what a relief."

"Clearly you believe I'm real enough if you're doing what I say," Hana pointed out.

"Well, this, this lead, the note — it's all real. *Actually* real. Not something a maybe-real ghost told me."

"Daisy," Hana said, and it sounded like an apology, an explanation, and a declaration of love all at once.

Daisy interrupted anything else Hana might have added. "What did Will really say?"

The silence between them was too loud, but Daisy hoped that holding the silence would make Hana tell her the truth.

"I ... don't know. It was too close to my death. I can't even remember what I had for breakfast, let alone talking to Will."

"Do you think if I solve this, you'll remember everything?"

"I don't know, maybe. Maybe I'll just go to heaven and none of it will matter." Hana rested her head back against the seat.

"And then I'll be left to deal with the consequences of your actions here on earth," Daisy said. "Isn't that just classic. You get to go into the beyond with no suffering and I'm stuck here with a broken heart. That is, if whoever killed you doesn't kill me too before I can figure this out."

"I wish I could help more, but I don't ... I don't know where I slipped up. I wish I could remember what happened that last day, how I got myself killed, so I could keep you safe, but ... I don't know what happened to me."

Daisy was silent for the rest of the drive, and Hana's ghost followed her on her walk to the water tanks.

"So, here goes nothing," Daisy muttered before she stepped into the tank, half to herself and half to the ghost.

She'd never wanted to venture inside before, and she still didn't want to, but this would never end if she didn't. Even if she made up her mind right now that Hana killed herself and the ghost was just a manifestation of her grief, the note Daisy found still said something was hidden for her. This tank might hold Hana's last words for Daisy, and she needed to know what they were before she could put any of this behind her. She couldn't move on without knowing.

She looked around the tank, wondering where she should start. Before she could even finish the thought, Hana's ghost walked forward. Her clothes were different from the other times she appeared — she was now wearing the green Wellington boots Daisy found along with her jean shorts and a New Paltz sweatshirt. She was constantly looking over her shoulder, but she was looking right through Daisy. Daisy needed to follow her, and she trailed behind the ghost, dodging weeds and rocks.

The ghost stopped in a spot near the edge of the tank and vanished, and Daisy knew that was where the note would be. She looked for anything out of place that could tell her where Hana hid something for her.

Daisy noticed a large rock poking out of the water, which wasn't unusual on its own, but there was dried mud covering half of it. It looked like the rock was once in the water and mud on its side but was yanked out of place and repositioned to stick straight up instead.

She shoved the rock with all her might, and after a few seconds of pushing it toppled on its side. She sprang back to try to avoid the splash and failed. She should have brought an extra set of clothes with her.

Water rushed in to fill the crater where the rock was resting, but when Daisy stuck her hand into the murky water, she felt something flimsy. She yanked on it, and when it didn't move, she took her shovel out of her backpack and started digging. After scooping away the mud, she pulled out a folder sealed shut in several Ziploc bags. It must have been Hana's attempt at waterproofing, and Daisy hoped it had worked as she lifted it up for a better look. She shook off the water, but the caked-on mud was rapidly drying and turning opaque under the August sun. She tried to wipe at the mud, but it only smeared into different patterns.

She trekked back to her car and contemplated where she could clean off her hands before opening the bags. She didn't want to go home. If Will was awake, he would ask questions, and she didn't want him there when she read whatever was in this folder. She walked back to her car and placed the folder on the floor of her passenger seat before trying to clean her hands with hand sanitizer and fast-food napkins, but she didn't have enough to clean all of the mud. She needed a real sink.

Daisy took a deep breath and called Noriko.

"Hi Daisy! How are you?" Noriko's voice was warm and soft despite the distant quality Daisy's phone brought to all her calls. She clicked the volume up a notch before speaking.

"I'm okay. I was just wondering if I could come over. I was looking for my favorite lipstick and I think I might've dropped it in Hana's room yesterday," Daisy lied. She really only wanted to know if Noriko was home, if she could use her house to clean up before reading the note.

"Oh, yes, of course. I'm running errands right now, but I'll be home in an hour or so."

"Oh, okay. I was already out and about, but—"

"If you're nearby you can go ahead and let yourself in. There's some lemonade in the fridge, too, if you want to come over now. I won't be too long."

"Okay, yeah, that sounds good. I'm not too far away, so I'll just pop in."

"Sounds good. Lock up if you leave before I get back," Noriko said. Daisy said a quick goodbye before hanging up, worried she might tell Noriko too much.

Parking at Hana's house held a sense of finality Daisy didn't expect. She took a deep breath to attempt to center herself before realizing no amount of oxygen would slow down her rapid heartbeat. She got out of her car to grab the spare key and let herself in the back door. She slid the lock closed behind her and ditched her muddy boots so she could make her way to the kitchen sink. The hum of the air conditioning was the only sound in the house, but the chill that ran down her spine was unrelated to the temperature.

She dropped the folder next to the sink and quickly scrubbed the mud off her hands and arms, drying herself off hastily before carefully opening the mud-covered Ziploc and pulling out the baggie inside, which was thankfully dry. She quickly opened the last two layers that were holding back the contents of the innermost bag — a manila folder with a lopsided drawing of a daisy on it. The design was the same one Hana used to draw on all the notes and letters she gave Daisy over the years. It was unmistakably for her.

Daisy's hands shook while she stared, frozen, at the folder. This was it. She'd already gone through Hana's room and her journals — all the pieces of life Hana left behind. This was it. After this, there were no more new words or messages from her. After this, it was just stories and re-readings, only wearing paths into familiar trails through Hana's life. Any secrets would be revealed by someone else, not by Hana herself. Hana, a girl who loved to hide things, was almost out of solvable mysteries.

Anything she could know about Hana was already out there. Whether it was in this folder, in the missing pages torn out of Hana's journals, or in the memories of other people — there was nothing new to know about Hana and there never would be. Anything Hana never told anyone was gone, taken to the grave to rot with her.

Daisy took a deep breath and opened the folder. It only contained two pieces of paper. The first was a note to her, and she read it quickly, hungrily, forgetting that she was supposed to savor this last scrap.

* * * *

Dear Daisy,

If you're reading this, I'm dead, and I'm sorry. I didn't solve this before it took me out, and I wish I was there to tell you everything I want to in person.

I'm sorry for cheating, and I'm sorry for weaponizing it against you so you wouldn't fight our breakup. I knew the truth was dangerous, and I couldn't have you close while I sorted this out. Clearly, I was right to worry since the only way you'll be reading this is if I'm dead.

As of right now, on June 18th, 2019, I believe my uncle was the one that hired Jake Hansen to kill my dad and then murdered Jake Hansen. You'll see all the evidence (and if my investigation reveals that my conclusion was wrong) if you log into the email. I made the password the month when we first said I love you, the day we broke up, and the color dress I wore on the date when we first ... you know. I hope this entire note is unnecessary and I'm showing it to you after I caught my father's killer, but there's a chance that won't be what happens.

I love you, even with all the ways I hurt you, and I hope one day I can explain why I did everything I did and try to make up for it. As a holder for my future penance, I will write it here for every year it's been true: I love you. I love you. I love you. I love you. I love you. I love you.

I will love you forever whether it's on heaven, earth, or somewhere in between.

You can find everything you need in the email account if I don't finish my work.

With love, always,

Hana

· · · ·

The second piece of paper was a small slip ripped from her most recent journal with the email address *hrh2019@gmail.com* on it. Daisy rushed to open her Gmail app and added the new account quickly, typing in *january9blue* for the password. There was only one email in the inbox, a welcome message from Google, but Daisy focused on the one unsent draft. Each tap on the screen reverberated through the empty home and harmonized with the slight rattle of the vents and the sound of someone down the street mowing their lawn.

The address bar of the email was empty, and Daisy figured that it was meant to prevent Hana from accidentally hitting send. She took a deep breath and started reading.

. . . .

To:

Subject: Evidence I've Collected (updated 6/18/19)
Hello,

I don't know why I used a greeting since I'm the only person reading this email. But that's unimportant, so ... moving on.

This is the best way I could think of to store this without worrying about it being hacked or easily destroyed, so this is it. Daisy if you're reading this, I'm sorry and I love you. I had this all in writing, but now that I'm getting close, I want a backup just in case something happens to my physical notes (or me).

. . . .

The email went on describing the evidence Hana had amassed, including attachments of the death threats against Mark she was referencing as well as pasted in photos of the specific parts of each threat she was referring to. She annotated the photos, using digital pens to circle and highlight portions that were noted in the body of the email. Daisy scrolled it slowly, trying to take in what she was seeing.

It was like a reflection of her notes on Hana's death, but with more diagrams and actual proof as opposed to Daisy's guesses and gut feelings. There weren't any lazy attempts to get alibis here like

Daisy in the graveyard. This was real evidence, the kind that could be shown in court and used to press charges.

Hana seemed to have a few suspects and theories, but the main ones were cases against Dennis and Noriko. In the section on Noriko, Hana detailed possible motives, ways she could've orchestrated her husband's murder, and notes on her reaction to the story Hana wrote. There was even a copy of Noriko's bank statements for the year before and after her husband's death along with information about his life insurance and their prenup.

Below the section on Noriko was a section on Dennis Holm. The motives were far more extensive than Noriko's, and there was more and more information that seemed to point to him as the killer.

• • • •

Motive: Wanted Noriko, jealousy, wanted more inheritance, less competition at work (made partner three months after the murder), stress from recent divorce.

Means and opportunity: *He had full access to all the case information, probably even knew about the threats Jake made after the victim got that murderer off. Knows how to use a gun. Was out with the victim the night of the murder. Allegedly home alone the night Hansen died.*

Evidence:
- Dennis went on a date with victim's wife before she met the victim.
- Dennis never really got along with the victim.
- No alibi for Hansen's death
- Divorce from his ex-wife around the time of the murder lost him a lot of money (no prenup)

Relevant Attached Documents:
- "Divorce Documentation"
- "Documentation of Dennis Holm Gun Collection"
- "Dennis Holm Financials"

• • • •

And below Dennis' section was another with other possible leads, ones with a lot less detail than the case against Dennis. There was some information about the cases her father was working on before he died as well as a note he had telling him he was a scam artist.

At the bottom, written in a font just a few sizes larger than the rest of the email, Hana declared her last guess at who was responsible for her father's murder.

• • • •

As of June 18th, 2019, I believe Dennis Holm is responsible for my father's death, and I believe it was murder, not an accident. After noticing the large cash withdrawal on 2/2/16, I'm going to ask him more about where he was when Mark died. Recording of the talk will be attached below.

See attached recordings:

- 6/18/19, 10 a.m. Dennis Holm and Hana Holm

• • • •

Daisy couldn't believe what she was reading, and she paused in disbelief and walked to the kitchen to get a drink before she could bring herself to listen to whatever recording Hana was referencing. Did this mean that Hana got to ask Dennis about her suspicions? Would the recording show unshakeable proof that Dennis did it, or proof that he didn't, and Hana didn't have time to make note of before she died? When did she write the note from the water tank? Was it before she updated the email with the new recording or afterwards?

Daisy poured herself a glass of the lemonade Noriko mentioned and drank all of it in one go. She didn't realize how thirsty she was until that moment, and she poured herself a second glass before hitting play on the recording.

At first, there was just some static and rustling, but then Hana started talking. She prodded Dennis with questions, and Dennis danced around them masterfully.

Did this mean that Hana was right? Had Dennis really played a role in Mark's death? Had Dennis killed Hana too? Was this conversation the point when Dennis decided Hana was too interested? If Hana thought he did it, thought he left the note, why would she talk to him about this at all? Did she think she was invincible?

Daisy didn't want to believe it — she didn't want this all to be true, to be real, to be anything at all. She needed time to mull this over later, so she typed in her email to send Hana's collected evidence to herself. Before she hit send, though, she contemplated adding Will. She wanted to keep him out of this, to keep him safe from this investigation that already cost her one person she loved, but she felt like she was in over her head. She needed someone in her corner that would always believe her. She wrote a sentence saying she had to talk to him when she got him, added him to the email, and hit send, hoping Will would hear her out when she finally told him everything about her investigation.

She tossed her phone on the counter and put her head in her hands, trying hard not to cry, not to be overwhelmed, not to lose it now when she now had a strong suspicion that she knew who killed Hana.

The man who she ate brunch with days earlier, the one who came to her house for Thanksgiving, might have murdered both her best friend and her father's best friend.

When she got home, she would talk to Will about all of this, and he would make sense of it. He always knew what to do.

She heard the key in the lock and got ready to face Noriko. She wasn't going to tell Hana's mother everything yet, so she hurriedly stuffed the plastic bags in the garbage and picked up the folder, holding it behind her back. She would tell Noriko about the note Hana left that her killer hid.

"Hey, Noriko, I'm glad you're back—" Daisy started, but when she saw who actually came in the door, she cut herself short.

"Hey, Daisy! How are you?" Dennis asked. He slipped off his shoes with a cordial smile.

He was dressed in one of the expensive suits he usually wore at the office, so Daisy figured he must have come right from work. He held a takeout bag from a Mexican place Hana used to love, and Daisy realized he was here to have lunch with Noriko.

Should she pray even though she didn't believe in God? If there was a chance she could be granted an act of mercy, she would take it.

"I was actually just going, Mr. Holm."

"Noriko mentioned that you might be over, so I got a burrito for you. Why don't you stay?" Dennis asked.

Daisy needed to act normal. "I forgot I have to do something for my dad," she said. Dennis was moving towards her now, and when he got into the kitchen his eyes caught on her phone, carelessly tossed a few feet away from her on the counter.

"Come on, Noriko told me which burrito is your favorite. You can tell your dad it was my fault if you're late," Dennis said, smiling his charismatic smile.

Daisy felt sick. "I ... I really appreciate that, but I have to get going." She smiled before walking towards Dennis and the exit of the kitchen, plucking up her phone as she went. She tried to subtly move the folder from behind her back to her front to keep it hidden, but Dennis noticed.

"What's that?" he asked.

"Oh, it's, um, the thing of Hana's I came to grab. Just some old poems she wrote me," Daisy said.

Dennis sighed and shifted to block Daisy from getting out of the kitchen. "If that folder is what I think it is, then I believe that we need to have a little talk."

Chapter 20

Hana — age 19

HANA'S UNCLE WAS RESPONSIBLE for her father's death. She didn't have proof yet, and she didn't know how hands-on he was, but deep down she knew.

Her ruse of acting like the perfect, doting daughter was working just as she planned. Her mother was thrown off, and her uncle didn't know how to act around her when they weren't at each other's throats. Best of all, Noriko and Dennis were letting their guards down. Hana was even able to steal their phones for a few hours while they thought she was locked away in her room. It seemed the lessons she gave them on cybersecurity when she was in middle school never paid off since they both had basic 4-digit codes for their lock screens. Noriko's was set to Hana's birthday, and Dennis' was the year he graduated high school. She went searching and was able to log into their bank and credit card accounts and send herself years' worth of transactions and delete all traces of her actions' notifications from their inboxes. There was nothing else telling in their messages or notes, but what she found before returning their phones was more than enough for her to dive into.

She realized that her journal would be too easy to discard if it was found, so she needed a digital backup that couldn't be easily wiped from existence. She created a new email account and only logged into it using an incognito window. She wrote everything into a draft, and she didn't send the email so there wasn't a digital trail.

After looking over all the evidence she'd accumulated, including a revised copy of her paternal grandparents' will, she was beginning to gather real evidence that wasn't just a sinking feeling in her stomach. She didn't know if Noriko was a coconspirator in any way, but after reviewing Dennis' bank statements, she was sure that he was a part of it.

In the weeks leading up to her father dying, Dennis made a series of cash withdrawals between $250-$700. The day he died he took out a final withdrawal of $3,500, and all together the withdrawals totaled $10,000. The same amount that Jake Hansen's mother said he set aside for his funeral. It couldn't be a coincidence.

Hana needed more concrete proof — she knew firsthand what a good defense attorney could do with evidence like this. No district attorney would pursue a case against a defense attorney as high powered as Dennis Holm without an airtight case.

Dennis was coming over for breakfast as he often did after one of Noriko's overnight shifts, but today he was coming before her shift instead of after. Noriko had traded a shift with a coworker who needed Tuesday afternoon off, so she was working a rare daytime shift today. Hana could count on one hand how many of those she remembered Noriko working since her father's death, and she tried not to think about whether Dennis inspired the change or not.

Hana made sure that she looked the part of a girl who grew up and was accepting her place in the world the way her mother and uncle wanted her to. She wore a pair of jean shorts with an oversized New Paltz sweatshirt tucked in at the waist. Her hair was meticulously brushed, and her lips had just the right amount of gloss. She was the picture of a casual college kid home for the summer.

When she came downstairs, she leaned against the doorway of the kitchen, taking in the scene in front of her. Dennis was in their kitchen already, wearing pajamas.

"Good morning, Hana!" he said jovially.

"Good morning." Hana worked hard to keep a contented smile on her face even though she hated the fact he must have slept over. He had stayed here playing house like they were that kind of family, like he wasn't involved in her father's murder. She was seething, but she kept it together.

"I hope you're in the mood for a big breakfast! I'm making up eggs and pancakes, and your mother ran out for muffins."

"Woke up with an appetite for some reason?" Hana asked innocently.

Her uncle blanched. "Uh ... yeah, I, um ... one of those mornings, I guess. Just in the mood for something sweet," he said, sprinkling chocolate chips on the pancakes.

"That's the same way my dad used to make them," Hana said, unable to stop the comment from slipping out.

"Oh, well, he and I learned from our dad," Dennis said uncomfortably.

"He never got around to teaching me, but I suppose I still picked up on it. It's almost the same," Hana said softly.

"Well, maybe I can show you sometime," Dennis said, though it sounded forced.

"Thanks, Uncle Dennis. That sounds good." Hana gathered things to set the table and left the kitchen without another word.

Noriko got home a moment later, and Hana gave her a half nod in greeting from where she was setting the dining room table. Her mother smiled at her before going into the kitchen to help Dennis, and Hana wanted to scream at her mother to run, to get away from the life-ruining man in front of her.

The two adults came out to her carrying breakfast a moment later, already wrapped in their own conversation.

"I wish I wasn't telling the truth, but really, that patient looked at me and started talking like I didn't speak English. It's ridiculous," Noriko complained.

"So, what did you do?" Dennis asked.

"Well, I let her know that I spoke English, and then every time I was close to her for the rest of the night, I muttered the few completely innocuous phrases in Japanese that I know so she would think I was talking badly about her." Noriko laughed. Hana laughed as well, even though she usually would use this as a start for a rant about how old racists need to just die off already.

"I can't even imagine doing what you do," Dennis said. Hana rolled her eyes.

"Well, I can't imagine doing what you do either. Anything big happening lately?" Noriko asked.

"No, nothing too important. Just the usual cases lately."

"Is it more interesting being a partner rather than just an associate?" Hana asked. Did her uncle think killing his brother was worth it?

"I think so. I have first pick of the interesting cases. Plus, I've always liked being busy, and I'm definitely busy as a partner," Dennis said wistfully.

"That's great," Hana said, not adding anything more as she began to serve herself. Dennis and Noriko exchanged a confused glance out of the corner of her eye, but she didn't comment on it.

She was elated. Clearly, they were buying her act, and if her pretending to be the girl who they wanted her to be would make them trust her she would lean in. If it meant getting one step closer to finding her father's killer, she would do anything. She would smile without her teeth and put on the clothes her mother bought her and rain down hell when she discovered the truth.

After breakfast, she helped clean up, much to her mother's relief. Noriko needed to get ready for work, and it left Hana and Dennis alone to do the dishes. Hana was loading the dishwasher and Dennis was handwashing a few in the sink. She paused, starting a voice memo on her phone before shoving it back in her pocket. She let the silence settle between them for a moment before she broke it.

"Uncle Dennis, can I ask you something?"

Dennis glanced over, puzzled, before focusing back on the pan he was scrubbing. "Yeah, kid, what's up?"

"So ... I was wondering if you could tell me more about how my dad died," Hana said slowly. Her pacing probably came off as uncertainty, but Hana knew exactly what she wanted to say. She kept loading the dishwasher, deliberately arranging and rearranging things while looking at Dennis out of the corner of her eye.

A look of anger came and went so quickly that Hana wasn't sure if it was actually there, and it was replaced by a mixture of confusion and sadness. His downturned lips fit the expression along with the crease on his forehead, but his eyes were too steady for the expression to look right. Had he ever done theater when he was younger or was his acting was an extension of his natural ability to lie?

"I ... I don't like to talk about it, you know that."

Hana fought against the urge to roll her eyes. "I know, I just ... I miss him, and I can't help but have some morbid curiosity about the whole thing."

"I ... Well, he went quick, Hana. The coroner's report said that the bastard hit him just right with one of his shots. Mark, he ... It was seconds."

"Do you think his life flashed before his eyes? Do you think — do you think he thought of me? And my mom?" Hana asked. It might be too far, but she wanted to make sure she pushed him. Surely her placid behavior at breakfast won her some leeway.

"I ... Well, I haven't died before, so I can't say for sure, but I'm sure he did. He loved you very much," Dennis said. Hana noticed how he left out mentioning how much Mark loved Noriko too.

"Yeah, he did."

She kept going. "I know you were in the restaurant when Dad was shot outside, but was it ... Where were you when it happened?"

"I was inside. It all happened so fast, and by the time I got outside, he was already gone." The way Dennis spoke sounded practiced, rehearsed, and was almost word for word the same as the original statement he gave at the crime scene.

"Do you think Hansen followed my dad or did he know where he'd be?"

"I don't know, Hana." Dennis's voice sounded exasperated. "I wish we could've gotten a trial, but Hansen killed himself before the police figured out he was the one who killed Mark. He took the coward's way out."

"Yeah, he did," Hana said. "Thank you for answering my questions. No one ever does." Hana closed the dishwasher and starting the cycle.

"No problem, kid. As long as you don't bother your mom with this stuff I don't mind."

"I won't. Bye, Uncle Dennis," Hana said. She left the kitchen and went straight to her room to add the voice memo to her email draft.

Hana had a feeling her uncle had already caught on to what she was doing and left the note on her windshield, but he couldn't know how much evidence she had. He was smart enough to cover up his involvement in his brother's death, but she was good at covering her tracks. Still, between the note and the way he was so insistent she didn't involve Noriko, Hana worried that something would happen to her and no one would be any the wiser that she was investigating her father's death. She needed someone to carry on the investigation if she was gone.

The only person she trusted wouldn't give up on this if something happened to her was Daisy. Hana didn't understand Daisy's obsession with detective stories, but it was convenient for now. Hana just had to figure out a way to give her the login for the email in a way that wouldn't be too obvious.

She wrote a note that she hoped someone would find in case anything happened to her. If she was gone, Daisy would want answers. At least, the version of Daisy from last week before Hana tore out her heart and stomped on it probably would. She just had to hope that even now Daisy would still care enough to look for her.

Hana wrote a note to anyone who might find it and included a short message to the three people she felt she still owed something to — Noriko, Will, and Daisy. She only gave a hint in the note about where Daisy's real letter would be, and she hoped Daisy would understand her cryptic message.

She wrote another letter, this one for Daisy, and tried to assure herself that it wouldn't come to this. Most likely these were all just unnecessary extra measures while she figured out the true next step in her investigation. She would be okay, and she would solve this mystery and get closure for her father's death. But just in case anything happened to her, she needed to hide this letter somewhere only Daisy would know to look for it — the water tanks.

After Hana heard Noriko and Dennis both leave, she went downstairs to grab a manila folder and a handful of gallon sized baggies she could use to hopefully waterproof the letter. She carefully packaged the folder in the baggies and pulled on an old pair of knee-high rain boots that could probably keep her dry while she hid Daisy's letter.

Hana sat in silence for half of her drive to the water tanks. When it finally became too much, she flipped on the radio to her favorite oldies station, and "Heaven is a Place on Earth" started playing. Hana smiled and nodded along to the familiar beat, wishing the song was enough to get her mind off everything going on.

She hiked to the water tanks quickly, pausing at the end of the trail to make sure no one was around to watch her. All she heard was the breeze rustling the trees and the distant bark of a dog, so she started to circle the tank, looking for their graffiti. She counted how many panels there were between the door of the tank and their initials to make sure she hid the folder in the right spot inside.

She circled back and listened carefully once more before stepping through the doorway.

The water was only about six inches deep, and Hana shuffled forward through it, kicking up the mud and making the water murkier with every step.

When she got to the area she wanted to hide the folder, she found a large rock that would be perfect to hide the letter for Daisy under. It was a few feet long and about half a foot wide, and she tucked the folder against one of the shorter sides of the rock before rolling it so the folder was now submerged in the water under the rock.

She took a step back to admire her handy work. The rock stuck straight up like a tombstone, and she hoped that if Daisy needed to go looking for the folder, she would be able to tell the rock didn't belong there. She slipped out of the tank and walked cautiously back to her car, happy to see that the trail was deserted and there was no one to give her odd looks about her mud-covered hands and clothes.

Her drive home was uneventful. She didn't turn on the radio, though she did roll down all the windows and open her sunroof to enjoy the early summer sun and the humid heat it brought with it.

When she got home, she was relieved to see that her mother and uncle's cars were both still gone. He mentioned that he had the day off to go to some doctor's appointment, so Hana worried he would already be back, but he must have still been out at his appointment.

She showered off the mud and made sure to really scrub at her legs and arms to ensure that no traces of her endeavor were left behind. She stuffed her muddy clothes and boots in a garbage bag and hid it in the back of her closet. She would figure out what to do with them both later, but for now she wanted to transcribe her conversation with her uncle.

She fished her laptop and journal out of her bag, but before she logged into the email, she ripped out the page with her could-be last words and placed it on her bedside table. She put a few things on top of it, but she made sure that it was easy to find if something did happen to her and someone needed to find it.

She was about to log into the email when the doorbell rang. She froze, figuring if it was some religious zealot or aspiring politician that would just go away if they thought no one was home. This idea was shattered a second later when whoever it was pounded on the door.

"I know you're in there, Hana! I see your car in the driveway!" Will Polo called, still pounding on the door. Hana cringed. He was probably there to make good on the series of shovel talks he gave her over the years.

She closed out of the email and shut her laptop before bracing herself to go downstairs and answer the door. She needed him to leave as quickly as possible, so she decided that she would keep up her docile doormat behavior for him as well.

She answered the door meekly, her eyes barely meeting Will's for a second before she opened the door entirely. "Hi, Will, come in," she said.

"Yeah, that's the plan," he said, walking past her and slipping off his shoes. Even angry, Will was always a gentleman.

"To what do I owe the pleasure?" she asked, shutting the door gently behind him. His breathing was harsh, and his face was red.

"I don't think this will be pleasurable," Will snapped.

Hana wilted like a flower in dried out soil. "Is this about Daisy?" she asked, trying to dive straight to the inevitable pain of the conversation.

"Yes. Of course it is," Will said.

"Do you want lemonade? My mom just made some yesterday," Hana said.

"I don't want lemonade. I want you to tell me what the hell is wrong with you," Will snapped. Hana walked towards the kitchen anyway, and Will followed at her heels.

"Where should I start?" Hana asked.

"Start with whatever is off in your head that would make you cheat on Daisy. Why would you do that?" Will demanded the answer to something not even Hana understood.

"I regret it, but I thought hiding it was wrong," Hana said tamely, pouring herself a glass of lemonade. She tried to put the pitcher back in the fridge, but Will got in the way.

"Doing it was wrong, Hana. What were you thinking? How could you do that to her?"

Hana paused, floundering for an answer that was both out of character for her and would possibly end this interaction sooner. Will wanted to know *why,* and he wouldn't accept that Hana wasn't thinking of Daisy when she cheated on her. Will would want her to say something reasonable, something that could satisfy his need for answers. Then it clicked into place, and her blood ran cold. She said a prayer for forgiveness for what she was about to say, and it suddenly struck her how long it was since she last went to church. Maybe she would go to mass on Sunday.

"I figured she was doing the same to me. I mean, why else would she not want to tell anyone we were dating?" Hana responded, nudging Will to the side to put away the lemonade.

"I — *what*? What do you mean you thought she was doing the same?" Will yelled.

"Well, her reasons for not coming out, they were always ..." Hana stalled while thinking of how to word it and hated herself for saying it. "Well, they always seemed like excuses. And she had so many of them, they came so easily, I figured she was telling some other girl the same thing. Or guy, who knows?"

"You're seriously messed up, Holm. What happened to all that talk about how you would never hurt her, how she was too good for you, how you would try to be the person she deserved?" Will demanded. She wished there was a way to do this without hurting Daisy and Will, but this was the only way to get them out of her life.

"All I did here was prove that I'm exactly the person you thought I was. Look, Daisy can fight her own battles, so why did you come here? Why today?" Hana finally looked up and met Will's eyes, wild with rage. The way he clenched his fists made Hana realize he really might hit her for breaking Daisy's heart.

Then again, maybe this treatment was what she deserved. She tried not to linger on that masochistic thought for more than a beat.

"She told me a few days ago, but she just left for her pre-calc final," Will said, "and I biked over here because I wanted to see your face when you admitted to it. I thought you would feel bad about this. I thought you could be better than this."

It stung to hear, even if she deserved it. She thought for half a second about dropping the ruse, about telling Will everything, but she wasn't sure that Will would help her even if he knew the truth. He loved Daisy more than he loved her, and he would always take her side.

"I'm the same person I've always been. It's not my fault you never noticed," Hana said after a beat. She turned and left the kitchen, and Will followed her. He pushed at her shoulder, and it sent her off balance enough that she nearly fell over.

"You never deserved her," Will spat.

Hana looked up at him, and she realized she'd never seen him so angry. "You should go, Will. I can't go back in time and become a better person, no matter how much I want to. I can't do anything to fix things between Daisy and I. I can't unbreak her heart."

"You should have been better. You should have known better. Your dad would be ashamed of the person you became," Will said.

"You don't know what you're talking about," Hana snapped. Will seemed spurred on by her anger, like he was feeding off it.

Hana was doing this wrong. Every part of her investigation was failing in one way or another. She couldn't find definite proof that her uncle paid off Jake Hansen, she didn't know who to trust and trying to keep the people she loved safe she was just hurting them. She was in so far over her head that she was struggling to breathe through it all.

She hoped that Will could forgive her eventually. Will knew what it was like to lose a parent, and maybe someday he would empathize with her burning need to know what caused her father's death. He was the one that came to Hana's house one day when they were eight and nine, fuming because Henry wouldn't tell him more about his mother's death. Hana sat with him and helped him look up articles about the accident she died in. They searched on the family desktop without clearing the history, and when Hana's mother checked it and asked Hana why she was looking it up, Hana told the truth. The next time Will came over, Noriko pulled him aside and promised she wouldn't tell Henry. Will had cried in her arms. What Hana remembered most clearly was Noriko saying that he needed to stop looking for answers to questions that didn't really matter.

Hana met Will's eyes and flinched back at his perfect picture of righteous fury. Something in his eyes made her blood run cold. He took a step forward, and she stepped back.

"Will? What are you doing?" Hana asked. Maybe if she could calm him down, he wouldn't do anything stupid.

"You think just because you're rich and beautiful you can do whatever you want?" he seethed, pushing Hana again. She stumbled but regained her balance quickly and continued backing up, Will matching her movements step for step.

"I, what? Will, look, you're scaring me. I can explain, please—"

"I told you I would kill you if you ever broke Daisy's heart."

Hana put up her hands in surrender. "Will, I can explain — I promise, I have my reasons for telling her now. I was — I'm looking into my dad's death, and I think there's something more. I got this note threatening me, threatening *Daisy*, and—"

"Bullshit!" Will yelled. "Mark's killer is *dead*. Stop trying to make up ridiculous excuses for breaking Daisy's heart."

"I promise — I can show you the note. I couldn't let her get hurt because of me."

"She's already hurt because of you," Will spat.

Hana flinched back, tears pricking her eyes. "But she's safe. I just wanted her to be safe. I promise, I'm not lying."

"Who sent it?"

"I don't know. There's something not right about my father's death, and I've been looking into it, but I haven't been able to find concrete proof yet."

"So you didn't cheat on Daisy, and you only told her that her to keep her safe?"

"I, well ..." Hana was never any good at lying to Will, and he saw it in her eyes right away.

"Oh, I see. You were going to just keep lying to her. If none of this happened, would you have just hidden this from her forever?"

Hana kept backing up, her hands raised defensively in front of her. "No, that's not it, and I — I was an idiot, okay? I made a mistake, and I wasn't brave enough to tell Daisy until it was for her own good. I didn't want to hurt her."

If she could just get to the back door, she could run to a neighbor. Will could cool off. But she only got one step into the living room before Will grabbed her around her upper arm, yanking her back in the hall and sending her falling into the hardwood floor. She cried out in pain when her head slammed into the wall, but she struggled back to her feet to face Will. It was like the boy she grew up with was completely gone, replaced with an angry man she didn't recognize.

"Well, you did hurt her the moment you cheated on her with some slut. You're just like all the other idiotic rich bitches in the world — you think you can do whatever you want without any consequences," Will snapped.

Hana was crying in earnest now. "What? Will, that's not me. I never — this isn't a consequence of my actions. Just — please, Will, I know you're better than this."

"You don't know shit about me! You have no idea what it's like to be me!"

"I don't. You're right. But I know the kind of person Daisy thinks you are. You're better than this. I'll hurt forever for what I did to Daisy. This — this will hurt her. If she finds out about this, it'll kill her," Hana said. She knew it was a mistake when she saw the stormy look on his face.

"You don't get to tell me about Daisy. You've taken yourself out of her life, and I'm just supporting your decision."

"Will, you'll destroy your future if anyone finds out."

Will wasn't going to listen to reason, though. Hana tried to make a break for the front door, but she wasn't fast enough.

Will caught up to her in seconds, grabbing her arm again and whipping hair around so fast her legs tangled beneath her. He shoved her away once she was facing him, but she was still off balance, and she fell backwards.

There was a moment as Hana fell when she realized her head was going to hit the marble plant stand in the foyer. Her stomach dropped, her reflexes too slow to react, and the swoosh of fear, of knowing, made her think of the first time she kissed Daisy. Her stomach dropped almost the same way, like it knew what was happening would change her forever.

DAISY, PLUCKED

The last thing she saw was Will reaching for her, anger replaced with fear.

Then, there was nothing.

271

Chapter 21

Daisy — August 2019

ALL OF DENNIS' USUAL casual, jovial nature was completely gone, like sidewalk chalk after a rainstorm. He sounded tired, as if confronting her was some sort of chore he needed to check off his to-do list. Daisy gripped the folder tighter, her knuckles flexing under the skin of her still-mud-flecked hands. Before she turned to face him, she started recording a video on her phone, which she shoved into her pocket and hoped it would at least pick up audio.

"I — this is just a few poems."

"There's no need to lie to me, Daisy. I know all about Hana's little note with that message for you. I should've figured you would find it even after I hid it. I didn't want to do this. Man, your brother is going to be pissed." Dennis put down the takeout bags and sighed, pulling a small handgun from his briefcase.

Daisy froze, and her vision went black around the edges for a second, but she managed not to faint from the panic. Her ears rang, and she was sweating like she just ran a mile outside in the humid August heat.

"Is this how Hana died?" Daisy blurted it out without thinking.

Dennis had the gall to laugh at her. "No, I didn't kill Hana. Cover up her death, yes, but that's just my specialty."

"So, you *did* hire Hansen to kill Mr. Holm. And you killed Hansen."

"Yes, I did. And here I was thinking you were too busy crying to figure things out. But you just had to see through my meticulous cover up, didn't you?" He took a step toward her.

"It wasn't that meticulous, clearly. Hana figured it out. I just followed her train of thought." Daisy just had to keep him talking and stall until she could figure out how to get help.

Dennis seethed and slid a butcher's knife out of the block on the island. Daisy's pulse hammered. Maybe her own body would make her heart give out before Dennis got the chance to do anything.

"Let's get this moving. Noriko will be home soon, and I don't want her to find you after you've used this knife to kill yourself. She still has nightmares from finding Hana. I'll take the first responder duties this time," Dennis said. He lunged forward and gripped her arm hard enough to bruise with the hand holding the knife, and when she tried to jerk away, he pressed the barrel of his gun to her neck.

"We're going to walk upstairs, and you aren't going to fight me, okay? I can make this easier on you," Dennis said. His voice was eerily calm, and an overwhelming sense of clarity washed over Daisy.

He would kill her, and the only way out of this would be going along with him until she saw an opening for escape. If she could hold him off until Noriko got here, she would be fine. Or maybe Will would wake up and see her message and decide to come find her instead of waiting for her to get home.

"How did Hana die?" Daisy asked. Her phone was still recording, and she hoped she would be around to turn it over to the police herself.

Hana's ghost appeared at the top of the stairs, vengeful anger on her face. Daisy wished Dennis could see her, but he didn't react to her appearance at all. Hana's ghost was still only seen by Daisy, her memory kept alive by the love they shared and Daisy's devotion to finishing what Hana started.

"She was too smart for her own good. Everyone else moved on from her father's death, but she had to go and stick her nose back in that closed case."

Daisy dragged her feet, forcing Dennis to slow down as he tried to force her up the stairs. "But you said you didn't kill her. What does the case have anything to do with it? Did you pay someone to do your dirty work again?"

Dennis growled in frustration and released Daisy's arm, pushing her toward the stairs with the barrel of the gun when she didn't immediately move. She fell, scraping her chin on the carpet of the steps. She let out a small cry of pain before scrambling back up to start her ascent. He'd just shoot her right here if she didn't comply at least a little bit.

"No, this time I got lucky. Someone did it for free. Good timing too. I doubt Hana had anything good on me yet, but it's better safe than sorry. I mean, hell, he thinks he owes *me* for helping with the coverup." Dennis laughed so coldly it sent a shiver through Daisy's body, and all the hair on her arms stood up.

She forced herself to stay calm. "And you saved ten grand."

"Well, yes, I guess I did. Plus, no mess this time. Getting Hansen drunk on expensive whiskey so he wouldn't fight back was also pricey. That man drank like a fish. But, in the end, worth it."

"Why? Why do any of this?" Daisy asked.

Hana's ghost moved aside when Daisy reached the top of the stairs, and Dennis walked right through her. He shuddered, and Daisy hoped he felt the anger and pain radiating off the ghost.

Dennis guided Daisy into Hana's room and closed the door. "Love, of course. I love Noriko, and she should be mine. I'm just clearing the path to her."

"Just for love? Not for the partner spot?"

"Oh, you are clever, aren't you? I didn't even notice that you were on the trail before today, so kudos to you for that. But you're a fool, just like Hana, for thinking you could outsmart me."

"I did outsmart you," Daisy said. She didn't know if it was wise to tell him he was caught no matter what, but she needed to say it.

"Why do you think that?" Dennis asked. His voice was condescending and sickly sweet, like he was talking to a toddler.

"Because I sent all the evidence Hana collected to Will. He'll be here any minute," Daisy said.

Dennis let out a real laugh at that statement. "Will? You think Will is going to take any of this to the police? Who do you think killed Hana?"

The words reverberated through Daisy's skull, and she looked towards the door, where Hana's ghost stood, also frozen in shock.

"Will ... No, Will wouldn't do that. Will wouldn't kill Hana. He wouldn't — stop lying!" Daisy shouted.

Dennis shoved her, hard, and she fell to the floor, dropping Hana's letter as she went. "It was a crime of passion, not premeditated at all if it makes you feel any better. When I showed up, he was still in shock, covered in blood. He'd ridden his bike here for some godforsaken reason, and I didn't even know he was here until I came looking for Hana."

Daisy remembered that day. Will let her take the car to her final to cheer her up because she was still brokenhearted over Hana.

Daisy stared at Dennis, still unbelieving. "And you ... helped him cover it up. Because he did you a favor, didn't he?"

"He did. I don't know exactly what Hana knew, but I had a feeling she was getting too close. I was going to come and reiterate what I wrote in my note to her, but Will beat me to it. And now, well, even Will would believe that you killed yourself after you discovered the truth. Your own brother killed the girl you loved. Who could blame you for it?" Dennis taunted, staring at his reflection in the knife for a second before setting his sights back on Daisy.

"No, no, no," Daisy chanted under her breath, looking around. Maybe Noriko would be home soon, maybe she could still make it out of this.

"And it's not as if your father won't be glad. Hell, he went on and on all morning about what a disgrace you are and how ashamed your mother would be of you. No parent wants a kid like you," Dennis spat.

Daisy flinched back at that. "That's not — you're lying. He'll come around."

"I'm sure he was planning on coming up with some placating thought about you coming out so he could sweep it under the rug and start dropping eligible bachelors in your path. He thinks you're obsessed with Hana's death, and he's right. Of course, he thinks you're obsessing over an open and shut suicide. Really, I'll just use all of this to make the story I tell about *your* suicide more plausible." Dennis waved the gun around as he spoke, and Daisy hoped that maybe she could disarm him by distracting him somehow.

"You should've been a writer," she said. "You're very good at making up stories." She backed up against a wall and stood up again. She needed to keep stalling long enough to come up with a plan or for someone to come save her.

Maybe if Will came, he could tell her the truth — he could clear up Dennis' terrible misunderstanding and make things right again. There was no way he really killed Hana. Daisy was still trying to process the possibility of her brother killing the girl she loved, but her struggle didn't stop Dennis from droning on, sounding unhinged.

"It's easy to make people believe something when it's all they want to hear. Those who are grieving just want to understand, and if they believe they know what led to someone's death, they move on. Mark's death was seen as an unthinkable, unpredictable, and unpreventable tragedy, when really it was a complete setup. It took me weeks to lay the groundwork for Jake Hansen to do it. I left him anonymous letters, cash, and eventually the entire price of the hit. He didn't even know it was me until the night he died when I showed up with his final payment and a bottle of whiskey. I couldn't have had it go any better if I wanted it to. Fate heard me and decided that it was my time! Finally, things worked out for me, the forgotten brother, always in second place!" Dennis declared, spit flying from his mouth as he yelled at her.

This was not any version of Dennis that Daisy knew. This was not the man who gave speeches at the holiday office party and made Noriko laugh at Thanksgiving. Maybe this was who he really was under his charisma and grandiose speeches. Daisy was too scared to respond, but this didn't stop Dennis and his tirade.

"And everything was going perfectly, so perfectly, until Hana went and dug her grubby little fingers into the case. She should've just left it, but instead she started her clumsy investigating. She wrote that stupid short story and made Nori and I read it as if I couldn't tell what she was doing."

"What are you talking about?" Daisy asked, unable to stop herself.

"Oh, didn't she tell you about it? About her little creative writing project where she wrote about her father's death without writing about her father's death? She probably thought she was being so clever, acting all innocent and using those doe eyes on me. Maybe if she looked more like Nori and not my stupid asshole of a brother it would've worked, but it didn't. I'm too smart for someone like her to bring me down, some embodiment of the wrong choice that Nori made decades ago.

"And it's kind of funny because I was going to kill her anyways before Will beat me to it. You Polos are always becoming unwitting accomplices to my murders. Your father was the one who made sure the police barely bothered me during the investigation of Mark and Hansen's deaths. And your brother did all the dirty work for me here. I mean, Hana helped too, of course. She was acting so strangely in the weeks leading up to her death; she was withdrawn, quiet, too placating, uninterested in her old life, distancing herself from her loved ones. After the fact, everyone said they never saw it coming, but they should have. There were so many signs that no one noticed. When we said that Hana's death was a suicide, of course everyone believed us. Hana was too damn paranoid to ask for help, so no one knew about what she was investigating. But then I found her stupid letter, and I knew I had to keep an eye on you," Dennis said.

"You knew about the letter?"

Dennis laughed, and the malice in the sound shook Daisy to her core. "Of course. Where did you think all her physical notes went? I took her notebook and ripped all the pages out after Will killed her. I found the note, too, but Noriko was on her way home so I just stuffed it in the journal and hid it with the others on her bookshelf so I could come back for it after the cops left. Noriko would never come in here, wouldn't want to read Hana's journals, but then you had to come and take it. Of course you did," Dennis yelled, gesticulating with the knife while still holding the gun steady, trained right on Daisy.

If Daisy was going to die, she wasn't going to roll over and take it. A fire burned in her veins she never felt before, and she took a steadying breath to stop herself from doing anything too brash. "I knew she didn't kill herself. I had to look for proof."

"And look where your little proof led you," Dennis laughed. "The same fate as your beloved little Hana." He mispronounced Hana's name, making the first "a" harsh and nasally, the way that substitutes and teachers would pronounce it before Hana would correct them.

Time was running out, and Daisy had no more ways to stall. "No one will believe I killed myself."

"Of course they will. It's a classic scenario, one for the ages — the poor star-crossed lovers take their lives. What a shame, that poor Daisy Polo. The final straw was that her own father didn't accept her, so she killed herself in her dead girlfriend's room. You'll be a cautionary tale of not accepting your children — you'll be martyrs. You'll be famous. Maybe you should be thanking me," he mocked.

He took a step towards Daisy, and she roared forward, pushing him with all her might. She managed to throw him off balance, but when she tried to run past him, he stuck out his arm and pushed her backwards. She screamed and fell, hitting her shoulder on Hana's vanity. Dennis clicked off the safety of the gun and raised it to shoot at Daisy, abandoning his original plan for her staged suicide. She closed her eyes, not wanting to look her death in the face. She didn't hear the footsteps of whoever darted into the room, only felt herself being pitched to the side as the gunshot rang out.

When Daisy opened her eyes, she thought for half a second that Hana's ghost was the one who knocked her out of the way and took a bullet for her.

"Oh no, no, no, this wasn't — Noriko, no, I didn't mean to," Dennis cried, watching in horror as Noriko staggered back against the wall and slid down it, clutching her side. Dennis lurched forward, cradling Noriko close to his chest even as she struggled against his grip. He took off his blazer and applied pressure to the gunshot wound in Noriko's side, murmuring apologies until they sounded like nonsense.

Daisy pressed herself back against the wall and watched the scene play out in front of her like a daytime television drama. Dennis was unworried about the gun that fell to the floor during their struggle, only focused on helping Noriko.

"What have you done?" Noriko asked, looking around wildly as if something in this room would explain the web that Dennis weaved, the one they were all trapped in now.

"Don't try to talk right now. You're losing a lot of blood," Dennis said, pushing harder against the growing bloodstain in his blazer. She tried to move again, but he held her in place.

"Hana didn't kill herself? And you knew?" Noriko asked, demanding an answer.

"I didn't kill her. I just helped cover it up so it would be easier to move on, so it would be easier for us to be together," Dennis explained, searching his pockets for his phone.

"Yes, so we can ... be together," Noriko said. She reached towards him, but instead of caressing him she picked up his discarded gun. His face turned stormy when she held it to his head with shaking hands, and he rocked back on his heels, his hands raised in the air.

"Nori, what are you doing? I did this for us, I did all of this for us, and this is how you repay me?" he said it as if he was a knight in shining armor, and she was angry at him for slaying the dragon.

Noriko clicked the safety off the gun and pointed it directly at his forehead. "Daisy, go," she said.

"You ruined everything, you stupid little girl, and I'm going to—" Dennis screamed, his face the picture of fury. Before he could do anything, though, the front door slammed open.

All three of them froze.

"Daisy! Daisy, I'm here!" Will called, his footsteps pounding up the stairs. He ran into the room and froze at the scene in front of him, dropping his bike helmet.

"What — what's going on? Daisy, are you okay?" Will asked, turning his entire attention on her, as if Noriko bleeding on the floor with a gun aimed at Dennis was inconsequential in all of this.

"She's fine, but she knows the truth now. She knows what you did," Dennis said, his voice cruel and dark. Will glared at the older man, and Daisy shrank back from the pure hatred and rage in his eyes.

"You tricked me. You told me you were helping me because you cared about me and cared about my future, not because *you* wanted Hana dead," Will bit out.

"What is he talking about," Noriko asked, her voice weaker than before. Daisy didn't know how much longer Noriko could hold the gun up for. Hana's ghost was back at Daisy's side, trying to urge her towards the door, trying to protect her once again from the chaos around her, but Daisy didn't want to run. She wanted the truth, all the painful parts of it laid out in front of her in unavoidable detail.

"I killed Hana," Will said. "Dennis found me afterwards and helped me cover it up. I just didn't realize how much experience he had faking suicides."

Dennis glared at him, and Noriko's gaze flickered over, trying to discern the truth of Will's statement.

In the moment of distraction, Dennis reached for the gun, and Noriko fired it, though she only managed to hit the round light on Hana's ceiling. The glass around the bulb shattered and rained down, making both Dennis and Noriko shield themselves while Will threw himself over Daisy. She dropped to the ground and lurched towards Noriko, grabbing the gun out of her weak grip and standing up again, backing towards the door. She felt in her back pocket for her phone, but it must have fallen out at some point during her struggle with Dennis.

"Has anyone called 911?" Daisy asked, her voice eerily calm. Will took a step towards her, but Daisy turned the gun on him, stopping him in his tracks.

"Daisy, what are you doing?"

The gun shook in her hands. "What am *I* doing? You killed Hana!"

Will held out his hands in a pleading motion. "It was an accident! We were fighting, and I just pushed her, and I thought — I didn't think she would fall over, and then she hit her head, and she wouldn't wake up. I just, she hurt you so bad. And she didn't even seem sorry. I got so mad. I just went there to try to find out why she did what she did so you could move on and find someone who could love you like you deserve and not treat you like shit," Will explained, as if anything he said would make what he did okay.

Daisy shook her head at him. "You killed the love of my life. She was my best friend, and even after I told you to leave things alone, you just had to come talk to her. I'm eighteen! I can stand up for myself. You didn't have to … you shouldn't have—"

"You said you wished for once she would deal with the consequences of hurting you. I was just going to yell at her."

"I also told you to stay out of it, it's amazing how selective your hearing is," Daisy snapped. Will flinched back, and Daisy took a deep breath, holding the gun steady and looking around the room.

"I didn't call 911," Noriko said. "I saw you through the window when I pulled in the driveway and came straight up." Noriko acted as though Daisy and Will's fighting wasn't happening. The color was draining from her face and her breaths were getting shallower.

"I did. I told them you were in danger," Will said.

"You're an idiot, just like your father," Dennis seethed. "You're going to get eaten alive in prison."

Daisy pointed the gun back at him. "Shut up. You don't get to manipulate any of us anymore. You're done playing your games."

"Am I?" Dennis taunted. "I'm the top defense attorney in the state. Do you know how many murderers I've gotten off? Do you know how flimsy a years old cold case is? Do you even know how much I can get a sentence reduced for being an accomplice who's willing to cooperate with the prosecution?"

Daisy didn't remember firing the first shot, only the expression on Dennis' face when it hit him square in the chest. Will lurched towards her, yanking the gun out of her hand. He fired the rest of the clip, hitting Dennis two more times before deliberately shattering Hana's vanity mirror with his other shot. He dropped the gun to the ground and sank to his knees, watching Dennis intently as if he was going to recover from the shot that hit him squarely in his throat.

"Why did you do that?" Daisy demanded.

"Your shot didn't land. He needed to pay," Will said. His eyes flicked towards Daisy's phone, which had fallen out of her pocket at some point and was now face up. The video was still recording, the screen only showed blackness from where the camera was pressed against the ground.

"He's right," Noriko said, her eyes fixed on Daisy as well. Before Daisy could respond, she heard the police announcing themselves and thundering up the stairs, their guns drawn. Will and Daisy put their arms up, and Noriko struggled to lift her arms before passing out cold.

The next two hours were a blur. Daisy and Noriko were taken to the hospital in separate ambulances, even though Daisy insisted she wasn't hurt and didn't need to go. One of the paramedics pointed out the gash on her shoulder she got from falling into the dresser, something she didn't feel until they mentioned it.

She didn't remember a single one of the questions the police asked or any of the answers she gave, only that once she handed them her still-recording phone the questions stopped. She could almost hear her father's voice in the back of her head telling her to lawyer up the second any cop started questioning her, but she didn't heed his advice. She was too numb to think through anything.

Reality snapped back with startling clarity when her father ripped open the curtain surrounding her bed at emergency room, his eyes wide with panic.

"Daisy, oh my god, you're okay," Henry said, running to her side and pulling her into a hug.

"You should see the other guy," she joked before promptly bursting into tears. Henry just held her while she cried.

"I'm glad that you're okay," Henry said gruffly once the worst of Daisy's sobs were done.

Daisy smiled weakly at him, still sniffling. "Will killed Hana. And Dennis, he ... he got Mark killed, and he—"

"I know, Daisy. They explained it all when they called me. Will used his one phone call for me."

"I'm sorry. It wasn't … Where's Noriko? Is she okay?"

"The doctors wouldn't tell me much, just that she was in surgery and that they'd ask her if I could see her once she wakes up. If she wakes up."

"I made a real mess of things, didn't I?" Daisy asked.

"This … this wasn't your fault. I'm gonna go find a nurse, see if we can get you discharged soon."

"Okay, Dad. I'll be here."

Henry strode away and Daisy curled her knees into her chest, startling when Hana's ghost appeared at her side.

"It's time for me to go. Thank you, Daisy," she said. She smiled Daisy's favorite smile, the one Hana reserved just for her. What would their life have been like together if Hana had never tried to investigate her father's death, if she never cheated on Daisy last Halloween, if things had gone the way Daisy used to think they would?

"I'm always going to love you," Daisy murmured, hoping no one bustling around the emergency room would hear her.

"I loved you from the moment I knew you until my heart stopped beating."

Daisy closed her eyes and sucked in a shuddering breath. Hana's ghost squeezed her hand, one last time.

When she opened her eyes, Hana was gone and Daisy was left, once again, with only the living.

Acknowledgements

WHERE DO I START! I came up with the idea for this book during my sophomore year of college while reading Hamlet for the third time. When I realized Ophelia was only in five scenes and still became such an iconic character in literature, I asked myself what it would look like if she had more agency and the ability to depend on herself and not the men in her life. This book was the result.

I couldn't have made this book what it is without the help of my incredible editor Raneé Clark. Your notes made me rethink my story in a new way and brought it to a whole new level that I couldn't have reached on my own. Thank you also to my beta reader, Jess, for your feedback and encouragement on an early draft.

Of course, I need to thank my friends and family who made me into the writer I am today. Mom, thank you for reading every draft and telling me it was better than the last — I hope you think this is the best one yet. Dad, thank you for actually reading my book and breaking your years long reading slump. Abby, thank you for listening to me rant about writing as if this isn't something I am fully doing of my own volition, and for always believing in me even when I didn't believe in myself. Cabby 13ever. Brianne, thank you for being the best travel buddy and for always cheering me up with endless memes, TikToks, and words of encouragement. I can't wait to see all the places we'll go together. Baylee, I am so glad the universe (via New Paltz housing) brought us together. I wouldn't be who I am today if I didn't meet you. Also, you were right, *Reputation* did change my life.

Thank you to Shakespeare, both the playwright and my dog. Neither of you can read this acknowledgement, but I couldn't have written this without both of you.

A special thanks also to the musicians who got me through writing this book. Orla Gartland, I couldn't have written the last two chapters without replaying "Over My Head" approximately 100 times. Taylor Swift, thanks for being an endless source of inspiration and joy — analyzing your lyrics has made me a better writer. Djo, thank you for creating *Decide*, an incredible album that always gets me into a creative headspace.

I'm sure I've forgotten people, so thank you to anyone else who encouraged me to write and not give up on my dreams of publishing this book even after rounds and rounds of rejections and setbacks.

And thank you, reader, for picking up this book. I hope you loved Daisy and Hana as much as I do.

About the Author

C. E. Witherow is a queer writer living in Rochester, NY with her border collie mix, Shakespeare. When she's not writing, she co-hosts a Taylor Swift podcast called *Swiftlore* with her best friend, curates hyper-specific playlists, and spends too much time on TikTok. This is her first novel, and she is so excited to finally share it with the world.

Read more at https://cewitherow.com/.